Torquere

Natural Disaster
TOP SHELF
An imprint of Torquere Press Publishers
PO Box 2545
Round Rock, TX 78680
Copyright © 2006 by Chris Owen
Cover illustration by Pluto
Published with permission
ISBN: 1-934166-63-4, 978-1-934166-63-5
www.torquerepress.com
First Torquere Press Printing: January 2007
Printed in the USA

Prologue

Fair Weather

In the pale light of early morning Jake Taggart told himself it was just another day, knowing full well he was lying. It was far more than an ordinary work day and everyone on the ranch knew it. He could see it in the smiles, the way all the hands stuck close to the main house and the barn even after he'd set out the work orders for the day. The men were lingering, and he knew why. He just wasn't sure that anything was really going to happen.

Tornado was like the rest of them, leaning indolently against the barn door, his arms crossed over his chest. "Be time for breakfast soon," Tor said as Jake wandered past, restless.

"Yep." As conversations went, it was a non-starter. Jake didn't want to talk about breakfast and Tor never could stop himself from talking when he was nervous. Jake shoved his hat higher on his head and looked around. "This lot is going to stick close until..." He trailed off, not precisely sure what would make everyone go to work like the good little cowboys they were. He shrugged one shoulder and kicked at the dirt. "Until."

Tor nodded slowly. "Yep."

"Don't know that anything special is going to happen," Jake said. He was actually pretty sure that nothing momentous was going to happen at all. The legal matters had all been dealt with at the lawyer's office and he and Tor already had the keys. They'd even moved most of their things over to their new home from their room in the bunkhouse.

"Don't know that it isn't," Tor said lazily. "And you know they'd hate to miss anything." He looked around, squinting a bit. "Know soon enough, I expect." His jaw lifted, pointing toward the big house, and Jake turned slowly.

Doug Gillian, the man Jake would always think of as The Boss even if he didn't own the ranch anymore, was standing on the porch of the main house. He was holding a suitcase and quietly looking out over the yard, not saying anything at all, his expression calm and contemplative. One by one, the hands noticed him and fell silent, then walked up to the railing, heads angled up to better see his face.

Jake and Tor joined them wordlessly, walking shoulder to shoulder until they were at the front of the pack.

"Mornin'," the Boss said with a faint smile. "Big day."

There was a murmur of agreement among the men, but Jake held his tongue. The day had been a long time coming, filled with negotiations and banks and long talks over the kitchen table. He and Tor had worked damn hard to get the money together to buy out the Boss, but they'd done it. Bought the land, the stock, the horses; hell, even the vehicles, bar the one truck waiting in the drive. Everything connected to the ranch was theirs, had been for a day and half while the Boss tidied up a few loose ends. And now it was time for the man to say his piece and drive off, leaving them to sink or swim.

Before Jake could even feel more than a little dizzy, Tor's hand landed on the small of his back. "Easy, Taggart," he said softly. "We'll be fine."

He nodded and backed up a few steps, watching as the Boss came down from the porch and tossed his suitcase into the back of his truck. Jake and Tor hung back as he then made his way through the group of ranch workers, shaking outstretched hands and saying a few words to each man. Jake knew that he'd also spent part of the day before talking to everyone and handing out discreet envelopes; it might have only been a few dollars each, but Doug Gillian was the kind of man who shared his good fortune and rewarded hard work.

Some of the hands had worked for him for more than a dozen years or more, the same as Jake, and they would be rewarded for their friendship.

Finally, though, the Boss was done, save Tor and Jake himself. But instead of going to them, he grinned and looked at Elias and Bobby. "Do me one last job?" he asked, his voice almost booming in the quiet.

"Yes, sir," Bobby said with a nod. "What do you need?"

The Boss gestured to the truck. "Got something in back I want put up at the end of the drive. Soon as you can manage it."

Elias and Bobby went to the truck and climbed up into the bed, then heaved a large wrought iron sign out, their grins growing despite its weight. "We'll take care of it," Elias called back, two more hands stepping up to help lift it down.

"Christ," Tor said in a low voice. "That sure is pretty."

Jake nodded, not sure what to say. The sign was big, big enough that he wasn't sure how it fit flat in the truck. The scrollwork wasn't fancy or elaborate, but the frame of it was arched and elegant. KaroJet Ranch was spelled out in swooping metal, and there was a flower in the lower right corner. "Apple blossom?" Jake finally asked, staring at the wrought iron sign.

The Boss nodded. "Arkansas state flower. Seemed right."

"It's right. All of it is right," Jake said, still looking at the sign. Elias and Bobby waited until Tor nodded, then started moving it to one of the ranch trucks. "Thank you," Jake said, turning to the Boss. "It's... it means a lot."

He got a nod and suddenly the three of them were standing alone, the hands backing off to give them their space. Jake noted it, appreciated it, but he had more appreciation of the way the Boss was shaking his hand.

"I'm glad it's like this," the Boss said quietly. "You've been here a long time, Jake, and I don't think it's going too far to say that it's damn close to leaving the place with family. You grew up here, and it's right that you and Tor bought it. I feel good leaving this spread in your hands."

Jake swallowed hard. There really wasn't anything he

could say to that, to the man who'd helped him put his life back on track and given him a home when he most needed it. "Thank you, Doug," he finally said, his voice tight. "We'll do our best here."

"Know you will." The Boss turned to Tor and shook his hand as well, smiling. "Keep him out of trouble, yeah? And make sure he doesn't work too hard."

Tor laughed quietly and nodded. "Set me an easy task, why don't you?"

"Hey, you picked him." The Boss's smile grew wider and he stepped back. "You got a ranch to run here. No more standing around now, you hear?"

Jake nodded and followed him to the cab of the truck. "Back to work, boys," he called, trying to keep his smile open and easy, though it was hard. "Don't make me regret this whole thing."

"Yes, sir, Boss," someone yelled, laughing, and Jake felt himself start to blush. Boss. Christ.

Doug Gillian got in his truck and looked around once more before starting it up. "Gonna miss this place, Jake," he said as Jake leaned on the truck. "Stay in touch."

"You know it," Jake assured him. "Got your number on the wall by the phone."

"Don't worry about using it."

Jake nodded and stepped back, thumping the door of the truck. "Drive safe."

"Ride safe," Doug said with a nod. Then he pulled away and Jake watched as he drove down the long lane and out to the road.

Gillian's spread was now KaroJet Ranch, and Jake stood blinking in the morning sun, his fingers crossed in his pocket.

The Calm

Chapter One

"You think you can get the fencing done in the next week or so?" Jake asked Tommy as they loaded up the truck. They'd spent the better part of two days searching for breaks in the fence that needed fixing. Jake knew that while Tommy and Tor could easily get it all done, Tor wasn't going to be around for the next few days, as he was sneaking a peek at some breeding stock a few towns away.

"Should do," Tommy said thoughtfully as he wiped his brow. He squinted into the sun for a moment and added, "Give me Elias or Fred for a day early on and that'll help."

Jake nodded and opened the cooler they had stashed in the cab. He grabbed a bottle of juice. "That should work. I'll check the sheet when we get back--"

"Who's that?" Tommy interrupted, pointing to a pickup truck coming their way, dust billowing around it in the sunshine. They were only three or four miles from the barns and were due back within the hour; there was no real reason for anyone to come out there for them instead of waiting or using the radio.

Jake squinted and shielded his eyes, then made out a flash of red. "Tor's truck. Can't tell who's driving, though."

They sat on the tailgate and watched the truck rumble nearer, conversation drying up in their curiosity as they waited.

"What's up?" Jake called as Tor pulled up next to them, his window rolled down.

Tor didn't shut off the engine, though he did put the truck in park. "Got a situation, Jake. Need you back at the house." His voice was quiet and serious and he was holding onto the steering wheel with a white-knuckle grip.

"Ah, shit," Jake breathed. He stood up and handed his bottle to Tommy. "See you in a bit."

"Sure, man. Hope it's nothing you can't fix."

"Me, too." Jake walked around the back of Tor's truck, his heart starting to beat a little faster. The sun went behind a cloud that hadn't been there a few moments before and he shivered, sweat suddenly cold and clammy on his skin as he climbed up into the cab. "What's up?"

Tor wouldn't look at him. He put the truck in gear and started driving, carefully doing a three-point turn to head them home. "Cath called," he said in that same tired, *old* voice.

"Fuck. She's not canceling, is she?" Jake demanded, throwing his head back on the headrest. He'd been trying not to get too worked up about his sisters' upcoming trip, but damn it, it was hard not to. It would be the first time he'd have his family on his land, and it had taken ages to arrange, between Cath and 'Lissa getting time off from work, Jacob's schooling, and getting the guestrooms redecorated. They'd owned the ranch for almost a year now, and he'd been eager for his family to finally visit.

"No." Tor shook his head. "I mean, it wasn't about that." He took a deep breath and Jake looked at him, looked hard, and started shaking his own head. "Jake, there's been an accident."

Tor was slowing down, stopping the truck.

Jake shook his head harder. "She called, so she's okay, right? But she can't come, which sucks, but there'll be other times--" He knew he was talking too fast but he had to, it was the only way he could stop Tor from speaking. He could drown Tor out with his own voice and then Tor would never ever say what Jake knew he was trying to.

"Cath's fine," Tor said in a soothing tone Jake had never heard before and didn't want to hear right then. "'Lissa was taking Jacob to--"

"No."

It was too hot in the cab of the truck and there was a fly trying to get out through the windshield, buzzing and fighting against the glass in a start and stop that had no rhythm.

"--with his friends and they were--"

"I said 'no.'"

The fly buzzed too loudly but not loud enough, and Jake's words were dry in his throat and he couldn't get them past his tongue.

"--didn't feel anything--"

"No, no, no--" It was possible to implode from repetitions of a single word, Jake discovered.

"--got a broken arm and Cath's there--"

"Please, no. Stop, Tor, just stop." And then there wasn't any air in the truck and Tor was wrapped around him, keeping his arms from lashing out, and Jesus Christ but Jake thought his chest would explode from the wrongness of it all.

"Baby, she needs you. Jacob needs you."

Jake wondered how he could hear the whisper of Tor's words when he was screaming so loudly. He opened his mouth only to find that the shrieks were in his head, that he hadn't said anything, hadn't done anything other than let Tor hold him.

The sun was behind a cloud. The fly lay on the dashboard, still.

"Okay," Jake said slowly, testing his voice. "Okay. It's going to be okay. I have to call Cath."

Tor looked at him uncertainly. "Okay," he echoed. Then he put the truck back in gear and headed for home.

Chapter Two

Part of Jake wasn't ready to get back to the house, back to where there were phones and people; back to where he was supposed to start coping. Part of Jake screamed out against calling Cath, refused to accept that he'd have to begin to deal with losing their sister.

Only a fraction of Jake was prepared for Tor to stop the truck, but when they rolled to a stop his hand reached for the door handle just like it had always done. Muscle memory. The truck stops, you reach for the door handle and get out. Habit.

He was almost in the house, Tor hurrying to be next to him, when Elias called out to them, yelling that he needed a word or two about something that Jake no longer gave a sweet damn about. Jake barely registered it when Tor broke away from him and simply kept going into the house, not sure what else to do. He didn't want to watch Tor tell Elias, didn't want to see sympathy appear in anyone's eyes. Not yet.

The house was silent inside, dull and muted. He could hear something outside, his puppy Barkley and another dog playing. Kip must have brought Winner for the day. Jake was holding the phone before he realized he'd crossed the room. He stared at it for a moment, his mind utterly blank, the numbers he needed gone, if they'd ever been in his memory. Someone, some time, had been thinking, though, and there was a neat little note next to the speed dial buttons. 1. Vet 2. Bunk 3. Becky 4. Melissa *ohgodohgodohgod* 5. Cath's cell. Five. Cath was five. One button dialing and he needed it now, needed it like he'd never needed anything before, except maybe the need he had for family, his family, so long gone and now ripped apart again.

He closed his eyes against the stab of pain and pushed the damn button, trying to breathe through the pressure on his mind. She'd found him, she'd changed for him, she'd accepted Tor, had welcomed Jake back, she'd actually looked for him after the lies and she... It was always 'Lissa. It was 'Lissa first; 'Lissa who wrote, 'Lissa who cared enough to keep trying when she knew all there was to know, 'Lissa who rebelled against her own upbringing and found a way to love Jake the way he was. 'Lissa had given him back his family and now she... she... Jake pressed his fingers to his eyelids, listened to the busy signal and disconnected, then pressed five again.

Busy.

Busy.

Jacob.

Jake groaned and sat down on the couch, still pressing five and then disconnecting. Shame welled up in him and he knew it was stupid. He was allowed to hurt about this. He was allowed to be upset and angry and he was allowed to be in denial. But there was a voice in his mind pointing out that there was a fourteen-year-old boy--almost fifteen--who'd just lost his mother, and Jacob had so much more pain to deal with, so fucking much more. It wasn't fucking fair.

"No, it's not," Tor said behind him and Jake jumped.

"Didn't know I said that out loud." Christ, he sounded pathetic, but Tor didn't seem to notice.

"Doesn't matter, you're right. It's not fair." Tor moved around the couch and plucked the phone out of Jake's hand. "Busy?"

"Yeah. Can't get through." Barkley came scrambling into the room, his feet sliding on the floor and his tail going a mile a minute. Jake scooped him up and buried his hands in the warm gray fuzz of his back, taking a bit of comfort from the pup but putting him down when Barkley just wanted to lick his face.

Tor nodded and moved to the desk. "Gimme a minute or two then, and try later. Gotta make some calls."

Jake didn't care. It didn't seem to matter at all, and he had no interest in the calls Tor was making. He didn't consciously listen to him either, just kind of registered that Tor was talking to a few people to let them know they were going out of town; that he wouldn't be able to get to Hally's to check the stock. Then Tor started calling the airlines and Jake was a little surprised at how easy it was to get them on a flight that night.

"... Is there anything sooner out of Little Rock?" Tor was asking. "...Nah, that's actually too soon, we'd never get there in time. Okay, leave us on that one, and make sure one ticket is open-ended, the other... say, five days."

Jake looked up at that, but didn't question it. It was enough that Tor was going with him. Then it was done and Tor was handing him the phone.

"I'll pack," Tor said gently. "You try Cath again. Elias will be over in a few minutes; I'm putting him in charge."

Jake nodded and pressed five. His finger floated over the disconnect button and almost pushed it automatically before he realized that the expected busy signal was actually a ring tone. Two rings, then three, and suddenly there was Cath's voice.

"Hi, you got me but you didn't. Leave a message."

He almost hung up, having no idea what to say, but his subconscious supplied a word for him. Screening. She might be screening her calls.

"It's Jake," he said finally. There was a silence then, unnatural and tinged with desperation, but he didn't know what else to say. "We... we're comin'. Tor's got a flight booked, but I don't know what the fuck's going on, and I need you to pick up, Cath. Cath? It's Jake. Come on, please be there."

"I'm here," she said, and Jesus, but Jake had thought he'd sounded bad. Her voice had lost its silky smooth sound, had mutated into something hoarse and raspy from crying and talking. "I'm here."

"Hey." Jake took a deep breath and realized he'd closed his eyes again. He decided that was a good thing. "How are you doing?" He thought that might just have been the stupidest thing he'd ever asked.

"As well as I can be, I guess," she said, and then it didn't matter if he'd been stupid to ask. "You?"

"Been better." God, wasn't that true? "What happened?"

She sighed. "They got hit side-on, on a cross street. As near as I can tell, it was an honest accident--the other guy's brakes failed on a hill, and he was trying to drive off the road to slow down, to hit anything other than another car. He actually crossed a lawn and slowed a bit, but not enough. Came through a low fence and... The doctor told me that she never knew."

Jake bit at his lower lip, his eyes still squeezed shut. God. "Jacob?" he asked hollowly.

"He's going to be okay. He's got a broken arm and a concussion. They're keeping him in the hospital for a few more hours, then I'll take him home."

Jake swallowed. "Have you seen him? Does he know?"

"Yeah," she whispered. "God, I never want to do anything like that again. They... they let me tell him. He said he doesn't remember anything, just driving and then being in the ambulance. Said that when he woke up and she wasn't there he knew she was hurt real bad, that his momma would always be there if she could be. Jake, he didn't cry."

Jake hadn't cried either, wasn't sure he could. "He will. And we'll be there."

"I know. Listen, I know this is going to mean huge changes for you and Tor, and believe me, I'll do everything I possibly can. I'll take a leave from work for as long as you need, do everything I can here to take care of the house and property. I'll do as much as I can to make this easier on you."

"Yeah, okay," Jake said, mostly from reflex. Someone promised favors, you said thank you; it was more muscle memory. But this was different, something wasn't sitting right. "What?" he asked, trying to engage his brain instead of floating on the cloud of not feeling.

"What, what? I mean, I know it's early and all, but it's going to take planning. I'm sorry, I'm pushing, we can talk about it when you get--"

"What planning? What're you talking about?" Jake sat up

and opened his eyes, heard the door open and Elias' familiar step in the hall.

Silence stretched out like a winding road. "She didn't tell you," Cath said softly. "Oh, God."

"Tell me what?" Jake could feel himself start to twitch and fought down the urge to yell. He could sense Elias behind him, and could hear Tor coming down the stairs. He held up a hand, for no reason other than it seemed like a good idea to grab Tor's attention.

"Jake, listen to me. You're listening?"

"Yes."

"I know this 'cause I'm the executor of 'Lissa's will. You knew that?"

"Yeah." No, he hadn't, but it didn't matter. She was executor of his will, too, it made sense. She was the smart one.

"When you and Tor bought the ranch and settled down, 'Lissa changed her will. She changed guardianship of Jacob from me over to you. She thought that it was a better atmosphere--a nice place in the country, two parents who would be there instead of one who works twelve-hour days and travels one week out of four. A better life for Jacob if anything... anything happened to her." Cath choked out the last words and Jake turned his head to stare at Tor, who was looking back with huge questions in his eyes, and Elias, who was leaning on the wall like he wanted to melt into it.

"She didn't tell me," Jake said quietly. "I'll have to talk to Tor."

"Yeah. Yeah, okay. I mean, I can take him if you want, I just thought you knew, and now I don't know if it's legal or what'll happen--"

"Cath, it'll be okay." He had no idea if it would be. "We'll sort it. Whatever is best for Jacob, that's what'll happen."

"Okay, Jake." She sounded so small and tired that Jake had a sudden memory of her as she'd been just before he'd left home. She'd been so small, playing in the mud in the backyard. She'd looked at him as he'd stormed out of the house that last day, him all of sixteen and her eight years younger, and she'd looked so serious, like she knew he wasn't coming back. "Okay."

Jake looked at Tor, held his uncertain gaze and nodded firmly. "We'll be there as soon as we can be; don't meet us at the airport. You'll be at 'Lissa's?"

"Um, yeah. I have to start the arrangements and Jacob will be there. I gotta make more calls, pick him up from the hospital."

"All right. We'll go there. Tell Jacob we'll be there as soon as we can. And Cath? We'll figure it out."

"Okay. I love you, Jake."

"I love you, too. See you soon." He hung up the phone carefully, like it might shatter, and stood to face Tor. "'Lissa made us Jacob's guardians."

A muscle in Tor's jaw twitched, but he nodded. "We'll figure it out."

Chapter Three

"Jake?" Tor's voice was soft, barely loud enough to be heard over the sound of the truck's engine. Low enough for Jake to pretend he hadn't heard if he wanted to continue his silence.

Jake kept looking out the window and wondered idly where they were, how close they were to the airport. It was the first non-family thought he'd had in almost two hours. "I wish she'd said something," he said quietly. "Just… anything. What do we know about raising kids? Being an uncle is one thing, taking them in is another." He turned his head suddenly and pointed an accusing finger at Tor. "And don't you dare say something about the hard part being over, and at least we don't have to deal with diapers, 'cause that's shit, and you know it."

Tor gave him a mild look and nodded. "Wasn't going there. Promise. I know this is going to be rough."

Jake narrowed his eyes and searched Tor's face for reluctance, resistance, for something to fight against, and found only the usual strength and weather-etched lines. He sighed and closed his eyes, his head rolling back against the seat. "I can't believe she didn't say anything."

"Jake, it was a safety measure. I doubt people make these arrangements ever expecting them to take effect. She probably thought that when Jacob was out on his own, or seventeen or whatever, she could just take the clause out. You know? And maybe she was going to tell us, ask us, when they were here, after she'd seen the place."

Jake sighed. "Yeah, I know. It's just… fuck. What do we know about teenage boys? Lord, between the two of us we're gonna screw this kid up so bad."

"Nah." Tor's objection was lazy and calm. "It'll be better than anything you had, better than me, with my dad just going. Think about it--we live on the same land that got you turned around. It's a good place to grow up. Same school Missy went to, people around us that we respect."

Jake opened his eyes and took another long look at Tor. "You want this. You never once said anything about kids."

Tor shrugged. "Didn't want kids. But this isn't the same. It's taking family in and making sure he's safe and grows up with his head screwed on right."

"But what about us?" Jake blurted, color rising on his face from shame about his selfishness. "What about you and me and the ranch? What about when you're off at auction and I'm riding fence? What about sex, for fuck's sake?"

Tor looked like he was going to smile, but he stopped just in time. "Take him on the fence with you. The ranch will be fine. You and me will be fine--even if we don't make out on the kitchen floor anymore. I can still drag your ass out to the barn in the middle of the night so you can scream. The rest will be the same; morning, noon, and at night, in our bed."

Jake just shook his head. "When did you become the stable one and the voice of reason?"

"When I wasn't the one knocked on my ass," Tor said gently. "Look, if 'Lissa had called us up and said, 'Hey Jake, would you and Tor take care of my boy if something happened to me?', what would you have said?"

Jake looked out the window. "Would've talked to you."

"Yeah. And then, after we'd talked about it?"

"Don't know, do I? Don't know what you would have said."

"Now you're just being stubborn. What would you have said, Jake?"

Jake looked out the window and wondered again where they were. Then he shrugged one shoulder and sighed. "Yes. I would have told her that we'd take him."

"There you go."

And there they were.

Natural Disaster

The Storm

Chapter Four

Jake's head was fuzzy by the time the plane landed. He'd resisted sleep and he felt like he'd been putting up hay for weeks, but with the added bonus of being an emotional mess. His hand shook as he picked up his bag, and he was glad it hadn't been that bad on the plane. Or maybe it had been and he hadn't noticed.

They walked through the arrivals terminal slowly, pacing themselves until the crowd thinned out a little. "Should we take a taxi or rent a car?" Jake asked as they approached the exit and the car rental kiosks.

"Already have one reserved," Tor said, pointing to a booth. "You'll be here for a bit, need something to drive."

Jake nodded then blinked slowly and stopped walking. "When did you do that?"

Tor took an extra couple of steps before he seemed to realize Jake wasn't with him. Turning, he reached for Jake's hand again and said, "I called the airlines. Packed. Talked to Elias. When you were checking to make sure you had enough clothes in your bag, I called and reserved a car."

"Oh. Thanks." Jake wasn't sure what the appropriate level of gratitude was for that sort of thing, but he was pretty sure that it wasn't supposed to make him want to cry. "I should have slept," he said stupidly, wondering if he was blinking too much or too little.

Tor's brow furrowed briefly. "Yeah, we both should have. Come on, let's get this done and get out of here, at least. Find some coffee."

Jake nodded and they stepped to the booth, where he tried to pay attention and be polite to the lady working there. He followed along with the basics, but by the end of it Tor had to prompt him to pass over the credit card and point out where to sign. The lady looked concerned and more than a little suspicious.

Tor leaned over the desk slightly. "Better sign me on as a second driver."

"It'll cost more." She reached for another form and tilted her head slightly, making her hair sway gently. "But I think you're right."

It took only a few moments to do up the extra paperwork and then she passed the keys to Tor. "It's in the first row; the tag number's at the top of the page."

Jake felt about five years old as Tor led the way to where the rentals were parked. It only took them a moment to find the car, a roomy sedan, and to throw their bags in the back, but Jake didn't get in right away. Now that they were there, so close to being with Cath, he didn't know if he could face it.

Any of it.

"I don't want this to be real," he whispered.

"Get in the car, Taggart," Tor said from the driver's side, and Jake had no idea if he'd heard or not.

Jake shook his head and opened the door, falling into the seat and closing his eyes. He waited while Tor got in and slammed his own door, the car vibrating from the uneasy impact. The silence stretched out for too long, making him turn his head and open his eyes. Tor was looking at him, and suddenly Jake could see the burdens Tor was carrying. The dark smudges under his eyes, the slump in Tor's shoulders, and the careful stillness; they drew Jake even closer to his breaking point.

"I ...-" He had no idea what to say.

"Got a choice here, Jake," Tor said gently. "We can go to the house right now, or we can find somewhere and get a room. Sleep first. Now, it ain't going to be easy, either way. You know that. It's going to be rough, hardest, when you first see them. Do you want to fill your tank first, or do you want to just go now?"

Jake tried to think about it, tried hard, but all he could bring to mind was that his sister and his nephew were dealing with the details alone, and that they were hurting by themselves. That he was hurting in a way he'd never felt before. That he was more scared of seeing them and making it real than he'd been scared of anything else in his life, maybe.

"I don't... Jesus." He rubbed his eyes and leaned back. "I need to be there, Tor. Take me to Jacob, let me hold my sister. Then we'll sleep. At least we'll be under the same roof." The car started and Jake left his eyes closed, feeling them burn. "Was it...when your mom passed, was it so confusing?"

There was only the sound of the engine and then the click of the signal light for a few moments.

"It wasn't...it was bad, yeah. But we knew it was going to happen." Tor sighed. "The arrangements had been in place, so there wasn't this kind of rush, you know? It hurt like fuck, and we were lost, but we knew what was going on."

Jake nodded, not knowing if Tor saw.

"There's going to be some other things we have to talk to Cath about right away," Tor said, and Jake could hear an unexpected edge to his voice.

"Like what?"

"Like we're going to have to talk to the lawyer damn soon, and it might be a good idea not to let anyone know that you weren't aware 'Lissa was naming you guardian. Could cause trouble."

Jake hadn't really thought of that, not from an outsider's point of view. Cath had said something, but he'd mostly been in shock. "Yeah," he agreed slowly. "We should talk to someone on our own."

Tor cleared his throat. "I... um, I called Becket. To find out if he can act, here in Texas."

Jake opened his eyes and stared at Tor. "You were busy."

Tor shrugged and looked faintly embarrassed. "It was just a thought."

"And?"

"And he can, but he gave me a number for someone local,

if we need help fast."

"Why would we? I mean, do you think we will?"

Tor looked at him out of the corner of his eye. "Depends on if your brother James knows yet."

Chapter Five

Cath looked like hell, Jake thought. She'd cut her hair since he'd last seen her, and he could only assume that under other circumstances the short blonde bob would look cute, and not so... wild. He and Tor walked into the small house that less than a day ago had been 'Lissa's home and stood in the kitchen, looking around them.

"You look like shit," Cath said bluntly, peering up at him. "Both of you." Then she leaned past Jake and tilted her head up to kiss Tor's cheek. "Did you sleep at all?" she asked, wrapping her arms around Jake's waist and hugging him.

"No," Jake murmured into her hair. "Did you?"

She nodded against his chest and pulled back. "A few hours, anyway. Come on in and sit before you fall down. Coffee?"

"Yeah. Thanks." He pulled out a chair at the table and more or less fell into it, steadied by Tor's hand before Tor seated himself next to him. "Where's Jacob?"

Cath nodded her head toward the short hallway and poured coffee into three mugs. "In his room. He was sleeping when I checked on him about fifteen minutes ago. The doctors said that the concussion was better, good enough to let him sleep if he needed to. Honestly, I'm glad he is; it's going to be a horrible few days."

They sat in silence for a few minutes, just sipping coffee. Jake had no idea what to do next, and Tor hadn't said a word other than his thank you for the coffee. Cath looked worn out, and she kept looking at the phone on the table next to her as if she expected it to come alive.

"How are you doing?" Jake asked seriously. He wondered

suddenly and absurdly why he was keeping his voice so low, why it just seemed the thing to do. Like he was talking to a skittish horse.

Cath looked up and met his eyes, her slight flicker of a smile forced and uncomfortable looking. "I'm holding it together. I have to. But eventually… it's gonna all hit me. I haven't stopped to think since they called me at work, and right now I'm just trying to keep busy, keep it away until after the funeral."

Jake could only nod at that; he'd been trying not to think for what felt like days. "What can I do? Make some calls, deal with the florists or something like that?"

Tor cleared his throat and they both looked at him, startled.

He looked faintly embarrassed again. "I don't mean to stick my nose in where it doesn't belong--"

Cath rolled her eyes as Jake snorted. "You're family now, Tor. That's your job," she assured him.

Tor acknowledged that with a duck of his head. "Yeah, well. Thing is, I think that it might be a good idea for the two of you--the three of us--to talk about… damn." Tor took a deep breath and looked at Cath. "You talk to James yet?"

Cath sighed. "James. Shit." She shook her head and leaned back in her chair, her hands wrapped around her coffee cup. "I called the last number I had for him, but it was a disconnect. He hasn't called me, so I don't know if Aunt Jess managed to reach him or not. Our wayward brother might be trying to stay wayward, if you know what I mean."

Jake closed his eyes. Oh, this was going to be hell in every way it could be. "Jess. She knows I'm alive?" He wasn't sure how many people still believed his mother's decades old lies; he wasn't even sure if he didn't want some people to just go on thinking he was gone.

He opened his eyes to see Cath wincing. "Oh, yeah. 'Lissa told her and the others when she found you. That's how James found out, you know. By then, I hadn't heard from him in almost eighteen months, and he and 'Lissa hadn't spoken in about four years."

Tor snorted. "Did the rest of the family take it as well as

James?"

Cath shrugged. "Jess didn't say much, just rambled about bad pennies. She didn't seem to care that she was the reason Jake ran in the first place, that it was her telling tales that got Momma to even say Jake died. James... well, James kept quiet after y'all tossed him off the ranch, but when he started in on Jacob... 'Lissa flipped out on him, you know? He's been warned off; he's not supposed to have any contact with Jacob."

"Legally?" Tor asked immediately.

"No," Cath said with another head shake. "Just by the wrath of a pissed-off sister. As far as I know, James hasn't tried to call Jacob since 'Lissa found out he was trying to turn Jacob away from you two. Jacob swears James hasn't called, and that he wouldn't listen anyway." She smiled at Jake then, the first real smile he'd seen since they'd walked into the house. "He's gone on you both. He told me once that James had to be wrong about God hating you, because you need all the love you can get, what with people that don't even know you hating you. That's God's job, he says. To love people who need it most."

Jake smiled and looked over at Tor. "He's a smart kid."

"Yeah," Tor said with a quick nod. He bit his lip and turned his coffee cup around twice before picking it up and draining it. "But still. We better get some legal stuff done soon as we can. And Cath--tell us what we can do to help you out, right?"

Cath nodded. "So, you're gonna take him, then? You've talked about it?"

"Yeah," Jake said, taking Tor's hand. "We're going to do what he needs. What we need."

"Good." Cath stood up and took her cup to the sink. "I'm glad for you, you know. Really glad. And I'll help as much as I can." She turned around to face them, studying them with a critical eye. "Right now, though, I think you both need to sleep, for a few hours at least. Then we can talk more."

"Does Jacob know?" Jake asked as he stood up.

She shook her head. "I didn't want to say anything, given

that you were… well, clueless. Didn't know what you would decide. And he hasn't asked."

"Okay." Jake looked around and picked up Tor's bag, handing it to him as he picked up his own. "Where do we sleep?"

The phone at Cath's elbow rang, a short, two-ring tone. "Got my home phone on forward," Cath said, reaching for the receiver. "You're in the guest room, is that okay?"

"No problem," Jake assured her, leading the way to the cheerful yellow room he and Tor had used on their only other visit there. Behind him, he could hear Cath start talking to someone she called Mary, saying that yes, it was a shock. He resolved to take over the phone as soon as he'd rested a bit. Cath shouldn't have to do that over and over again.

He and Tor had just put their bags down when the door opposite theirs opened. A slender figure was framed there, one arm in a cast and his hair sticking up in ragged tufts. "Uncle Jake?"

Jake put his plans for sleep on hold and paused only long enough to squeeze Tor's shoulder before moving forward, hoping to hell he had the strength to manage this. "Hey, Jacob."

Jake had only a moment or two to marvel at how tall Jacob had gotten in the past few months; 'Lissa had said that the boy was going through a growth spurt, but Lord, he must have shot up two inches. He looked gangly and awkward standing in the doorway, like his limbs didn't quite fit yet, which Jake vaguely remembered it actually felt like. The bright blue cast didn't help much.

"When did you get here?" Jacob asked, glancing past Jake into the room. "Hey, Uncle Tor."

"Hey, kid," Tor said, flopping onto the bed still dressed.

Jake took another step forward, unsure if he was supposed to reach out or hold back. "Not even half an hour ago." He looked back at Tor, hoping to hell for a little bit of guidance.

Tor closed his eyes and draped an arm over them. "Jacob, you send him back in ten minutes, yeah? He needs his beauty rest."

"Okay," Jacob said, sounding as relieved as Jake felt. "Sure. You bet."

They went into Jacob's room, leaving the door open. "How's your arm?" Jake asked, looking around the room. He was still twitchy, his hands acting on their own and taking his arms with them in frequent, abortive movements.

"Hurts. And my head aches." Jacob looked around too and sighed, then sat on the edge of his bed. "How're you?" he asked tentatively.

"Been better," Jake admitted, still looking around. It was a kid's room, but at the same time, not. There were posters on the wall of guys skateboarding, and a couple of awards from school. A trophy for soccer on the desk. Clothes all over. But there were CDs too, and the clothes weren't the little boy jeans and shirts that Jake had seen months ago. The stuffed animal that Jacob had seemed both embarrassed by and reluctant to give up was now high on a shelf and Jake could see the dust on it.

Finally, Jake sat next to his nephew on the edge of the bed. "Want to talk about it?"

"Nope. And I don't want to cry."

Jake looked at him, startled. "Pardon?"

Jacob's cheeks colored. "I heard one of the nurses, when she thought I was sleeping. She said that I hadn't cried yet and that it wasn't natural."

"She was full of shit," Jake said immediately, offended that anyone would judge any of a boy's reactions to his mother's death as unnatural. "Crying... crying is good, don't get me wrong, and you'll do it at some point. But don't you let anyone tell you that you have to do it--that's as much crap as the entire 'boys don't cry' bullshit."

"Yeah?" Jacob looked relieved but after a short moment his eyes clouded again. "It's okay to cry and it's okay not to cry?"

Jake nodded and felt impossibly old. "Yeah. It's all good, kid. It's... it's the way you feel things. Nothing wrong with feelings."

Jacob nodded slowly and seemed to think about that. Jake

had no idea if he'd made any sense at all and he wasn't really sure if it mattered. Clarity of thought had long since abandoned him, and he was just trying not to fuck things up beyond what they were. He glanced up at the posters and then at the CDs on the floor, wondering with a small part of his brain why there weren't any posters of girls up. Shouldn't a kid Jacob's age have pinups from magazines on the walls? That Spears chick, or that scary girl Tommy liked--Pink? Stupid name for a girl. He tried to remember what was on his walls when he was Jacob's age and drew a blank. Still though, should be something up, maybe actresses, unless Jacob wasn't into--

Jake's brain froze and he blinked. "Don't borrow trouble," he whispered to himself.

"What?"

Jake shook his head. "Nothing, just thinking. Sorry."

"Oh."

They sat in silence for a few moments longer and Jake was just about to get up and tell Jacob he needed sleep when Jacob said, "I'm worried about Aunt Cath."

"How come?"

Jacob shrugged. "She's got too much to do. I mean, you're here now and that'll help, but there's just so much. She's been callin' and callin' and dealing with people and making arrangements and I can't help. And after… I just think it'll be too hard."

Jake took a deep breath. "Well, now. You don't have to worry about any of that, Jacob. I'll help with everything, so will Tor. That's what we're here for--we're older, for one thing, which means that we can legally do what you can't. It's nothing you have to worry about, I promise."

Jacob looked at him, his face impassive. "Then what *am* I supposed to do?"

Jake had no idea what to say. "Try to get through it as best you can. We're here for you, we'll do everything in our power to make this--" not easy "--less horrible for you."

Jacob shook his head, but didn't seem to be really disagreeing. "What's going to happen to me?" he whispered, staring at the floor.

Jake sighed. "You don't have to worry about this right now."

Jacob stood up. "I do have to. No one will tell me anything, and I don't even know who's going to take care of me!"

The utter agony in Jacob's voice cut through Jake like an ax through pine. He stood up and eased Jacob back onto the bed, then knelt down in front of him, holding his gaze steadily. "You're right. That was damn stupid of me, and I apologize. I guess we're just trying to keep you from worry, and instead we're causing more."

Jacob just looked at him, blinking rapidly.

"You know what a will is, right?"

"Yeah."

"Okay, your momma has one. And in there, she's got a plan laid out about what we're supposed to do--about the money, what to give to people, what to sell, and what to do with her savings and such. It's yours, of course, but it'll most likely go into an account until you're a certain age, or for your schooling or something. I haven't seen it yet, so I can't say for sure."

"Okay. But what about--"

Jake held up his hand. "She also made a plan for what to do if she... if something happened to her before you were old enough to live on your own." Jake swallowed hard, willing himself to get all this out before he finally had to give in to his own need for catharsis. "Which means that she named a guardian for you. And that's me."

Jacob stared at him, his eyes wide with disbelief. "You?"

He nodded, unable to speak.

"I'm supposed to go live with you and Uncle Tor?" He looked horrified now, his eyes narrowing.

"Your mom thought that it would be best--that we could give you a good home and watch out for you." He paused for a moment and then plunged on. "If you're upset 'cause me and Tor are together, then we'll have to talk some more."

Jacob literally waved that away. "Nah, whatever. I don't care about that. It's just... it's..." He was looking more and more upset by the moment, his hand shaking a little as he reached up to rub his other arm above the cast.

"What?"

"It's Arkansas. My friends are here, my school, my team... everything!" He stood up again, suddenly, and strode to the door. "You can't take everything from me. I won't go."

Jake could barely breathe, his throat was so tight. He banged his head against the mattress and went after Jacob, only to meet Cath in the hall. "I gotta talk to him," he said tightly, trying to pass.

"No you don't, big brother." Cath suddenly sounded a lot like 'Lissa. "You need to sleep. He needs to think. It'll work out, I promise. We'll all talk later but right now, hon, you need to crash." And with that she pushed him hard into the guest room and closed the door on him.

Jake stood for a brief moment, trying to decide if he should go out to Jacob anyway. He had his hand on the doorknob when Tor rolled over on the bed and said his name.

"Taggart? You talk to Jacob?"

Jake could only nod, so he sat on the bed and pulled his boots off. He was shaking, the day crashing over him like a spring storm, violent and fast.

Tor pulled him back, tugging at his shirt sleeves until they were lying on the bed facing each other. He didn't say any-thing, just looked at him, and Jake closed his eyes, burrowing his head into Tor's neck.

"He doesn't want to come with us," he whispered, and then he let it all fall apart, let the storm start to break over him as he lay in Tor's arms.

Chapter Six

When Jake woke up, his eyes were gritty and a headache loomed just behind his forehead. He was too warm, too restricted, and it took him a moment to realize he was tangled in a blanket, fully clothed. He wrestled the blanket off and lay still for a long moment, letting the cooler temperature soothe him a little.

Tor wasn't there on the bed next to him, and Jake had a vague memory of a soft voice saying something about coffee. He definitely remembered an embarrassing moment of clinging before Tor broke away.

Jake rubbed at his face and sighed, unable to convince himself that staying in bed for the next few days was a real option. He had strong doubts that everything would just work out on its own, or that this nightmare was going to fade in the warm light of day no matter how long he put off getting up.

By the time he'd taken a shower the headache had retreated enough for him to think with reasonable clarity, and his watch was telling him that the warm light of morning was actually showing up in mid-afternoon. He followed the sound of voices into the kitchen, mildly surprised to find people there. It wasn't a crowd, but there were two women at the table with Cath, and Tor was leaning on the counter, reaching for a mug and the coffee pot as Jake appeared. The sound of a video game drew Jake's attention as he passed the living room, and he glanced in to see Jacob staring intently at the TV screen, the control braced on his cast and the fingers of his good hand flying as he tried to play despite his injury.

"Jake, this is Tracy and Laura, friends of 'Lissa's," Cath said softly.

Jake nodded, accepting their murmured words of sympathy and the mug from Tor. He was about to ask Cath what he could do to help when the house phone rang, Cath wincing as she reached to answer it.

"Hungry?" Tor asked beside him, and Jake shook his head. He wasn't, or at least he didn't feel like it, but common sense told him that he really should eat something. Tor seemed to be in his head, smiling slightly as he pulled the fridge open.

"Maybe a sandwich," Jake said, sipping his coffee, hoping the caffeine would kick in nice and fast. The two strangers at the table talked quietly to each other, apparently making a list of names between them. Or maybe it was a shopping list; one of the neatly written names looked like 'Rice Crackers'.

"Gonna have to be something simple," Tor said, pulling out a small brick of cheese. "There's not much here. I'll go shopping in a minute."

"Oh, we can do that," Tracy or Laura said. "We have a list of things. For… for after."

Jake swallowed thickly, Tor's hand suddenly on his shoulder.

"It's okay," Tor assured them. "I can get it all. Maybe you can stay here for a bit, though? Make some calls for Cath? I'm sure there are people who'll need to know, and Jake doesn't know any of 'Lissa's friends. Or the parents of Jacob's friends."

Jake was almost obscenely grateful for Tor at that moment. He still felt useless, but where he would have expected to rail against Tor taking over, he found only comfort. He listened with half an ear to Cath tell someone when the funeral was, happy enough to melt into the background as Tor finished making the sandwich, and then went over the list with 'Lissa's friends.

"Jake."

He blinked, not really aware how long Tor had been trying to get his attention. "Sorry," he said, feeling his cheeks heat. "Not real awake yet."

Tor just smiled at him, gently coaxing him into the conversation. "Do you remember which dip got eaten first after my mom's funeral?"

"Yeah, that shrimp and onion thing, with the cream cheese," Jake answered immediately. He'd been pretty much in charge of the food distribution after Maureen's services, and Tor had been out of it; he wasn't sure how Tor knew what Jake had been doing, but apparently he'd taken the time to find out. Or, more likely, Becky had made a point of telling Tor that Jake had been helpful. In any event, Jake was just happy to have an answer to something, anything. It made him feel a tiny bit less shell-shocked.

Cath hung up the phone and sighed, picking up her own cell phone. "Two lines going is a bit much," she commented, pushing the power button. "What's the plan?"

Tor picked the rental's keys up off the counter and waved the list at her. "I'm off for food."

"And we're going to make some calls for you, honey," the Tracy/Laura creature said. "Why don't you go lie down?"

Cath looked at Jake.

"Go," he said, pointing down the hall. "Even until supper. I'll make some calls, if I can use your phone?"

"Okay," Cath said, sounding surprised. "If you're sure."

Jake shrugged. "You got an address book or something?"

Cath stood up and handed him the cell phone. "I called all the family; mostly people are just calling me back at this point. Might be a stray cousin or something, but I wouldn't worry."

Jake looked at the door to the living room. "How about things for Jacob? The school and stuff?"

Cath looked stricken, her eyes shutting. "Damn it--"

"Go rest," Jake ordered, aware of the two women watching calmly, ready to offer a shoulder if needed. "I can handle it. Gonna need the practice, yeah?" He offered her a weak smile.

She gave him a ghost of a smile back, then said a few words to Tracy and Laura. Jake was already looking through the phone book and dialing from the list of numbers in 'Lissa's handwriting at the front.

When a pleasant voice answered the phone at the school, Jake had to take a deep breath. "Hello. My name is Jake Taggart; I'm Jacob Taggart's uncle."

There was a very brief pause before the female voice said, "Of course. I'm deeply sorry for your loss, Mr. Taggart. We were all so… sorry to hear about the accident."

"Thank you," Jake said calmly. "We're all a little thrown at the moment, and I apologize for not being in touch sooner."

"Oh, don't worry about that, Mr. Taggart. Really. How is Jacob?"

Jake's gaze slid to the living room. "As well as can be expected, I guess. His concussion seems better, but his arm's gonna be in a cast for a while. The rest isn't really sinking in yet." Or maybe it was, and Jake was still in denial too much to see it.

"That's understandable. The poor child." She paused for a long moment and Jake was struck by the woman's genuine concern. Suddenly, he wondered if he really could take Jacob from these people.

"Um. I just wanted to let the school know that Jacob will be out for the rest of the week, and possibly a little longer. Is there a way that someone, maybe one of his friends, could bring him his assignments so he doesn't get too far behind?"

"Of course. I expect that Tressa will be stopping in anyway, and I'll make sure that Miss Keene knows to send his homework with her. And if, for some reason, Tressa isn't able to be there, don't you worry. There will be a certain amount of latitude and leeway for Jacob, given the circumstances."

Jake found himself nodding. "Thank you. Could you give me some information while I have you on the phone?"

"If I can." She was still warm and polite, but Jake could almost see the little flag of warning shoot up.

"I just need to know when school is done for the year, and if Jacob has exams or anything," he said gently.

"Oh! Well, no, he doesn't. I mean, considering the circumstances. There'll be tests, but they aren't run at special times or anything, just in regularly scheduled classes, and there will be a bit of leeway for him, of course. And the school year ends on May twentieth this year, so another three weeks."

"Okay, thank you," Jake said, writing the date on a slip of

paper. "And after the twentieth he doesn't have to go back for anything?"

"No, he'll be done for the year then. May I ask a question, Mr. Taggart?"

"Sure."

"Has someone been named Jacob's guardian yet? Has he got... someone?" She asked it tentatively, and even though Jake knew next to nothing about the school system he was pretty sure she was just asking because she was worried, and not for any official reason.

"His mother named a guardian in her will," he assured her. "Jacob's going to be well cared for."

"Oh good," she said, and Jake smiled at her relief. "I was worried, to tell you the truth. A single mother, and all. It was on my mind. I'm glad that Jacob has family."

Jake bit his lip, suddenly aware of the silence in the living room, the game shut off. "Yeah. Family is important." He took a breath to steady himself and then said his thanks, once more checking that Jacob's assignments would find their way to him. Finally, he hung up and placed the phone on the counter.

"You did that really well," Laura said to him, her voice soft. She had a necklace on; it said 'Laura' in script, the gold catching the light. "Now, eat that sandwich your man made you and go be with your family. We'll take care of the phones. Promise."

Jake nodded and picked up his plate. "Thank you. Both of you."

"Not a problem," Tracy assured him. "Wish like hell we didn't have to do it."

"Yeah. Me, too." And then Jake went to see if Jacob would eat anything.

Chapter Seven

Jake had gotten only a few mumbled words out of Jacob by the time Tor got back with the groceries. Jacob said he wasn't hungry, which Jake both fully understood and knew was probably not entirely true--he seemed to remember being constantly hungry at that age, but he didn't press the matter. So they sat in the living room together and flipped through TV channels without paying any attention to what was on, lost in their own misery.

Jake knew he should be talking about something, but he had no idea what. Feeling utterly helpless and lost, he chose instead to let Jacob lead the way with his blank stare and re-flexive channel changing. It might have been a cop-out, but somehow it seemed better than trying to fill the silence with meaningless chatter that would just annoy them both. Jake wasn't sure he was even capable of creating chatter; talking just wasn't something he did easily. He was immensely re-lieved when Tor came back and he could go help unpack the groceries.

Jacob turned on his video game again, the soundtrack a far too happy background noise, but Jake was glad he'd stopped with the remote. Tracy and Laura helped with the groceries, setting aside the things they'd requested, and said they'd make up as many things as they could; Jake, Cath and Tor were not to worry about food for after the funeral.

"Honestly, y'all will probably be swamped with food in the next few days," Tracy promised as she got her things together. "People will be dropping off all sorts of dishes any time now."

Jake and Tor nodded, remembering the casseroles and pans

of food that had appeared at Becky's. Meals seemed to be something that people easily offered as a way of support. Jake, for one, would be grateful; anything to take a bit of pressure off.

It wasn't until the women had gone and Tor had started chopping peppers for a stir-fry that Jacob roused himself from the couch and appeared in the kitchen. "You're cooking?" he asked, somewhat dubiously.

"Sure," Tor said with a grin. He reached for an onion. "Food doesn't get cooked by itself. You want chicken or steak?"

"Um, chicken, I guess." Jacob moved closer and watched as Tor quickly sliced the onion. "You cook a lot?"

"Well, sure," Tor said, his gaze on the knife. "We share, but now that we're not in the bunkhouse it's a matter of every other night, instead of once or twice a week. Plus, you know. Lunches, breakfast... sometimes a fourth meal if we're doing hay or working long days."

Jake smiled as Jacob's head tilted. The expression felt odd, like his face was stretched, but he let it happen.

Tor caught the look on Jacob's face and chuckled for a moment. "That's the way it is, kid. No one else is going to cook for us, so we do it. Been feeding myself since I was about nineteen--Jake's been doing it longer, but that's just 'cause he's old."

Jake whapped Tor gently on the head. "Not old." Plus, it wasn't true--he hadn't started cooking for himself until he wound up on the ranch, and he was twenty-two then. At least he'd gotten better at it as the years had passed.

As if reading his mind, Jacob asked Tor, "Are you good at it?" He picked up a mushroom and studied it curiously.

"What, cooking? Yeah, I guess so. Better than Taggart, anyway."

Jake whapped him again and Tor made a show of being injured, his free hand flying to his head. "Don't be so mean! You'll rattle my brains if you keep hitting me."

Jake snorted. "They've been scrambled for years now."

"And yet, you keep me around."

"Yeah, well. You can cook. Now if you only mopped the floors I'd be a happy man."

Jacob was eyeing them, looking bemused. "You mop the floors?" he asked, pointing to Jake.

"Only when I have to," Jake admitted. "I'm better at laundry."

Jacob looked around the kitchen and set the mushroom back down carefully. Jake watched his hand shake and sighed inwardly, then reached out and gave Jacob what he hoped was a reassuring squeeze on the shoulder.

"Guess I... I guess there's a lot of stuff that has to get done around a house," Jacob said, blinking rapidly.

"Yeah." Jake watched carefully, not sure if this was the next step of Jacob's mourning or not, but utterly determined to do whatever Jacob needed. He had no idea what that would be, and Lord knew he wasn't the greatest at taking nonverbal cues, but he'd try his best anyway.

Jacob sat at the table and was quiet for a long moment. Tor had apparently noticed the change in his mood and glanced back at Jake, his eyes questioning until Jake nodded at him to keep cutting. And Jake waited, his ass braced on the counter, his stomach in a knot.

Jacob stared at the table top, his teeth worrying at his lower lip. "She did everything for me," he said quietly. "I can't take care of myself. I can't cook, or do my laundry, or anything like that."

"You don't have to." Jake moved to the table and pulled out a chair. "And you're not really supposed to know that stuff yet. I mean, some kids do, yeah, but it's not something that's required, you know? You're fourteen--"

"Almost fifteen."

"Yeah, all right. You're almost fifteen. Your job right now is to grow up. You're supposed to be playing soccer and going to school and learning how to think. You're supposed to be doing kid things, not worrying about if you have clean shirts or what you're going to make for dinner. Right?"

Jacob shook his head. "It's just that... she did it all. I didn't help her much, just mowed the lawn when she told me to, and cleaned my room once in a while. She worked so hard, and I didn't even think about it."

He looked up and Jake was fairly surprised to see that Jacob's eyes were dry. He sounded sad, of course, and guilty, but he wasn't breaking yet.

"Baby, she wanted it that way," Cath said from the door to the hallway. "She wanted you to be a kid, like we didn't get to be."

Jake leaned back in his chair and watched Cath come in and sit down. She looked a little better, rested, but nowhere near the woman she'd been a couple of months ago--hell, a couple of days ago, he was sure. It was going to get worse, he knew.

Right then, however, there was yet another small hell to go through. No matter how things had turned out for him and for his family after their long separation, nothing would change the way they'd grown up or the fact that he'd left 'Lissa and Cath there. All he could do was sit and acknowledge the shitty way things had been and accept it as a part of all of them.

Cath sat across from Jacob and looked at him with serious eyes. "Your mom wanted you to have everything, you know. And when she couldn't give you a lot of material things, she decided that you'd have the less tangible things we didn't have. A family who loves you, a chance to have a happy childhood, a home where you knew you were loved and wanted. Look at us, honey. Look at me and your uncle. When he left I wasn't even as old as you, and I didn't see him again until I was damn near thirty. And when he left us, when he walked out because he couldn't stay anymore, he was only two years older than you are now. That's what your mom came out of, the kind of place she never wanted you to see."

Jacob looked at them both, his brow furrowed, and appearing far older than he should have. "Okay," he said, nodding.

Jake sighed, out loud this time. Jacob was trying, he knew, but so many things were conspiring against him really understanding. "Jacob, you don't have to feel badly about anything. You'll learn those things as you get older. Just keep being who you are, and try not to worry about it. You're young, and you're not going to go out into the world without knowing how to take care of yourself--it's our job to teach you those things now, and you've got to know that your mom would have. I swear, she never thought you were anything less than what she wanted you to be."

"Yeah, okay," Jacob said quietly, his eyes fixed on the table again. "I just don't want to be a burden for anyone, and I am now."

"No, you're not," Cath said, patting his hand. "You're not, baby. We love you, and we're going to take care of you."

Jacob didn't look very reassured.

The Flood

Chapter Eight

The next few hours descended into the sort of madness that Jake really disliked. Jacob retreated to the living room once more and the sounds of his video games filled the small house, setting everyone's teeth on edge, though that might have had more to do with a collective inability to know how to deal with a hurting teenager. Shortly before Tor finished the stir-fry, a small whirlwind in the form of a tiny Asian girl descended upon them and breezed through the kitchen with the calm statement of, "I'm Tressa. Jacob needs me."

Jake and Tor blinked at each other and then turned to Cath, who merely shrugged and said, "Never met her. Heard her name, though."

The three of them waited a few minutes before curiosity got the best of them and they oh-so-casually looked into the living room. Tressa was sitting almost in Jacob's lap, one small hand on his cast as she spoke earnestly and quietly into his ear. Jacob had his good arm around her shoulder, his eyes fixed dead ahead although he appeared to be listening. Neither of them looked up at their audience, and after a moment Jake and Tor went back to the kitchen.

"What do you think?" Tor asked, adding the chicken to the pan. "Girlfriend?"

"Like I'd know?" Jake shrugged and forced the entire thing out of his mind.

Tressa left a few minutes later as quickly as she'd come, pausing only long enough to shake their hands and assure them that she'd be back the next afternoon with Jacob's homework.

Supper was subdued, the table conversation limited to passing the salt and pepper and compliments to Tor. Jacob excused himself as soon as he was done, saying he was going to go lie down, and Cath left for her apartment, promising to be back in a few hours.

"Why don't you stay there tonight?" Jake suggested. "Sleep in your own bed, get some rest."

She shook her head. "I don't want to be alone."

So Jake let her go and went out to the backyard. He *did* want to be alone. But some things weren't meant to be, and he hadn't been sitting outside for even half an hour when he heard a car in the drive. He assumed it was Cath coming back earlier than she'd said, until he heard two doors slam. It was only because he didn't want Tor dealing with absolutely everything that he stirred himself to wander around front to see what was going on.

He rounded the corner of the house just in time to see two figures mount the stairs to the front door and immediately had to fight the urge to turn tail and run. It had been a lot of years since he'd last seen the woman, and he had no idea at all who the man was, but he knew trouble when he saw it. He knew he couldn't avoid it, even though he'd assumed he wouldn't have to deal with family until the funeral--he'd been counting on it, actually. Counting on ceremony and common decency playing a part in making everyone behave. There were no such guarantees outside of that.

Jake squared his shoulders and walked toward them, hoping he looked non-threatening or at the very least, calm. "Hello, Jess," he said, his voice devoid of any friendly overtures. He couldn't be any better than he was, and he wouldn't make a mockery of his life.

They turned as a unit, the man looking curiously at him, the doorbell unrung. Jake only had time to note that the stranger appeared to be a couple of years older than himself before he gave his full attention to his aunt.

She was peering at him over the top of her glasses, her mouth set in a thin, straight line, just as he'd always remembered her. "Huh. You're here. I didn't think you'd come."

Jake stopped where he was, a few feet away, and shrugged one shoulder. "Sorry to disappoint," he said blandly.

The man winced and sighed, looking like he did it a lot. "Mother."

Jess snorted and looked at her son. "Nothing wrong with the truth, boy. Jake there's always been a bad penny, no use in pretending otherwise."

"And you've forgotten that rudeness isn't one of your better traits. Maybe being civil to the man would help," her son snapped, turning away from his mother before she could do much more than open her mouth. "Hello, Jake."

Jake looked at the strange man and tried to pull a name out of his memory. He'd forgotten that Jess even had a son, let alone what his name was, but now he thought it might be a good time to remember. Anyone who'd tell the old bitch off was someone to know more about, even if he was her son. "David?" he finally asked, only about fifty percent sure he'd gotten the name right.

It earned him a half smile and a nod, and then David was stepping off the stoop, his hand out. "Yeah. Long time-- haven't seen you since you were about ten, I think."

"I don't even remember that," Jake admitted, shaking his cousin's hand.

David didn't seem to care, shrugging it off easily. "How are you doing?"

"Been better."

David nodded. "I bet." He sounded sympathetic, which Jake appreciated more than Jess' impatient noises in the background. "I'm sorry for your loss," David added.

"Thank you." Jake gestured to the house. "Come on in, we'll put some coffee on."

Jess reached for the door handle. "I'm sure Cathy already has it on--that girl was raised right."

Jake wondered what would happen when Jess called Cath 'Cathy' to her face and said, "She's not here. She'll be back in a bit, though."

Jess stopped, halfway through the door. "Where'd she go?"

she demanded.

David had almost run right into her and barely managed not to fall off the step. "Mother!"

"Stop your fussing," she scolded him, and then glared at Jake. "Where?"

"Her apartment, if it's any of your business. I'll call and find out how long she'll be." He could use the reinforcements.

Jess stormed into the house, making Jake and David rush to keep up before she could get too far.

"Where's the boy?" she demanded, staring around the kitchen like she expected Jake to have him tied to the stove or something.

"Sleeping." Tor stood in the entry to the living room, staring at her, his eyes cold. "Please lower your voice."

Jess pulled up short and Jake caught David grinning before he could turn to study the edge of a cabinet with careful attention. Jake had to admit that Tor looked pretty imposing like that, all wide shoulders and broad chest, his head held high.

"Who are you?" Jess asked after a long moment.

"Mark Flynn. And you are?" Tor's voice was like ice.

"This is my Aunt Jess," Jake said easily as he stepped around her to stand next to Tor. "And that's my cousin, David."

David immediately leapt forward to shake Tor's hand, and Jess sniffed. Tor glanced at Jake, looking a little confused. "Problem?"

"No more so than usual," Jake said, pulling out a chair and sitting down. "Jess, would you like a cup of coffee?" he asked with exaggerated politeness.

Jess seemed to rally a little and her mouth once more assumed its straight line. "I would like to know, Jacob Matthew Taggart, why your sister left a young child here alone with you and this... this man."

Jake froze, intensely aware that Tor had become as still as stone beside him. David looked furious, but unsurprised.

"Excuse me. Did you just say that we're likely to abuse my nephew?" Jake asked quietly, but unable to hide his anger.

Jess looked momentarily flustered, like she'd not expected

him to object to the slur. "She shouldn't have left him here," she stated again, as if saying it over and over would make it true.

Jake suspected that she was very used to people just agreeing with her, whether she was right or they just wanted her to shut up. Not this time. Standing again he stared at her and put a hand on Tor's elbow. "We're gay. That means we like cock, not kids. Got it?"

David looked like he was either going to laugh or pass out; it could have gone either way in Jake's eyes. Jess, on the other hand, merely looked disgusted. She narrowed her eyes. "I know what you like--I saw your filthy perversion right in my own store, damn you. Your parents must be spinning in their graves."

Jake snorted. "Yeah, like them telling the world I was dead didn't get their point across. Do you think I worry about them? I worry about Jacob and Cath and Tor. No one else matters. Not you, not anyone."

"I think you better go," Tor said quietly. He was looking at David, not Jess. "We have trouble enough right now."

David nodded and pulled car keys from his pocket. "Come on, Mother. It's time to leave."

For a long moment Jake thought that she would refuse and the situation would get completely out of hand. Then David touched her arm and she spun on him, her face growing pale.

"Don't you ever tell me what to do, boy. I'm still your mother."

David met her eye and nodded. "You are. Nothing I can do about that. But I won't stand here and watch you do this. The car is leaving now. Are you coming with me, or are you going to stay here?"

Jake could almost see her thinking; she certainly didn't want to leave, and she looked like she was about to reach for a strap to take to her grown son's ass, but the alternative to leaving brought her up short. With a flash of horror, Jake realized she was actually worried that he and Tor would hurt her, never mind Jacob. Bile rose in his throat and he swallowed thickly, grateful for Tor's hand suddenly at his waist.

Jess turned to face them, already walking to the door. "You tell your sister that I was here. And you tell her I'll be calling after the funeral--she's going to need help raising that boy, and I aim to make sure she gets it."

"I'll pass that along," Jake said. And he would, as soon as he was sure Jacob wouldn't be around to hear him losing his temper.

David held the kitchen door open for his mother and looked back at them for a long moment before nodding once and leaving.

"Jesus," Tor breathed in Jake's ear. "Your family is fucked."

Jake sighed and nodded. "Yeah. It is."

He went into the living room and fell onto the couch, suddenly exhausted again. Tor followed him in and sat next to him, pulling him around so they were curled up more or less comfortably.

"Sleep, Jake. You're gonna need it."

A long time later, Jake slept.

Chapter Nine

When Jake awoke, he was still on the couch with Tor, but somehow he'd managed to shift around enough that his head was resting on Tor's chest and he was being held gently in warm arms. He came awake slowly, not moving, and when he heard quiet voices he was glad he'd stayed still; Tor and Jacob were talking.

"She looks like she's been crying," Jacob whispered, and Jake assumed he meant Cath. Vaguely, he wondered what time it was.

"Yeah," Tor agreed easily. "Wouldn't surprise me. Don't worry about it, kid. Going to be lots of tears over the next while."

There was a long pause. "Has Uncle Jake cried yet?"

Tor shifted a tiny bit, one hand rubbing over Jake's side. "Well, now. He has, yes, but not for your mom, I don't think. Sometimes things just pile up and a body can only take so much missed sleep and strong emotion before things spill over. But, yeah, he's cried."

"I haven't," Jacob said, a little louder.

Jake could imagine Tor's face as he thought about that; no judgment, no sign of any worry, just mulling Jacob's declaration over at face value.

"Does that bother you?" Tor finally asked.

There was a soft sound of fabric rubbing, like Jacob was moving in the easy chair. "Should it?"

"Not really. I expect you'll cry sometime soon, but it's not a big deal that you haven't yet. You're still kinda shocky, I expect."

Jake almost smiled. Tor was in fine form, being as calm as

he could be and just letting Jacob start to deal with things. There was another long pause, long enough that Jake almost fell back to sleep listening to Tor's steady heartbeat.

"Why are you still out here?" Jacob asked. "There's a bed."

Tor laughed quietly. "Yeah, I know. Didn't want to wake him up once he was asleep, I guess. Plus, it's comfortable here, and if I try to move him, he'll be up all night."

"Oh."

Tor rubbed at Jake's side again and Jake would have smiled if he'd been turned the other way. For some reason he didn't want Jacob to know he was awake; it would end whatever was going on with him and Tor. Jake was almost certain that if that happened, Jacob would close off again, maybe for days. He needed this, the silence and a sympathetic ear to listen to him.

"Do you do that a lot?" Jacob asked suddenly, curiosity strong in his voice.

"Do what?" Tor asked back, clearly baffled.

"That."

Tor laughed again, amusement and possibly embarrassment in the sound. "Lie around like this in full cuddle mode?"

"Well, yeah. Do you? It looks... different. Sort of unexpected."

"I'm sure it does." Jake could feel Tor suppressing more laughter. "Not exactly what you expect from a couple of middle-aged cowboys, huh?"

"Something like that," Jacob allowed. "I mean, it's not bad, it's kind of nice, actually. Just different."

Tor nodded, his chin brushing the top of Jake's head. "Yeah, it's nice. And I don't know if I'd say we do this a lot... but sometimes, sure. Watching TV and stuff. You gotta remember, we got together when we were sharing a house with three other men, so we didn't really get in the habit. Wouldn't have been fair to make the guys we were living with uncomfortable. They had enough to deal with."

That seemed to close the subject and another long silence followed. Jake was fully awake by then and wondering if he should move when Tor cleared his throat. "So. Tressa seems nice," he said so casually that it was all Jake could do not to laugh. Sometimes Tor missed subtle by a mile and a quarter.

"She's all right," Jacob said, sounding disgusted. "She used to be really cool. We hung out all the time, played soccer and video games... just stuff. Now she's all weird and girly and she never stops talking about Bill Donnelly."

"Ah. He's a jerk?"

"He's sixteen and has a car," Jacob said, like that was all the explanation needed. And it was, Jake supposed.

"Oh." Tor agreed, apparently. "Nice car?"

"Nah, he bought it from his grandmother." Jacob seemed to settle after that, satisfied that Bill Donnelly's car wasn't really that great. "Bill's okay, I guess," he added generously.

Jake felt Tor nod again, and once more silence fell over them, for what could have been five minutes or twenty. Twice Jake decided to move, to 'wake up' and go get ready for bed, but he was too comfortable to really make the effort.

"Uncle Tor?" Jacob suddenly asked, his voice both quiet and tense.

"Yeah, kid."

"I hate the man who killed my mom."

Tor sighed. "I know, Jacob. He probably hates himself just as much. Hopefully you'll both be able to let go of that, eventually."

"I don't think so," Jacob whispered, his voice rough. "It's not fair."

Jake moved slightly, more to warn Tor that he was awake than anything else. He didn't want Tor to deal with this on his own, but was unsure how to join the conversation at this point. As he shifted, Tor squeezed his arm and then rubbed the spot in acknowledgment. At least, Jake hoped that was what it was.

"Nope, it's not," Tor said to Jacob. "Ain't fair at all. No one should lose anybody like this, especially not their mother. But you know in your head that it was an accident--your heart's just going to take some time to figure that out. It's okay to be angry, kid. Be mad, be furious and upset, be sad. Just don't let the anger be stronger than loving your memories of your mom."

Jake listened to Jacob breathe for a moment, a long shaky breath that he let out slowly. He found himself wishing that Jacob would just let it go, start to let out the pain, but the boy wasn't ready for that, apparently, or at least wasn't willing to start crying in front of an audience. Jake heard him stand up, the springs in the chair protesting for a moment.

"Yeah. Okay," Jacob said, his tone dismissing the topic. "I'm going to get a drink of water and go to bed. You really should take Uncle Jake to your room, though. That couch is lumpy."

"I'll do that, kid." Tor took a deep breath, his chest pushing Jake up. "Try to sleep, yeah? And if you need to talk, you know where we are."

"Okay, thanks."

"I mean it, Jacob--you need to talk, we'll listen. Doesn't matter what time of the night."

There was a pause, and then the sound of steps on the carpet, sneakers not quite lifted high enough. "Thank you," Jacob said, his voice tired. "Good night, Uncle Tor."

"Night, kid."

Jake waited until he was sure Jacob was gone before sitting up. His back ached, and he rubbed at it with one hand, the other going up to smooth his hair. "Hey."

Tor's hand joined his own, rubbing at his lower back with soothing strokes. "Hey. How much did you hear?"

"Most, I think." Jake groaned and turned, letting Tor get a better angle. "God, I'm getting old. That kid's in a world of hurt."

"Yep."

Jake shifted around, stretching. He really should have known better than to sleep like that, he figured. He was far too old for anything but a bed. "We have to help him, you know."

"Of course."

"It would be easier if he decided on his own to come with us," Jake said, thinking out loud. Not that it would change any practical arrangements, but it would be a world easier for Jacob if he saw that going to live with them was best for all of them, given the situation.

"Yeah. Maybe he will." Tor swung around and sat up next to him. "Have you had time to think at all?"

Jake nodded. "Yeah, about a couple of things. I called Jacob's school; he's got another three weeks of classes. Think I better stay here. Cath'll have to get back to work, and we'll need time to sort out 'Lissa's things."

Tor nodded slowly. "Got hay coming in."

"Yeah. You'll have to hire on more hands, no way around it."

"Going to be strapped this summer, then. Lots of money going out." Tor was just stating facts, his tone easy and his voice smooth.

Jake nodded; it was true, this was going to be a lean year and they could ill afford for him to be off the ranch for a month. There wasn't any help for it, though, and Jake was pretty sure they'd find a way around it. They had to.

"I'm going to call that lawyer tomorrow, too," Jake added. "My blood relatives aren't going to be a help. Best head that off as best we can, get the paperwork started."

Tor nodded again and suddenly touched Jake's jaw, his hand gentle. The gesture was tender and wildly out of character, but Jake found himself nuzzling Tor's fingers, needing it. Needing the loving.

"Your kin might raise a fuss, but your family will help," Tor said softly. "Count on it."

Jake knew he could.

Chapter Ten

The next two days were a bit of a blur for Jake. He talked to a lawyer and managed to stay focused long enough to make sure that the paperwork was going to get started and that everything was on track. Outside of someone filing to contest the custody arrangement, the process would go quietly and smoothly, but it would take months.

His big question; whether he and Tor would be able to take Jacob home to Arkansas, was addressed early in the conversation. Then he kind of tuned out, his mind racing ahead to which room they could give him, what needed to be done about transferring schools, who they had to talk to, and all kinds of things that he really didn't have any control over.

Jake's sense of control seemed to have utterly vanished. He had no power over anything anymore, it felt like. He didn't know what was going to happen with Jacob, with 'Lissa's home and belongings, with money… he didn't even know what was going to happen to 'Lissa's remains. Every time he asked a question and got an answer, the answer slid through him, over him, and he found himself wanting to ask again a few hours later.

He dragged Tor into their borrowed bedroom at one point, shaking in confusion and fear of everything he didn't understand. He needed something solid to hang onto, something and someone he knew he could count on. Tor held him and whispered promises that everything was going to work out, that they had answers that would make sense when Jake had a chance to deal with them.

"You're just not ready yet, not ready to think clearly, and that's okay," Tor told him. "I'm doing it for you, Jake. It'll be okay, I promise. Let me take care of it for now. Let go."

Jake nodded because he didn't really have any choice. Burrowing into Tor's arms he closed his eyes and tried to breathe. "It's horrible," he whispered. "Never felt like this. Not even when we had our trouble."

Tor kissed him and sighed softly. "I know."

Jacob was floating around the house, his eyes distant. Jake and Tor both tried to talk to him about moving, but after he retreated to his room again they let it rest. Cath said that she'd try to talk to him, but the closed door kept them from him and the three of them agreed to just let it go until after the funeral, at least.

The phone stopped ringing off the hook but every time it *did* ring Jake wound up with a tension knot in his gut, worried that someone had managed to reach James. He didn't really want to think that he was the sort of man to deny a brother the chance to say goodbye to a sister, but Jake had no doubt that any sign of James would spell trouble for them and Jacob. By the morning of the funeral, however, there had been no word from James, and Jake forced himself to put his brother from his mind.

It occurred to him that the amount of things he was deliberately not thinking about was about the same size as the pile of things he actually had to deal with as soon as he could get his brain to function properly again. The problems weren't going to go anywhere, and by not thinking about them he was simply pushing things aside, letting them fester. But he couldn't seem to make himself deal with them. Not yet.

The funeral itself was the easiest part, in a way. He didn't have to do anything other than sit and listen and hold onto Tor's hand on his right and Cath's on his left. He didn't have to talk or share or think. He stared blankly ahead of him, his eyes on a framed photo of 'Lissa, seeing only the months and years ahead of him as he tried to raise her son up to be a good man.

He looked away to glance at Tor when the fingers around his squeezed harder. He assumed someone had said something especially poignant, but didn't know for sure; he wasn't listening. He only knew that the smell of the flowers was getting cloying and that the sunlight streaming in a side window did nothing to illuminate and only served to show off the dust motes floating through the air.

When the hymns were done and everyone who was supposed to say something had done so, Tor left him to help two cousins, a neighbor, and two people Jake didn't recognize carry the coffin out to the waiting hearse. Jake held onto Cath's hand and followed, Jacob on her other side, and they left.

Jacob didn't cry. Cath did.

They got into the funeral home's sedan and followed 'Lissa to the place where she would be buried, none of them talking, Cath still sobbing quietly. Jake grabbed hold of Tor's hand again as soon as he could, and they stood at the head of her grave, listening to the minister commit her to the earth. When he was supposed to, he lifted a spade full of dirt and watched it cascade onto the polished, gleaming wood of her casket, the sound of each grain hitting it like a hollow thump in his ears.

Then there were people, milling about, walking carefully up to him and Cath and Jacob, offering words and hands and more than a few hugs. Jake did what was expected, murmuring soft words again and again, until it felt like a constant stream of nothing, his numbness made vocal.

At last, the words were done, the people were leaving, and the minister was shaking Jake's hand. Tor led him away with a hand at the small of Jake's back, and when they were in another car, just the two of them, Jake broke down and clung to his man as he finally started to say goodbye to his sister.

Chapter Eleven

The house was full of people. There were groups gathered in the kitchen, in the living room, out on the lawn. Jake had expected it, even welcomed it. It meant he could sort of float, say a few words to people, and move on. He didn't have to maintain an entire conversation with anyone.

He'd gone right to the bathroom when he and Tor had arrived, spending a few moments with a cold washcloth so he didn't look quite so trashed. He studied himself in the mirror, told himself he needed sleep, and realized with a shock that he felt a little calmer, a little more like he'd survive the day. Possibly.

Cath was in the kitchen talking to a group of women whom Jake assumed were 'Lissa's friends. He caught her eye long enough to make sure that she was okay, and moved onto the living room, looking for Tor. Jacob was in there, sitting on the couch and talking to a few adults who looked uncomfortable, as if they were just as clueless about what to say to the boy as Jake was. Maybe more.

Tor wasn't there, though, so Jake paused only long enough to accept condolences from people who offered them and to nod to David, who was keeping a careful eye on his mother. Jess was talking quietly to a man Jake vaguely remembered from the distant past, and otherwise ignoring Jake and Tor. She'd spoken to Cath at the graveyard, but she'd passed him right by.

Thank God for small mercies, he thought.

Outside, Tor was sitting on the front step, talking on the phone and wearing the half smile he seemed to save up for his niece. "Gotta go," he said, looking up Jake. "I'll call you in a couple of days." He paused and nodded. "I'll tell him. Hug your momma for us. Bye."

Jake sat down next to him and leaned in a little. "How're they?" he asked.

"Good. Said to give you their love and tell you they'd be in touch real soon. If there's anything they can do..."

Jake nodded. "Thanks."

Tor slipped his arm around Jake's waist. "How are you doing?"

"Better." Jake inclined his head. "Thanks," he said again. "Sorry I--"

"Nothing to be sorry about."

There wasn't, and Jake knew it. "Okay."

They sat there for a few minutes, listening to the hum of voices from the yard and through the open windows next to them. There was a round of laughter and Jake found himself smiling a tiny bit; it had been days since he'd heard anything like that. A car pulled in and a few more people arrived, nodding to him and Tor before being joined by a man from the lawn.

Jake closed his eyes and rested his head on Tor's shoulder; was just opening his mouth to say he was feeling tired and like he could sleep for a year, when there was a shout from inside the house.

"You nasty old bitch!"

Jake sat bolt upright and Tor was already on his way in, throwing open the screen door just as Jacob said it again.

"You bitch! How dare you say anything about them? How dare you say anything at all? My *mom* chose them, you old cow, and you have no right!"

Jake pushed past Tor and looked around the room. Stunned faces looked at Jacob, who was standing in the middle of the room, his good hand clenched into a fist. Jess was on the couch, her mouth open as she stared at Jacob.

"David, take her out of here," Jake said quietly. "You're not welcome here, Jess. Go poison someone else."

Jacob turned and fled, stomping off to his room. The slam of the door shook the walls.

Jess stood up, looking at the people watching her. "If you think for one moment--"

"Get out." Jake took a step forward. "You have no say. Melissa made plans for her son, and everyone is going to honor her wishes. Period. You are an evil, nasty old woman, and I won't permit you to--"

"Jake." Tor's hand landed on his shoulder. "Go see to Jacob. I'll deal with this."

Jake didn't even look back as he left the room. He had no intention of seeing any of those people ever again. He was about one word from just taking Jacob and heading to Arkansas, the law and school and everything else be damned.

At Jacob's door he knocked once and opened it, not willing to be blocked out this time. There was too much pain and upset, and he wasn't going to take silence for an answer, not when he needed to see Jacob's eyes. He slipped into the room and leaned back on the closed door, waiting.

"She's evil," Jacob said, staring the floor. He was sitting on the edge of his bed, rocking back and forth, cradling his cast.

"She's... ignorant," Jake said. He sighed and added, "And a mean old bitch."

"You going to make me apologize?" Jacob asked dully.

"I probably should, but no. I told her to get out."

Jacob looked up at him, his eyes damp with angry tears. "She said she was going to take me!"

"Not going to happen," Jake said with every ounce of conviction he had.

"She said that Aunt Cath would need help raising me and she was going to take me. That she was sure Uncle James would help, too. I said I was going where my mom wanted, and that you and Tor would do fine by me. She said--" He stopped suddenly and threw himself back on the bed.

"I can imagine." Jake walked to him and sank down on his heels, kneeling by the bed. "Forget her, Jacob," he pleaded. He wanted to ask about Jacob and Arkansas, and if that meant he was willing to come with him and Tor, but he didn't know if that would add to the stress or not. He left it alone and reached out, put his hand on Jacob's shoulder and gave it a squeeze. "I won't let her say anything more to you."

Jacob nodded and closed his eyes tight, sniffling a little bit. He was trembling under Jake's hand, obviously trying to keep himself together; anger and hurt radiated from him and he opened his eyes, looking up at the ceiling.

"Can I have a horse?" he asked, tears starting to flow, running down the side of his face and into his ear.

"After you learn to take care of one," Jake said, his voice suddenly tight. The weight on his chest was back.

"Okay." Jacob shook and Jake moved to the bed, gathering the boy up in his arms, his own tears forcing their way out again. "God, I miss her," Jacob gasped, sobs wracking him.

"I know." Jake held on, let Jacob cry in his arms until they were both shaking with it. His face was wet, his own tears going almost unnoticed as Jacob finally let go and cried for his mother, and for himself.

It was a start, and an end, and Jake hoped he had the strength to carry them both through to the other side.

The Dark

Chapter Twelve

There wasn't any light in the room when Jake woke up, just a lighter shade of black around the window to let him know that night had fallen. He was stiff and sore, his eyes gritty in the aftermath of his sorrow, and his arm was asleep where Jacob lay across it. It took a moment for Jake to figure out what had woken him up, other than the discomfort of sleeping with his body curled protectively around Jacob's.

A sound from the hallway came, a soft murmur of voices and quiet steps which reminded him of the guests in 'Lissa's home. Most would be long gone, even those who hadn't fled in the wake of the scene with Jess, and Jake assumed that only Tor and Cath and a very few others still remained.

Carefully, slowly, he untangled himself from Jacob and pulled a blanket over his nephew's sleeping body, ignoring the way the nerves in his arm zinged as circulation was restored. Numb to the point of calmness, he kissed Jacob's forehead and made his way to the door, braced for the light in the rest of the house after the dark of the room.

Squinting, he shut Jacob's door behind him and turned to the living room, only to bump right into Tor. "Hey," he said softly, automatically, wrapping his arms around Tor and leaning into his body, soaking up the warmth.

"Hey, you," Tor whispered. "Okay?"

"Okay. Everyone gone?"

"Just about. Hungry?" Tor's hand rubbed on Jake's back, slow and soothing.

Jake shook his head. "What time is it?"

"About nine. Do you think he'll sleep through the night?"

"No idea," Jake said with a sigh. "He's exhausted, though. Cried for a long time."

Tor nodded. "You?"

"Yeah." Jake sighed again and moved a little closer to Tor, his head resting on Tor's shoulder. "Can we...? Do you think...?"

Wordlessly, Tor moved them down the hall and into their borrowed bedroom.

"We should help clean up," Jake protested weakly, not in the least bit interested in being anywhere other than where he was going. Still, though. He had to offer, even had to go out in the kitchen and help if that's what was necessary.

"We will. Later." Tor's voice was low and steady, and every move he made only put them closer to the bed.

"I just..." Jake paused and tried to find a few words to describe what he was feeling, what he needed.

"I know," Tor told him, easing them both down onto the bed. "You're tired, you're sad, and you just need to forget for a little while. I know."

"Do you?" Jake asked, rolling away only far enough to unbutton his shirt and peel it off. "Need to forget?"

"Some things." Tor kissed him, helped with Jake's shirt, and then tugged his own off. "But mostly I just hate the thought of leaving. Leaving you here, hurting."

Jake nodded. "I'm not thinking about that yet." He undid his trousers and sat up, pushing them off awkwardly.

"Don't," Tor told him, his hands skimming over Jake's body. "Waste of time, thinking about it. Talking about it."

Jake nodded, not really able to do anything else. He felt like he was under a mountain of blankets, everything distant and unable to reach him. Even Tor's touch felt muted, like it was a memory already and not an experience. "Be here," he whispered. "I need you to be here. Now."

"I've got you," Tor told him, sounding sure and strong and dependable. "I'll take care of you, Jake."

"You always do." Jake closed his eyes and opened his mouth, taking Tor's kisses and his words, sure that Tor would do exactly as he promised. With mouth and hands and words, Tor took charge and made Jake forget for a while, made anything not there in the room with them fade away until Jake thought he himself would float away and not come back. He was anchored, though, tied to Tor in an infinite number of ways, and when Tor finally slid into his body, Jake was right there with him, holding onto life and hope and joy.

Chapter Thirteen

Jake was alone in the bed when he woke up, but by the way the light was hitting the walls from the window, he was sure it was still early morning. He couldn't hear anyone moving around in the house, but long experience told him Tor would be up and sitting somewhere with a cup of coffee. The thought of coffee was enough to get him mobile; the promise of a few quiet moments with Tor was an added blessing.

Dressed, but promising himself a shower before too long, he made his way to the kitchen and ran his hand over Tor's shoulders as he passed him. Tor was sitting at the table, his mug in front of him as he read the morning paper.

"You're up early," Jake said as he poured his own coffee.

"Fell asleep early." Tor smiled at him as Jake joined him at the table. "We were out by ten, you know."

"Really?" Jake's concept of time had gotten a little shaky over the past few days. "God, poor Cath. We should have helped her clean up."

Tor nodded as he sipped his coffee. "She left some of it," he said, nodding to the dishwasher. "I emptied it and ran another load. We'll vacuum and stuff later."

Jake didn't find that eased his conscience much, but it would have to do. "Is she still in bed?" he asked.

Tor nodded. "Jacob's still out, too. He's exhausted."

"Yeah." Jake got up and went to the counter, bringing the pad by the phone back with him, along with a pen. "Help me out here," he said, sitting down and starting a list. "I have to find out when Jacob has to get back to the doctor about his arm." He wrote 'Doctor/Jacob' down and looked at Tor.

"Rent on this place," Tor said, leaning back in his chair.

"We have to call the owner and find out how long it's paid up, how much notice they need."

Jake wrote it down, nodding. "Have to go over 'Lissa's will, or talk to the lawyer again about that. Figure out what to sell, and how." He took notes, reaching for the phone book on the edge of the table. "We should make a list of anything big we might be able to use--or Cath--and what Jacob might like to have with him. Rent a truck."

Tor shook his head. "I'll bring mine, and a trailer if it comes to that. Jacob's bed, desk... whatever."

"Yeah, okay. And we'll have to see if we can refund the open-ended ticket for the airline--we'll be driving back with you. Lost cause, most likely." Jake added a couple more things to the list, about Jacob's medical and school records and settling the bank accounts. "Which room should we give Jacob?"

"We can figure that out after I get home and take a look. The one at the end of the hall is the biggest, but--"

"We just painted it for our sisters to use and it's girly. Right."

Tor grinned. "It'll keep him busy if we make him paint it again."

Jake snorted. "He'll be busy enough in the barn, learning to take care of the horses."

"True enough," Tor said easily, standing up. "Breakfast?"

Jake smiled. "Yeah, thanks. I think Cath and I'll spend a good part of the day starting to go through the house. Maybe get Jacob to help out, if he wants to. He might have opinions we should take into account."

Tor got out the eggs. "Yeah," he agreed, rummaging for a mixing bowl. "I'll do what I can on the phone, too." He paused. "I'm heading back tomorrow, cowboy," he said softly.

Jake set the pen down and sighed. "I know. I'm trying not to think about it."

Tor came back to the table and kissed him. "It'll be okay," he said. "We'll all be okay."

"Eventually. I just... I don't like being without you." Jake felt like a fool saying it, but it was true.

"I know," Tor whispered, kissing him again. "We have the phone, though. And I'll be back as often as I can swing it. Maybe you and Jacob can come for a weekend before school lets out."

Jake nodded, although he doubted it, given there were only three weeks left of school. "And there's today."

"And tonight."

A cough from the door startled them both into jumping and Cath smiled at them. "So, I'm thinking it might be a good idea for me to take Jacob out to the movies tonight. Or dinner. Or anywhere where you two aren't saying goodbye."

"Sounds like a plan," Tor said before Jake could protest. "Want some eggs for breakfast?"

"Uh-huh. And then you can make another pot of coffee, Romeo."

Jake snickered and went back to planning their day, ducking to avoid the whap on the head Tor aimed at him.

He felt almost normal for the first time in nearly a week.

Chapter Fourteen

The day seemed to pass both quickly and impossibly slowly by turns.

Doing a tour of the house with Cath at his side, Jake made notes about which pieces of furniture to move and which to donate or sell, then enlisted Jacob's reluctant help to pick a tentative date for a yard sale. He told himself that he wasn't trying to be deliberately cruel and that involving Jacob in the inevitable process was going to give Jacob a sense of power and control in the long run, but it still felt shitty.

Jacob, however, seemed to share his own odd feeling of energy in the aftermath of the funeral. He talked more, stacked books and things he didn't want to take with him, and measured his bedroom furniture for Tor. Jake was well aware that it was likely fleeting; he hoped that Jacob knew it, too, and wouldn't be devastated when he was once more feeling weak and lost.

"Time will tell," Tor whispered as they passed in the hall around noon. The sentiment seemed to come out of nowhere, but it made Jake smile to know that they were so in tune with each other, sharing the train of thought.

In the afternoon Jake spent some time on the phone when he could pry it away from Jacob, who had taken up residence on the couch, his bad arm propped on a pillow and his good hand rapidly dialing friend after friend and touching base with them in quick succession.

That, too, was a good sign, Jake knew, and he would have happily let Jacob go with it if he didn't need to be doing, moving, calling, dealing with things himself. When Cath pointed out that he could use her cell phone he felt himself start to blush, embarrassed that the thought hadn't even occurred to him. Wordlessly, he handed the phone back to Jacob, got a half smile in reply, and took Cath's cell to the kitchen with him.

The landlady, who had heard what had happened through the paper and had not called out of respect, was more than pleasant. She expressed her sympathies, agreed that it would be best for Jacob to stay where he was for the remainder of the school year, and told Jake that there wouldn't be any need to change the lease.

"I can put your name on it and have you sign until the end of May, Mr. Taggart, that won't be any trouble, but I'm fine with leaving it as is. It's only a few weeks, after all, and given the circumstances..." She trailed off and then added, "Ms. Taggart's lease was due to be renewed in October, but it's void and you don't have to worry about it. Just let me know when I can show the house--after you've moved out, even. Don't you worry about a thing dealing with that, you understand?"

"It'll be before the end of the month," Jake assured her. "I expect we'll stay through the weekend after school lets out, so he can see his friends for a bit, but then we'll be off. I can't be away from home too long past that."

She made more sympathetic noises and that was one more thing crossed off his list.

By the end of the afternoon he'd paced and made calls and drafted yet more lists. Tor and Cath sat in the kitchen and made lists of their own, and at some point Cath got out 'Lissa's jewelry box and went through it, setting aside the very few pieces that had special significance.

"You might as well keep it all," Jake said, sitting down. "Not like we'll have much call for any of it."

She smiled and shook her head. "I'll take care of it, but some day Jacob might want to give some of it to his wife. This ring," she said, picking up an opal set in silver, "is worth less than seventy dollars. But it's the first thing 'Lissa ever bought herself just because it was beautiful and she wanted it. These earrings were a gift from a man she loved very much."

She pointed to a pair of small gold cross posts and dropped her voice. "Not his father. After that."

Jake raised his eyebrow and Cath smiled. "I liked him."

"What happened?" Tor asked, undisguised curiosity in his voice.

"He moved out of state--well, was transferred. 'Lissa wasn't cut out to be an army wife. But she loved him anyway, and he loved her. I'm actually kind of surprised he wasn't there yesterday."

"Maybe he didn't know," Jake suggested.

Cath shook her head and put the earrings next to the opal. "I called him myself. He's in California. Doesn't matter. Point is, I'll take care of it, perhaps even use some of this... but it's all Jacob's when he wants it."

Jake could only nod. It made sense, and there really wasn't anything more to say about it.

In the late afternoon he found himself wandering aimlessly around the house like a restless cat. Tor was watching him, and every once in a while Jake caught him smiling a little, looking amused and a little exasperated. Finally, Tor got up and stood in front of him and Jake absently tried to step around him. Tor moved with him, blocking the way. Jake apologized and stepped to the other side. Tor moved with him again, starting to grin.

"Am I missing something here?" Jake said, almost stumbling in his effort not to run Tor down.

"Yep." Tor's grin grew. "I'm hungry."

Jake took a moment to switch mental gears and nodded slowly. "Pizza?"

Tor beamed at him and shook his head.

"That's our cue, kiddo," Cath told Jacob with a wink. "Come on. Ribs, sugar, and then a movie." She scooped up her keys even as Jacob was pointing to his cast and insisting that ribs were a bad idea, and then they were gone out the front door and Jake was left feeling more embarrassed than he'd been since the last time Tor had been so obvious in mixed company.

"Do you have to do that?" Jake asked, fighting off the urge

to smile as his blush began to fade.

"Nope," Tor said easily. "But it's fun."

Jake shook his head to himself and asked, "Any interest at all in pizza?"

To his mild surprise, Tor nodded. "I think there's one in the freezer. How about you get that going? I'm going to take a fast shower."

"All right," Jake agreed, letting Tor move past him and down the hall. Amused and a little confused by Tor's change-able notions, Jake went into the kitchen and turned on the oven. He added cheese and a few more mushrooms to the mostly unremarkable pizza and waited for the timer to tell him the oven was preheated. When the sharp beep roused him, he realized he'd been staring into space thinking about Tor's ass, weighing its merits against Tor's mouth.

"Got it bad," he said under his breath as he put the pizza in to heat.

Tor arrived in the kitchen just as Jake was getting plates out and watching the timer again, peeking in to check the browning of the cheese.

"Almost done," Jake said, not looking up, just aware that Tor was there. "Few more seconds. Your showers are getting longer and longer, you know."

Tor snorted. "Says the man who routinely leaves me with-out hot water."

"I figure if you want a long shower you can haul your butt out of bed and join me," Jake said with a grin. "But we should take a look at a bigger water heater, what with Jacob and all." He turned off the oven and the timer just before it could beep at him again, and turned to grab a couple of pot-holders off the counter. "Nice dinner attire, sir," he said, not really object-ing to the towel clinging to Tor's hips.

Tor shrugged and winked at him, but didn't say anything at all. His hair was damp and a little curly over his forehead, and there were still occasional drops of water splashing onto his skin; he was obviously turned on as well, his erection nicely distorting the towel. All in all, it was rather distracting.

Jake dished out the pizza slices and graciously let Tor walk in front of him into the living room where they both sat on the couch, probably closer to each other than was absolutely necessary for optimum TV viewing. Jake didn't care at all.

They flipped through a few channels as they ate, but Jake spent more time looking at Tor than he did watching the evening news. Tor knew it, meeting Jake's gaze now and then and smiling, his eyes frank with invitation. But that was all he did, and it confused Jake. Tor was still hard, his legs splayed and the towel all but falling off, but he didn't actively do anything at all.

Jake looked at him more and more frequently as they finished eating, waiting. Tor's skin was starting to flush, his breathing had picked up, and as far as Jake could tell from years of reading the signs, Tor was more than ready to move on. And yet, he didn't so much as reach out for Jake or even offer a kiss.

Slowly, because by that point he was more than a little excited himself, Jake moved their plates to the coffee table and sat back, leaning against Tor's side. "Hey," he said softly, turning his head to look at Tor's face.

"Hey, yourself." Tor winked at him, and Jake leaned closer, fitting his mouth over Tor's.

The kiss was intense and deep, Tor falling into it with a quick hunger that made Jake that much harder, but it was clear from the first that Jake was in charge of it. He thought about that as he plunged his tongue deeper, forcing Tor's mouth to open wider. It wasn't like Tor to not even play at taking control; he wasn't usually so passive.

As soon as the thought occurred, Jake knew what was going on. Tor wanted him in charge, wanted to be taken care of. He was offering himself up, with a great deal of anticipation, apparently, to be… manhandled. Dominated. Controlled. Possibly even sweetly loved, although Jake doubted it, given the way Tor's body was in overdrive and his lust was leaking out around the edges.

Jake didn't even have to think about the last week, about how well Tor had cared for him and protected him, to know that if Tor wanted it that way, he could have it. Tor could pretty much always have Jake any way he wanted; Jake wouldn't ever turn down something Tor needed. Tor needed Jake to be boss, so Jake would. The obvious perks were nothing to give up, either.

"Bed," Jake said, standing up and pulling Tor along with him by the hand. "Now."

"Uh-huh."

Jake dragged Tor down the hall and more or less shoved him onto the bed before falling mostly on top of him and ripping the towel away. "This what you want?" he asked, biting down on Tor's neck and starting to work the skin there. "Want me to be in charge? Take what I want?"

Tor gasped and arched his back off the bed. "What you want, I give."

"Goes both ways."

"I know."

Jake nodded and buried his head in Tor's neck, teeth marking him. He was braced on one arm, his other hand raking over Tor's chest and belly and leaving score marks before wrapping around Tor's cock. He played with Tor's Prince Albert piercing with his thumb, stroking and tugging aggressively. "Give and take. Right now I want to give it to you. Take you. Shove my dick in your ass and give you--"

"Oh, fuck!" Tor bucked against him and grunted, his cock swelling even harder.

Jake grabbed for Tor's balls fast, then changed his mind and squeezed just under the head of Tor's cock. "Tor?" he said as they both panted. "Ask you something?"

"What?" Tor sounded like he was concentrating very, very hard on something.

"How long have we been together?"

"Uh. About six years? I think. God, Jake."

"Right. Six years. So how come I didn't know that filthy talking like that would make you come before I'm ready?"

Tor shook his head. "Don't know. Never tried it before, have you? Not like it's my fault."

Jake carefully let go of Tor and rolled away to start getting undressed. "Not saying it's anyone's fault--just a little surprised that there's still stuff we don't know. That's not a bad thing." He tossed his shirt onto the floor and undid his jeans. "So, what would happen if I started talking about pushing you into walls and how I want to pound into you and fuck you raw? How I'd like to think about you having trouble sitting on that plane tomorrow? How I sometimes wonder if I could fuck you into coming and then jerk off on your face, coat you in--"

Tor had rolled over, his knees spread wide and his ass high.

"Jesus," Jake croaked, shoving his jeans to his knees and climbing onto the bed between Tor's feet. "Jesus Christ."

"Please," Tor whimpered, lifting his ass.

Stunned, and harder than he knew he'd been in a while, Jake nodded and moved closer, taking his prick in his hand and guiding it to Tor's ass. "Shit! Lube." He looked around, his heart starting to thunder harder and faster.

"I left it in the bathroom," Tor said in a rush. "Just do it, now." He sounded like waiting was agony, his voice harsh and broken.

"In the bathroom?" Jake poked a finger into Tor's hole and found him wet and open. "Oh, you slut," he breathed. "My slut. Ready and wanting and now you're going to just offer up your ass to me."

Tor nodded frantically. "You."

"Me. Want it now?" Jake didn't think he'd be able to hold off for more than a moment or two in any case, but he was starting to see the upside of both teasing Tor and of this new kink to explore. "Want my cock in you so deep you'll be able to taste it? Want to feel me splitting you? How about the way I'll pound against you with this pretty bit of metal?" He rubbed his own piercing around the slick opening.

"Yes!" Tor yelled, and shoved back, impaling himself.

Jake didn't waste time being startled, just grabbed Tor's hips and pulled him back even faster, ramming into him and starting to fuck him in hard, rapid thrusts.

It was rough and dirty, and Jake couldn't form the words to tell Tor everything he wanted to do. Part of it was that he had to actually think to be as filthy as Tor seemed to like, but mostly it was because talking required breath he needed for other things, like fucking. He did manage to get out a few words about how tight Tor felt, and how he wanted to do it dry some time, just bend Tor over the table or couch and ride him until they were both aching, and then Tor was damn near screaming as he came on the bed.

Jake pulled out and flipped Tor over onto his back, watching as Tor kept coming, his hand pulling the last of it out in a slick puddle spreading over his belly, streaks of come sliding down his side like stripes. "Yeah, like that," Jake said, reaching for his own cock.

"Up. Please," Tor said, tugging on Jake's thigh, then higher to grab at his hips.

Jake let him pull and moved awkwardly up the bed, stopping to kick his jeans the rest of the way off so he could straddle Tor's chest as he pulled his dick. He watched Tor's face, his eyes, and his sweat-slicked curls, and then the pretty, pretty mouth. "Oh, God," he whispered, balls pulling up tight. He shoved two fingers into Tor's mouth and hissed when Tor sucked hard. "Coming. Going to fucking come on your face."

Tor sucked again and closed his eyes, and Jake's orgasm slammed into him, rocking him and taking his breath like being kicked by a horse. He cried out, squeezed his cock, and arched, watching as his spunk made tracks in Tor's hair, over his face, and splashed over his own fingers. Tor started licking it off, letting it drip from Jake's hand down into his mouth, and Jake shot again, the last of it coating Tor's jaw.

It was almost half an hour before either of them spoke; Jake had actually fallen asleep almost immediately, curled possessively around Tor's body.

"That was intense," Tor said mildly.

"Uh-huh."

"I liked it."

"You don't say."

"You liked it."

"Uh-huh."

"So..."

"So?"

"Think maybe we can do that again?"

Jake realized he was grinning. "Oh, yeah. I think so."

Tor kissed him and gave him a shove. "Good. Shower time, cowboy. They'll be back soon."

Jake nodded. "Think we have enough time to conserve some hot water?"

Tor shrugged. "I think they'll live, either way. Come on, get wet with me. I'll even let you wash my hair, seeing as how you got it all dirty again."

Jake laughed and rolled off the bed. "Bitch, bitch, bitch."

"It's what I do best."

"No," Jake said softly, suddenly unwilling to let Tor leave at all, let alone in less than twelve hours. "It's not."

Tor didn't say anything, just pulled him close and held him for a long time before they went to shower.

***

At the airport they waited outside the security area as long as they could justify it, but when Tor started checking his watch every thirty seconds Jake knew it was time to send him off. He personally didn't object to Tor missing his flight, but he didn't really want to deal with Elias about it, especially over the phone.

"Take care of my horse," Jake said, avoiding Tor's eyes. "And Barkley."

"You take care of you," Tor said softly.

Jake nodded and sighed. "Yeah." He stepped closer to Tor and rested one hand on Tor's arm. "I'll talk to you--"

"Day after tomorrow." Tor moved quickly and kissed Jake's mouth hard, pulling back almost immediately.

"Right." Jake squeezed Tor's arm and let him go. "Day after tomorrow."

Tor picked up his bag and backed away, toward the line for security. "Hey, Jake?" he called when he was a few feet away.

Jake waited as a woman moved between them, blocking

his view for a moment. "Yeah?"

"Take care of our boy."

Jake swallowed and nodded sharply. "You know I will."

"I do," Tor said, turning away and walking faster. "I know you will."

Chapter Fifteen

On Monday morning Cath left early to go to her apartment and then to work, and Jacob roused himself with enough time to shower and make his lunch for school.

"I can do that for you," Jake said, leaning on the kitchen counter and sipping his coffee.

"I know," Jacob said, carefully constructing a sandwich with his good hand. "But I can do it, too."

Jake nodded and gave him an apple, then stood in the doorway and watched as Jacob set off to walk to school. He wasn't sure how he felt about Jacob leaving. Mostly he was pleased Jacob felt up to it, but a small part of him wanted to keep him home, with him.

He finished his cup of coffee and then had another, wandering absently around the house. He had a vague idea he should be doing something, getting something accomplished, but he had no idea what that would be. It felt very wrong to start boxing things up; too soon. He and Jacob had to stay there a while, and he doubted that living in an empty shell of a home would do either of them any good.

It was less than a week since 'Lissa had died. It wasn't time yet to strip the house of her touch, and it was far too soon to make Jacob start his goodbyes.

He walked around in the silence and then he went outside to ramble there. He was more comfortable out of doors anyway, and even if there weren't horses to feed or cattle to tend to, he could at the very least weed the garden and mow the lawn.

By noon he was done and staring blankly into the refrigerator looking for lunch.

When Jacob came home there was a bit of relief; conversation with his nephew was far preferable to listening to the radio and resisting the urge to do foolish things like take apart the stove to scrub it down.

"School okay?" Jake asked, once more leaning on the counter and watching Jacob build a sandwich.

"Boring. Everyone kept looking at me, you know? No one knew what to say." He moved to the table and shrugged. "We got any milk?"

Jake nodded and got two glasses down from the cupboard. "It'll get better," he said, pouring them both a drink. "They'll relax."

"I guess." Jacob picked up his sandwich awkwardly with his good hand. "Can I go to soccer practice?"

"If you want. They won't let you on the field, you know."

"I know." He shrugged again, the tomato in his sandwich sliding out a little. "Just want to go."

"What time does it start?" Not that it mattered to Jake; he had nowhere to be.

"Six," Jacob said, working the tomato back where it belonged. "I hate this damn thing," he added with a growl, lifting the cast.

"I bet."

"What did you do today?" Jacob asked, finally taking another bite from his sandwich. He looked up at Jake with apparent interest.

Jake drained his milk glass and turned it upside down in the sink to rinse it out. "Worked in the garden. Mowed the grass. Not much." The real question was, what was he going to find to do the next day, or the one after that. He stifled a sigh.

"Cool, that saves me part of the weekend," Jacob grinned. "I hate mowing the lawn."

Jake had to chuckle at that, if only because Jacob's grin was infectious and so damn good to see. "Right. You can vacuum instead."

"Hate that, too." Jacob shot Jake a hard glance. "You got lots of carpets at your place?"

"Hardwood. You get to sweep. And trust me, kid, we track dirt all over the place."

Jacob rolled his eyes. "Figures." He finished his snack and took his plate to the sink. "I'm going to go kick the ball around the backyard for a bit. Tressa might be over later, too."

Jake nodded and watched Jacob head to the door, wanting more than anything to hear Tor's voice.

Chapter Sixteen

As expected, the coach didn't let Jacob on the field, but he did let him sit with the rest of the team, which seemed to be enough for Jacob. Jake watched him for a few minutes, saw the kids gather around him for the first few moments, and relaxed. Jacob would be fine. He was showing off his cast and telling them how long he'd have to wear it, and when the coach produced a marker, Jacob let his teammates sign their names all over the blue fiberglass. To Jake's inexperienced eye it looked like any reluctance Jacob had was all for show, as he made sure everyone had a chance to sign or draw.

Jake wandered around the sidelines for a few minutes and figured out which side of the field was populated with parents of Jacob's teammates, then sat in the grass near them. He didn't impose himself, but then he hardly had to; he'd been sitting for less than a couple of minutes when delegations of mothers and fathers wandered over to him.

He introduced himself to the first few, even tried to remember a few names, but when they started pointing out which child on the soccer field belonged to which parent, Jake gave it up for a lost cause and contented himself with being polite and answering questions. After the first tentative questions about Jacob were answered, everyone seemed to relax a little; they were surely checking him out as a parental figure, but it was clear that all they wanted was to make sure Jacob was going to be okay.

The game wore on and the looks he got lessened, everyone's attention either on the field or on each other as they compared notes about the players, made plans for the weekend, or just gossiped. Jake kept his eyes on the game, his own attention split between Jacob on the bench and the action on the field, only listening with half an ear to the conversations going on around him.

"So, how are you holding up?" a new voice suddenly asked, and a man dropped down next to Jake.

Jake glanced over at Jacob and then to the man looking at him. "All right," he said. Then he added, actually thinking about it, "Better than I expected, actually. Last week was rough."

The man nodded sympathetically and offered his hand. "Tim MacPhee. I lost my wife about two years ago--don't re-member a thing about the week she died. Suddenly raising a kid alone... it ain't easy, Mr. Taggart. But you can do it."

Jake shook his hand and searched for an appropriate re-sponse. "Thanks," he finally said. "I'm sorry to hear about your wife. And it's Jake."

"Tim." Tim nodded and looked out at the game. "Our boy was eleven at the time. He took it hard, but seemed to come around pretty well. A few months later he had a down swing, got really angry. We're doing okay now, though."

"Yeah," Jake sighed. "I figure there's a lot of stuff yet to come. Between his mom passing and having to move out of state and being fourteen... it's going to be a trial."

Tim looked at him, his eyes searching. "Hard work."

"Work we want."

"Good enough. Got people around you to help?"

Jake nodded. "Got a ranch full of good people, a commu-nity. Got a sister, a sister-in-law, mess of ranch wives at-tached to helping out."

"You'll need them," Tim assured him, not unkindly. "Only advice I can give you is to hang on. Let people help, but don't let them push you into anything you think isn't right. That boy is going to be looking to you, even when he's fighting against you. If you believe, don't back down... you'll be ahead of the game."

Jake offered his hand again, grateful that this man, this stranger, had taken to the time to share a little with him. "Thank you," he said sincerely. "I think I needed that."

Tim smiled and stood up. "Not a problem. You need any more, just call. We're in the book." He smiled again and moved off, leaving Jake to watch the game and gather his thoughts.

Chapter Seventeen

For the rest of that week Jake carefully planned his time so he had something to do each day. He grocery shopped and tended to the yard, made appointments and visited Jacob's school and doctor, and went back to the lawyer's office a couple of times to sign papers and fill out yet more forms. He carefully figured out how many boxes he'd need to move Jacob and how many he'd need to pack things in for donations. He made signs for a yard sale and finally started packing a few things away, almost tentatively. There was still time left, but he told himself that waiting until the last minute was almost as bad as pushing too fast. He looked at the walls a lot.

He was bored to tears and trying his level best not to go stir-crazy. His body wasn't used to the physical inactivity and his mind wasn't used to having no one to organize. His skin missed the weather and his stomach missed actually working up an appetite. He missed Tor more than he'd thought possible, given that they'd been apart before.

They'd had a couple of quick phone calls, fitting their relationship in among talk about Jacob and the ranch and how Barkley was doing without Jake there to keep him in line. They'd never really been given to long goodbyes, and Jake found himself reaching for reasons to get off the phone because being on it with Tor, hearing his voice, was underlining how horrid it was to go bed alone each night and to wake up cold.

Tor seemed to know it, and he didn't seem to mind, but Jake was hardly surprised when the phone rang at almost eleven Friday night.

"If you didn't call by eleven-thirty," he said as he picked

up the phone, "I was going to call you."

"You didn't even know it was me," Tor replied, a hint of laughter in his voice.

"Of course, I knew it was you." The ring of the phone sounded happier when it was Tor.

"You're nuts."

"So you've said." Jake couldn't keep from grinning, something hard and tight in his belly letting go for the first time in what felt like forever.

"Kid asleep?"

Jake glanced down the hall from where he sat in the living room. "Yep," he said, leaning over to turn off the lamp. The TV was already off, Jake's interest in the movie he'd been staring at long gone. "Out like a light about an hour ago."

"He all right?"

"Yeah," Jake sighed, stretching out his legs. "He's okay. Been in school all week, gone to soccer three nights. Friends have been dropping by... he's busy, you know? Seems to be holding it together. Which isn't to say there ain't a storm coming--I just think he'll hold it off for as long as he can."

"Family trait," Tor said, and by his tone Jake knew he meant it. They'd been through enough that Tor was well aware of Jake's tendency to keep things close until they more or less exploded out of him. Tor was the same way; it really was a family trait.

"I know," Jake agreed. "All we have to do is be a safe place for him to land."

"That's it, huh?"

"Yep. Easy." Hardest thing in the fucking world, but they'd kill themselves making sure it happened.

There was a short pause and then Tor asked softly, "And how are you, cowboy?"

Jake closed his eyes. "Well, you know. Hanging in. Getting some stuff done, watching out for Jacob. I washed the walls yesterday."

"That bad, huh?"

"Fuck, I'm bored. And I miss you."

"I miss you, too, Jake."

Jake smiled to himself. "Yeah?"

"Yeah. I miss having a decent meal I didn't cook, and I miss you yelling at the hands. I miss you feeding the damn dog, and taking River out."

"Poor baby," Jake teased. "I miss Barkley. And River."

"As much as me?"

"More. They don't make me cook."

Tor laughed. "But they don't take care of you the way I do..."

"And how's that?" Jake asked innocently. "River gets me where I'm going and Barkley gives pretty good cuddles. When he's not busy running in circles, anyway."

"Ah, but I'm a better ride than River and I don't drool as much as the dog."

"I don't know--"

"Shut up!"

Jake laughed, the sound of Tor's voice warm in his ear. "All right, you don't. But he can do things you can't."

"Like what?" Tor demanded, his voice still happy and teasing.

"Well, he can lick his own balls."

"I lick yours."

"Good point." It was. And it had been a long time since Tor had done that, had been able to do anything at all, and Jake missed him so much it was like a canker. "You want to do this?" he asked, not really sure if he was up to following the flirting into phone sex or not.

"What I want, Jake, is to see you. I miss you. I want to touch you."

"Yeah," Jake breathed. "I want that, too. I hate being apart from you. I... I'm doing okay. But it would be so much easier if you were here."

"I know. Soon, cowboy. Soon you and Jacob will be home and we can start to settle in. Soon you'll be back where you belong and we can all breathe a little better. Things just don't... it's not right with you gone. The house is empty and the bed's cold, and I keep turning around to talk to you."

"Maybe we can make a fast trip next weekend," Jake suggested, knowing that it wasn't practical, that it wasn't really possible.

"Yard sale," Tor reminded him gently. "But..."

"You could..."

"Yeah."

"Do you think?"

"I'll talk to Elias," Tor promised. "If nothing else, I can help move some things."

"If nothing else?"

"And fuck you stupid."

"That's better."

There was a long pause and Jake took a deep breath, was about to speak when Tor said, "I love you, Jake."

The breath left him in a rush, the shock of the rarely heard words flowing through Jake like a wave of heat. "I know," he said, his voice suddenly tight. "Love you back."

"I know." Tor cleared his throat and did it again, like he couldn't quite get air properly. "I should go."

"Okay," Jake said softly. "Good night, Tor."

"Take care of our boy. Take care of yourself."

"I will."

"Night, Jake."

Jake gently hung up the phone and slid onto his side on the couch, holding a pillow to his chest. "Night, Tor."

Chapter Eighteen

Jake was fairly sure his time management skills had utterly gone to shit when Jacob came home from school and fixed him with a piercing look.

"Uncle Jake, what did you do today?" he asked, his tone almost aggressive.

Jake blinked and said, "Um. I washed the car."

"I was gone for over seven hours." Jacob's eyes narrowed. "You aren't watching soap operas, are you? They'll rot your brain."

Jake grinned. "No, I'm not watching stories on TV."

Jacob nodded sharply. "Good. So. What were you doing? Because I think you're getting a little stir-crazy."

No shit, kid, Jake thought. However, he didn't say it, opting instead to ask, "What makes you say that?"

"You meet me at the door and ask me about my day before I'm halfway in. At first I thought it was because you were worried, but Tressa says you could be bored. I said I didn't think so and she said that you're usually a really busy man and there's nothing for you to do here. So now I want to know. Are you bored?"

Jake bit his lip, half to keep himself from grinning and half to keep from blurting out that he was barely clinging to reality, he was so hard up for something to do. "I'm fine, Jacob," he said, sounding unconvincing even to himself. "It's okay."

Jacob snorted, the sound so much like an adult Taggart that Jake was tempted to glance around to see if Cath had snuck in. "Right." Jacob went to the fridge and pulled out a bottle of apple juice for Jake and then the milk carton for himself. "Well, we don't have horses or cows here for you, but there's got to be something."

Bemused, Jake shrugged. "Friday I'll get everything sorted for the yard sale. Next week I'll be taking anything we're not moving and get it dropped off at the donation places. Then it's packing up and a day of house cleaning."

"Right," Jacob said, giving him that piercing look again. "So you have four days of nothing to do."

Four more days that stretched out like an eternity. Jake grimaced. "Yeah."

Jacob poured his milk, carefully balancing the carton on his cast. "What do you do at home when you have free time?" he asked.

"Only get about two hours in a day," Jake said gently. "And there's always something to do. Between the animals and the house and the paperwork, I never get real free time."

Jacob sighed and nodded. "Okay. Pretend then. What would you do for an hour or so a day, if you had the time?"

Jake's first thought wasn't anything he was about to share with Jacob, but unfortunately the idea had fully formed before he could stop it. He felt himself blush and said, "Watch TV, I guess. Or read. But I can't do that for four days."

Jacob, thankfully, had been putting the milk away and missed the blush. "Why not?"

"It's just not who I am, Jacob. Can't sit still that long."

"Well, what did you do before you went to the ranch?"

Jake rolled his eyes. "You know I was in jail, kid."

Jacob's eyes widened. "Oh, right. Forgot. Well, they didn't have horses there, did they? What did you do?"

Pulling out a chair at the table, Jake sat. "Do you really want to know this stuff, Jacob?" he asked. Did he really want to talk about it, was likely the real question.

Jacob shrugged. "You must have had free time, right?"

Jake nodded. "Worked most of the day, but I was taking classes and getting sober, so I had a lot of things to do. Did schoolwork, went to see the doctors, spent some time in therapy sessions. Not every day, but there was structure. I went from one thing to the next."

Jacob merely nodded and drank his milk.

"There was time in the gym or out in the yard--you lock up all those men, you make sure they exercise. And at night there was TV and reading and talking and card games." There was a hell of a lot more than that, but there wasn't any power on earth or in hell that would make Jake tell Jacob about that.

"So... you can read for a while," Jacob said. "Then go outside and do something. Play solitaire for a bit. Go shopping. Maybe it's not so much that you can't read all day as it is you miss having a list of things to do. Sure, you're not busy here, but there's stuff to fill time with. Just don't watch the soaps. And don't beat my high scores on the PlayStation."

Jake stared at his nephew. "Who are you and where did that kid go?" he asked. Jacob's ability to reach out and touch him wasn't exactly unexpected, but this particular expression of the boy's love for him was something Jake hadn't seen coming. He'd been prepared for a hug, for maybe--eventually--a serious talk about serious matters. He hadn't once thought that Jacob would have the urge to take care of him.

Jacob flushed but didn't look away. "I don't... I want you to be happy, Uncle Jake. Not crazy."

Jake laughed and nodded. "Okay. I don't blame you. I'll make myself a schedule, then."

"Yeah," Jacob said with a grin. "Too bad we don't have a time clock. No slacking off when you're on duty, y'hear?"

"I hear you, Jacob," he agreed with a grin. "I hear you."

Chapter Nineteen

Friday evening Jake was putting the second of two takeout orders of Chinese food in the oven to reheat when Cath came out of 'Lissa's room, a box in her arms and her eyes watery.

"Okay?" he asked gently, taking the box and moving it to the pile by the back door. Most of 'Lissa's things would be donated on Monday, both Jake and Cath agreeing that they couldn't bring themselves to sell her clothes and more personal items. Picture frames and knick-knacks that didn't have a lot of sentimental value were fine, but there was just something about the idea of watching strangers try on her coats that made them both wince.

"Yeah, fine," Cath said with a sigh. "Everything's out of her room now, except the furniture. You get to move that in the morning, unless you want to bring people in to see it."

"We'll see how it goes." Jake reached out and tugged her into his arms. "Sit awhile, Cath. Have something to eat."

She nodded and rested her head on his shoulder for a long moment. "When's Tor getting here?"

"Soon, I think. He said he'd be around to help take the tables outside so we can just set up in the morning."

Cath sighed again and hugged him hard. "All right, then. I'll get Jacob and we can eat; he's making sure he's got everything he doesn't need in the next week ready to be boxed. I think he's hoping Tor will take some of it back with him."

Jake was hoping so, too. It would mean less boxes he'd have to help take into the house, and the fact that Jacob was actively participating in moving was something he wanted to encourage. They'd had a week of slowly sorting things out and Jake thought that both he and Jacob were ready to be done so they could move on a bit.

The three of them ate in near silence, the kitchen and living room an organized chaos Jake tried to ignore. He'd been working steadily toward the upcoming yard sale all week, but living in the disorder was unpleasant.

It just wasn't right. Nothing about the two weeks he'd just lived through was right.

He took the plates to the kitchen sink and was running the water when Jacob silently passed him, his soccer ball braced between his cast and his side. Cath, just as silently, joined Jake at the sink, drying cloth in hand. He wanted to say something, anything, but they all seemed stuck in limbo, each of them lost in their own heads.

The dishes were done and Cath was putting the last of the glasses up in the cupboard when the kitchen door opened and Elias sauntered in, a broad grin on his face.

Jake stared at him, then at Tor who was following in Elias' wake. "Exactly who the hell is running my ranch?" he demanded, something tight in his belly letting go. He grinned right back at Elias and shook his hand, then tugged him closer. "It's good to see you," he said quietly.

"You, too. Holding up all right?" Elias patted Jake's shoulder and gave it a squeeze, his eyes suspiciously bright.

"Yeah," Jake nodded. He let go of Elias and nodded his head to Cath. "Cath, this is Elias. My sister, Cath."

"Miss Taggart," Elias said, swiping his hat off his head. "I'm sorry for your loss."

Cath looked a little bewildered, but she smiled. "Thank you. Please call me Cath. And Tor, you get your ass over here and give me a hug."

Tor snorted and tossed his own hat on the counter and headed to her, but veered suddenly and wrapped himself around Jake. "Hey, you."

"Hey, you." Jake wrapped himself right back and probably wouldn't have let go in any rush if Jacob hadn't come in, calling Tor's name.

"Later," Tor whispered and let him go, opening his arms to give first Jacob and then Cath both tight hugs.

It took a few minutes for everyone to get sorted out and settled down, for Cath to get snacks out and order up some dinner for Tor and Elias, and for Jake to get the coffee pot on. Jacob and Elias introduced themselves to each other, Elias being a little stand-offish and quiet and Jacob a little shy, but then Tor settled it all by telling Jacob that Elias was going to be in charge of Jacob's barn work.

They both looked a little terrified at that, and Jake hid a grin. His man was brilliant, really.

"So, what are you doing here?" Jake asked, glancing at Elias. "And seriously, who's running the ranch?"

"Kirk and Tommy, but Bobby's really taking care of things," Elias said. He shrugged a shoulder. "Nothing major going on, just their usual work--it'll be fine."

Jake nodded and looked at Tor. "So?"

Tor sighed. "Got a mess of things to do next weekend, Jake. Vet's coming out, got fence to fix and cows to move to fresh pasture. Be real hard to get away."

"Impossible," Elias said softly. "Could spare Tor, but not the truck, not without--"

Jake waved a hand. "All right. I hear you. So I take it you have a plan of some sort?"

Cath and Jacob were sitting at the table, eyes and heads turning as they tried to follow the conversation, looking like they were at some fancy tennis match.

"Got my truck out there," Tor said, pointing toward the driveway, "with the trailer. We're going to help out with the sale tomorrow, deliver all the donations, take what Cath wants moved to her place, and take everything Jacob needs back with us. His bed, desk, all that."

Jacob looked at Tor, but didn't say anything.

"And then," Jake drawled, "Jacob and I get to stay in a house empty of everything but a few dishes and our clothes?" Well, that sucked.

Elias winced. "Brought you a nice tent," he mumbled. "And sleeping bags and air mattresses. Least you have running water."

Jacob's eyes widened. "Seriously? Cool!" He grinned and

looked at Jake. "You can sleep in the house. I'm going in the tent."

Chapter Twenty

After Elias and Tor had eaten, and after Jacob had claimed a few more empty boxes for his stuff, Cath headed home to get a good night's sleep. "I'll be back by seven in the morning," she said, rolling her eyes. "So you make sure everyone is up and the coffee is on. I wasn't born to keep these hours, you know."

Jake showed Tor and Elias all the separate piles of things, pointing out everything that had to be moved out to the yard in the morning and what had to be loaded for drop-off, and then the three of them sprawled out on the couch, half watching Jacob play his video game and half sleeping.

Jake was hardly surprised to find himself leaning into Tor's side, though he didn't remember doing it. Tor didn't seem to mind, one arm sliding over his shoulders as easy as anything, fingers petting Jake's arm.

"You'll be home on Friday?" Tor asked quietly.

Jake nodded. "Yeah. I'll make sure we can drop the rental off in town on the weekend, though we might have to go out to the airport to do that. It'll work out."

"I'm done with school on Thursday at noon," Jacob put in, glancing over his shoulder at them. He was sitting on the floor, his good hand flying as he manipulated the joystick tucked up against his cast. "We can go then, can't we?"

Jake shook his head. "Could, but we won't. I want you to have at least the afternoon to see your friends."

Jacob shrugged. "Doesn't matter to me."

"It will."

Jacob shrugged once more, his attention going back to his game, but the silence felt heavy again. Jake looked at Tor, not sure how to fix it, or if it needed fixing; he just knew he didn't like to see Jacob hurting.

"Got something in the truck for you, kid," Tor said, his foot reaching out to nudge Elias' leg.

"Going," Elias grumbled as he levered himself up. "This old body wasn't made for sitting in a truck that long. Lord." He groaned and headed out the front door, both Jake and Jacob watching him go before turning to look at Tor.

"Just hold your horses," Tor said. "It's not much, not a real present, just something he might like to see."

Jake was almost as eager to see what Elias had when he came back in, his curiosity growing when he saw it was a big, flat envelope.

"You want to do this?" Elias said, holding it out to Jake and Tor.

"Go ahead," Tor said before Jake could reply. "I'm comfortable right here."

Elias snorted and sat on the floor next to Jacob, both of them turning to face the couch. "Your uncle will die of curiosity if he doesn't get to see," Elias said to Jacob as he reached into the envelope and pulled out a pile of photographs. "Me and Tor were thinking, when we realized we'd have to get your stuff to the ranch before you. It's only fair you get to pick your own room, and you can't do that right if you don't know what your choices are. So we took a mess of pictures, then we went for a ride and got pictures of the rest of the place." He pointed up at Tor and added, "Even found someone with a little prop plane and went up and got some aerials."

Jake turned his head to stare at Tor. "You what?"

"Got some pictures from the sky."

"Yeah, I got that part." Jake grinned and kissed Tor, hard and fast. "Great idea."

Tor's ears turned pink.

On the floor, Elias started spreading out photos, grinning from ear to ear. "This here's the house," he said to Jacob, who had abandoned his game. "And this is the bunkhouse, where I live."

Jacob twisted around to lie down, to get a closer look. "Neat."

Jake watched, moving closer to Tor as Elias and Jacob went through the pictures. There were photos of every room in the house, including various views of the two spare rooms, and pictures of the barns, the cattle and one each of all the horses. He had no guilt about reaching out to steal the one of River, and he all but snatched the photo of Barkley sitting pretty on the middle of the couch he wasn't allowed up on.

The aerial photos showed most of the ranch: the herd spread out in a pasture; the river looked full and high, which wasn't quite right for the time of year, but Jake decided not to worry on it yet. There were pictures of most of the hands at work, and a group shot of Elias, Kirk, Tommy and Fred outside the bunkhouse, the four of them grinning happily and waving.

Jake decided it was odd, feeling homesick and happy all at once.

He kept his peace while Jacob went back to the pictures of the spare rooms, and let Tor and Elias fill in details about sunlight and actual measurements. He didn't tell Jacob that the bigger room, the one with the pretty white rose wallpaper, had been decorated for his mother, but he thought Jacob knew. He wasn't at all surprised when Jacob chose it over the smaller room, despite the decorating.

It fit. They all fit.

There was hope in those pictures, in the way Elias knew how to talk to Jacob, in the way Tor knew what to do.

There was also a fair amount of knowledge in Elias' face when he finally stood up and asked Jacob to help him pitch the tent in the backyard, his grin knowing as he looked at Jake and Tor curled up on the couch, almost on top of each other. "Think we can see to ourselves," he said with a wink. "Leave you two in peace."

"It's early," Jake protested.

"So we'll talk a bit," Elias said. "I'll teach him to play poker."

Jacob went all wide-eyed again. "Really?"

"Sure, kid," Elias said with a broad grin.

Jake struggled to get up but Tor held him fast. "Let them go," Tor said, not quietly. "I think we deserve it, cowboy. An evening in front of the TV..."

Elias snorted. "Come on, Jacob. You don't need to be hearing those lies."

Jake smacked Tor's arm and hoped he'd lose the ability to blush in the week he had before his family was all living in one place. "Do you have to do that?"

"I didn't do anything!"

Jake rolled his eyes and watched Elias and Jacob head past a stack of boxes, both of them giggling like fools. "Christ." He glared at Tor. "You're all a bad influence."

Tor laughed and nodded. "Yep. And I debauch cowboys," he added as the door slammed behind Elias and Jacob.

"Thank God for that, anyway," Jake said, not able to keep up the glare. "Planning to do that soon?"

"Oh, yeah."

Oh, yeah. Jake grinned and shoved and then they were off the couch and moving to the hall. "About time. You've been here for hours."

"Impatient?" Tor teased, his hand skimming over Jake's ass. He gave it a squeeze and a push, and then they were through the bedroom door, falling toward the bed.

"More like needy and pathetic," Jake admitted, rolling over onto his back. He reached up with one hand and tugged on Tor's arm. "Come here."

Tor went to him easily, stretching out beside him on the bed and molding to his body. He didn't say anything at all, just wrapped himself around Jake and kissed him gently, arms looping around Jake to hold him close.

Jake let out a long breath and sank into it, into the feel of Tor there, with him. No long miles in the way, no telephone line, just the press of his body, warm and close. "Been missing you something fierce," he said. He closed his eyes and inhaled the scent of Tor's shirt; mostly Tor over the fading smell of laundry detergent. It was comfortable and as necessary as breathing.

"Yeah," Tor said, one hand smoothing over Jake's hair. "Had better weeks."

They lay on the bed for long minutes, trading slow kisses and unhurried touches. Jake was content to simply get to know Tor's body again. It wasn't like he'd had time to actually forget anything, but his hands liked to map the contours. He took his time unbuttoning Tor's shirt and even longer to push it off, his mouth and tongue joining in on the slow exploration.

Outside, the sounds of Elias and Jacob talking and laughing mingled with the muted roar of someone's lawn mower. Inside, Jake was able to tune it out, pleased to find that knowing Jacob and Elias were there wasn't distracting in the least. Tor had once more utterly captivated him.

He hoped that never stopped.

Tor was hardly passive, eagerly taking his turn to relieve Jake of his shirt, and once they were both down to just their jeans, Jake allowed Tor to push him into the bed, their kisses growing hungrier as they touched smooth, warm skin.

Jake sucked on one of Tor's nipples, drawing out a moan that turned into a groan as he lowered a hand to grope between Tor's legs, squeezing him through his jeans. Jake growled right back at him and lifted his head to grin. "Think I'm ready to get past cuddling," he said.

"Just waiting on you." Tor pushed his hips up against Jake's hand and grinned right back.

Jake didn't like to think they still scrambled out of their clothes when they were getting naked, but they certainly didn't waste a lot of time. Tor caused a few problems, all grabby hands and unhelpful tugs, but Jake put up with it; it was all fun, and they took to laughing at strange moments, just happy to be together.

The laughing died off as soon as they started moving together, hips pushing and cocks rubbing, the metal of Tor's Prince Albert catching and then slipping on Jake's hip. They moved with purpose then, mouths biting at shoulders, kisses sharp and rough as their passion built. Jake's hands were almost fused to Tor's hips, guiding him into the fast fast quick

quick rhythm he wanted, fingers digging in deep enough to bruise.

Tor went with it, followed him, pushed back just as hard. His teeth were sharp points on Jake's skin, his breath damp and panted out with each moan and grunt of effort. His hands floated from Jake's face to his chest and down to his cock, never resting long, teasing and tugging and inflaming.

"Too fast," Jake protested weakly, his voice almost too rough to be clear. "Too much." But he didn't stop, didn't think he was able to even slow a little, and then it didn't matter at all. Heat blossomed in his belly as Tor flipped them over and ground down onto him, pushing Jake into the bed.

Jake watched Tor's face and let it happen, let Tor drive him and push him and pound him into the mattress, skin suddenly slick with sweat and come. He watched Tor's eyes as they came, one after another, the knife edge of wanting making his gut tight and then loose. He watched Tor watching him, and knew that it didn't matter if it was too soon; there would be more. It didn't even matter when they would be able to make love again--it only mattered that right then he was with Tor and they could hold onto each other and sleep in the same bed.

"Glad you're here," he whispered, still under Tor's weight. "Stay for a while, yeah?"

Tor nodded. "Yeah," he whispered back. He licked his lower lip and nodded. "I'm staying." Slowly, he lowered his head to Jake's chest and there he stayed, a welcome weight right over Jake's heart.

Chapter Twenty One

When Jake woke up it was still dark. At some point Tor had rolled off him, but Jake must have rolled, too, as they were tangled together, legs and arms wrapped tight.

"Hey," he whispered quietly.

Tor mumbled something back at him and shook his head.

"Pardon?" Jake asked, smiling into the dark.

"Said I'm not awake and if I was, we'd have a problem." Tor's voice was rough and sleep slurred. He didn't move away, though, didn't stretch or twitch at all.

"What kind of problem?"

There was a long pause and Jake thought Tor might have drifted into sleep again, but finally he said, "We're disgusting and... well, kind of stuck together."

Jake laughed; he couldn't help it. "Yeah, I noticed. Need a shower worse than anything."

"Now, there's a good idea." Tor nuzzled his neck a little and goose bumps broke out all over Jake's skin. "What time is it?"

Craning his neck to see the clock, Jake winced. "Five-thirty."

With a sigh Tor tried to peel himself off Jake. "Least it gives us time to shower before Elias and Jacob get up."

Jake nodded, then nodded again, starting to grin. "You get the best ideas."

This time it was Tor who laughed. "I do, indeed. Come on, then; let's get clean and I'll take care of that problem that's just popped up."

"I've got a couple of ideas about how you can do that," Jake said as he followed Tor into the bathroom. "Missed out on lots of stuff last night."

Tor flashed him a grin and a lingering look as he turned on the water for the shower. "Hey, I had to sleep. Long drive just to mess around with your ass, you know."

"Worth it," Jake said, grinning back and shoving him into the spray. "Lord, you're a mess." They really were, both of them covered in flaky patches. "Should work on your aim."

Tor snorted and pushed him against the wall, just enough spray reaching them to rinse them off a little. Tor helped with his hands, which Jake had absolutely no objections to, and in moments they were well on their way to greeting the morning properly.

Jake kissed Tor with a hand fisted in his hair, right at the back of Tor's neck, keeping him there. He could taste the water, running down the side of their faces and into the kiss, and he could feel it, strong on one shoulder and glancing off his belly where it followed Tor's hand. The tile was cool on his back, but he had no intention of moving, not while Tor was kissing him like that, hands caressing and touching.

He braced himself, feet planted as well as he could, and shook his head when Tor reached for the shampoo. He didn't want bubbles and slippery soap; it was going to be hard enough staying upright without turning the shower floor slick.

Tor laughed into the kiss, his hand finally closing around Jake's cock and stroking lightly. "Wanting something specific?"

"Uh-huh." Jake didn't see any point in being coy. He tugged on Tor's hair and started pushing him down. "Guess what."

"Oh, this is a hard one," Tor said, stopping on the way down to lick at Jake's chest. He was smart enough not to stop with his hand, something Jake appreciated.

"Very," Jake agreed, his hips rocking a bit.

Tor looked up at him, his eyes twinkling. "Lame."

"Don't care." Jake gave him a harder shove, his hand heavy on Tor's shoulder, and pushed him down to his knees. "C'mon." He looked down at Tor and shuddered; there was something incredibly sexy about Tor kneeling there, water pouring over him. His hair was wet, dripping curls lying on his forehead, and his eyes looked darker than ever as he met Jake's gaze.

Jake was just about to demand that Tor get on with it and stop making him wait when Tor winked at him and licked at the head of his cock, his tongue playing with the ring at the tip. "Yeah," Jake said, the word more a moan than anything else.

"Yeah," Tor agreed, doing it again. "Fucking love the way you taste."

Jake whimpered, one hand slamming back to the wall, the other gently brushing at one of Tor's curls. "Give me more. Please."

Tor nodded and the sense of playfulness morphed into something a little more serious as Tor licked at him, teasing the ring. His hand stroked Jake slowly, root to head, and Jake's legs spread, giving him better access. Tor took it, the heel of his hand brushing over Jake's balls.

Water ran into Jake's eyes and he closed them, concentrating on the sensations Tor was layering over him. A hand rough from work, tongue warm but not as hot as the water, and finally suction when soft lips closed around him. Jake's breath sped up and his fingers curled against the tile as he held himself still; years had taught him that there were times it was just better to let Tor do what he did for as long as Jake could stand it.

Moments later his hand was flat again because if he was keeping his hips still then something else had to give; Tor wasn't taking the time to tease, maybe was having a hard time holding back himself. He was sucking Jake's cock like it had been months rather than a few long days, and Jake's eyes flew open. "Don't you make me fall over," he warned. He knew exactly what would happen if Tor was going to give him the kind of blow job that had earned him his nickname.

Tor came off his cock and stared up at him, eyes more glittering than twinkling. "Hang onto something solid, then," he said, then dove back down.

"Fuck!" Jake grabbed at Tor's shoulders with both hands as

Tor went down on him, sucking hard and then playing his tongue on the underside of Jake's dick. The next thrust was Jake's, it had to be, and he had to drag his cock against the suction, almost quivering. When he plunged back into Tor's mouth it happened, that weird, slippery, twisty thing Tor could do with his tongue, and Jake was gone. He managed to hold on for two more thrusts like that before his head tipped back and he shot, his entire body tight and tense and then suddenly floating.

He was panting as Tor eased him down, both from his orgasm and literally to the floor of the tub. "Want to fuck me?" he whispered, hands shaking as he reached for Tor's face, kissing him sloppily.

"Yeah," Tor whispered back. He groaned, though, and pushed Jake's hands down, dragging them to his cock, hard and leaking. "Can't though, not gonna--"

Jake knew, he could feel it in the way Tor was shaking almost as hard as he was. He ran his fingers over Tor's cock once, then jacked him hard, with one purpose. "Don't worry," he said against Tor's skin. "I got you."

Tor lurched, his hips bucking up, and Jake didn't tease any more than Tor had. He stroked with one hand, the other digging into Tor's thigh, and flicked his hand over Tor's ring on the upstroke.

"Yes," Tor hissed, and as he started to come Jake kissed him hard, tongue pushing into Tor's mouth. Tor spilled over his hand, hot and wet, and the shower took care of the mess, almost to Jake's regret. He liked it when there was evidence for a few moments at least.

Tor laughed softly into the next kiss, his arms wrapping around Jake. "Damn. We need to try that again later."

Jake grinned, happy enough to stay where they were for a few minutes. The water felt nice, almost like rain. "Sounds like a plan."

"We'll fit it in around the other plan."

Jake raised an eyebrow. "What other plan?"

"The one about yard sales and breakfast and coffee. And other people wanting to use the bathroom."

Jake sighed. "Oh. That plan. They can wait a bit."

"It's not even six. They can wait a lot."

That sounded about right to Jake, so he kissed Tor again and didn't think about anything other than being warm and naked and mostly clean.

Chapter Twenty Two

By nine the sale was in full swing. The yard was full of people and the amount of things had diminished by half. Jake wasn't surprised by the turnout; aside from people who knew 'Lissa and wanted to stop by to wish him and Jacob well, there was the usual crowd of dedicated yard sale aficionados, hell-bent on finding a bargain.

What did surprise Jake, however, was that people utterly ignored the prices he and Cath had put on everything. Those who knew what had happened pressed money into his hand, five or ten dollars, and took things priced at two dollars. The family who bought the kitchen set paid double and wouldn't take no for an answer. Others, Tim MacPhee included, merely handed Jake money and shook his hand before walking away with nothing.

He could hear quiet conversations all around him, people talking about 'Lissa and what she'd meant to them. There were long conversations about her books, about times that she'd made coffee for someone and spent an evening talking about movies or stories or telling them about some little happening. Those people would come to him with shining eyes and pay for the book or cut glass dish and walk away with their own little memento of what his sister had meant to them.

He felt horrible when that happened, and tried to refuse their money, but each person protested. They wanted to help and he had to let them; it was healing, in a way.

Cath was wandering around and helping people sort through boxes when Jake and Tor took a man and his teen-aged daughter into the house to look at some of the bigger furniture. She was getting ready to go to college in the fall, and her daddy figured she might as well have as much as they could afford--and he wasn't about to give up his own couch and chair. While Jake was happy that the young lady had a father who wanted to set her up right, he couldn't help but be a little envious; his own family had hardly been as kind to him. He made a mental note to make sure Jacob was treated well when he went off to college and left Tor to work out the details about pickup or delivery.

He joined Cath, standing in the sun, and draped an arm around her shoulders. "It's going well," he said, more to say something other than 'are you okay?' again.

Cath nodded and beamed up at him. "Jake, I've got more than three hundred dollars in my pocket. These people... they've been so *kind*."

Jake looked at her, almost stunned into silence. He knew damn well he had about that much in his own pocket. "That's incredible," he said weakly. "Shit, Jacob'll be able to buy his own damn horse if this keeps up."

Laughing, Cath turned and hugged him quickly. "Put it in an account for him."

"I will," Jake promised. He shook his head and looked around at the people who were being so generous to Jacob. "Damn." He had no idea what else to say.

A heavy hand landed on his shoulder. "Taggart." Tor's voice was low and serious, and Jake immediately turned to see what was wrong.

"Calm yourself," Tor said, still talking quietly. "And stay that way. I need you to take a look across the street at the man standing there. And then I need you to tell me I'm seeing things."

Jake turned, but not as fast as Cath. Her face went from confused to pale and worried so fast Jake thought she might fall over. "Shit," she hissed.

Tor's hand tightened on his shoulder, but Jake shook it off, eyes on the man who was smoking across the street, leaning on a beat-up old wreck of a car. "Take Jacob in the house," Jake said to Tor, stepping forward. Cath was right there with him, her shoulders back and her eyes narrowed. "And you."

"Yeah, right," she snorted, matching him step for step. "He's my asshole brother, too, you know."

Jake sighed and glanced back at Tor who was watching them go with a worried look. When Jake waved a hand at him in a shooing motion, Tor rolled his eyes, but he shooed. Across the street, James tossed his cigarette down and stepped on it, watching Jake and Cath come to him.

Cath got there first. While Jake made sure his arms were down by his sides and his hands were relaxed, Cath had her arms crossed across her stomach, every inch of her showing her rage. "You missed her funeral," she said coldly, standing right in front of James. "Where the hell have you been?"

"Florida." James' voice was faded and dry, like his throat was closed and unused to speaking. "Just found out the day before yesterday. I'm sorry." He looked at Cath, then back down at the ground. "You look good, Slip."

"You look like hell, Scrap."

He did. He looked old and worn out, his face lined and gray, his hair lank and lifeless. He looked like Jake had felt for the days around the funeral.

James appeared to ignore that, his eyes fixed on his boots, as far as Jake could tell. "Did she… was it fast?" he asked quietly.

Cath's face lost some of its rage, morphing into mere pain. "She didn't hurt," she said. "It was quick."

"Good," James whispered, and his gaze darted to Jake's face before dropping again. "Where's Jacob?"

"In the house," Jake said, not looking to make sure.

"Can I see him?"

Jake looked at Cath, unsure of what to do. His first reaction was to say no and leave it at that, but he wasn't unbiased. Not that Cath was, but she had a better way about her, and James was still family.

Cath sighed. "Why?"

James finally looked up, his lined face full of a pain Jake couldn't name. "Because he's her boy. Because no matter what happens, 'Lissa was my sister, too."

Cath nodded slowly, but Jake found himself shaking his

head. "James," he said, trying to keep his voice calm and even and low. "Do you know I'm his guardian? That he's coming to live with me?"

James nodded slowly, his hand dipping into a pocket and pulling out another cigarette. "Yeah. Think it's wrong. Think you're wrong, right to your bones. But there ain't nothing I can do about it."

Jake willed his hands to stay loose. "Why not?"

James made a disgusted sound and put the cigarette between his lips. "Look at me, Jake. I ain't got nothing. I don't have a house, a job, or any hope of getting one. I'm sick, I'm an alcoholic, and I've abandoned three kids. What would I do with him? No way I could take him, no way a court would give him to me. Jess is too old." He looked at Cath and away again. "And Slip doesn't see things the way I do."

"Don't call me that," Cath said, her voice catching a little. "No more."

James sighed again and looked at Jake, his eyes cold and blank. "I hate you. I hate that the girls love you, I hate that you screwed up and still got a good life. I hate what you are. But that don't take away the fact that Jacob is my blood."

"No, it doesn't," Jake agreed. "But I can't have you poisoning him."

"I just want to see him. Once more, before you take him away."

"Don't make me get a restraining order against you," Jake said softly. "Because I will. You say one wrong thing, James, and so help me God, you'll wish you never left Florida."

"Already wish that," James mumbled. "I just want to look at the boy, go see where 'Lissa's buried, and then I'll leave. You'll never see me again."

Jake could only hope that was true. "Stay here," he said. "I'll go see if he'll talk to you." Without waiting for a reply, he turned and walked back to the house, nodding to Elias who was standing guard by the door. "If Cath starts to cry," he said, "deck him."

"You got it," Elias said with a nod, his gaze firmly across the street.

Jake found Tor and Jacob in the kitchen, Jacob looking furious and Tor looking stressed. "He wants to see you," Jake told Jacob. "I said I'd see if you wanted to."

Jacob frowned. "What did he say to you?" he demanded. "Is he going to try to take me away?"

Jake shook his head. "No. And he couldn't, even if he tried." He ran his hand through his hair and stifled a sigh. "Look," he said, meeting Jacob's eyes. "James is... well, he's broken. He's not doing well, and I think he's pretty messed up. He just wants to see you before he leaves town."

Jacob looked at Tor for a long moment, then back at Jake. "Will you come with me?"

"Yes." Lord, yes. No way he was letting James be alone with Jacob.

Jacob nodded once and took a breath. "Okay. But if he's mean about anything, I want you to hit him or something."

"Not a problem."

Jake and Jacob went back outside and across the lawn, ignoring the furtive looks from the people still wandering about the yard. James and Cath were right where Jake had left them, but Cath moved to Jake's side, both of them just behind Jacob, like guards.

James swallowed and stood a little straighter. "Jacob," he said, his voice still cracked and ragged, a rasp more than anything. "I'm real sorry about your mother. She was a good woman," he said formally.

Jacob nodded and looked at Jake, uncertainty in his face. "Yeah," he said to James. "She was. I miss her."

"I'm sure you do. You always will, most likely. But try hard to remember her, and try to grow into a good man. Just like she knew you'd be. Study hard, okay? Be more than any of us. Well, be as smart as Slip, anyway. Stay out of trouble." He took a step back and looked at Jake. "That's all I've got to say."

Jacob looked bewildered, and Jake put an arm around his shoulders. "It's okay, kid," he said softly.

James opened the car door and looked at them all once more. "Take care of each other. Be a family, for 'Lissa if not me." He climbed in the car and slammed the door, the engine turning over almost immediately.

Jake, Cath, and Jacob stepped back out of the way and watched as James pulled out and drove away.

"That was..." Cath waved a hand in the air.

"Weird," Jacob said, shaking his head. "He's not coming back."

"No," Jake agreed. "I don't think he is." He looked over at 'Lissa's house and what was left of her things. "Come on," he said. "We have work to do, then I think we should get ice cream and go do something fun. Maybe torture Elias and Tor with mini-golf or something."

Cath nodded, her smile forced but there. "Taggarts against the rest?"

"You know it." Jake smiled at her and nudged them both back to where they belonged, on the right side of the street.

Chapter Twenty Three

Elias kicked their butts.

Even when Tor abandoned him and teamed up with Jake, Cath, and Jacob, Elias kicked their butts. The four of them would play the hole, take the best score, and match it against Elias'. In the first nine holes, they beat him on one. On the second nine, they didn't even come close, and Elias managed to get a hole in one four times.

"Want to explain to me how a ranch hand got so good at mini-golf?" Jake asked when they were returning their putters.

Elias grinned and winked at Cath. "I've always been good with my hands."

"Oh, that's nice," Cath said sweetly as Jake's jaw dropped open. "I've always been pretty good with a shotgun."

"My sister!" Jake slapped Elias' arm.

Tor laughed and slapped Jake's arm right back, before Elias could do it. "Think your sister can take care of herself, Taggart."

Cath beamed at Tor and slipped her arm through his. "Now, Jake. You didn't have it in your head that I'm innocent, did you?"

Jake shuddered. "I don't want to know. And stay away from my cowboys--they break easy."

Elias smirked at him and took Cath's arm from Tor's. "I think it's best if Jake takes a few moments to gather his thoughts, Miss Cath. He's obviously lost his mind and confused me with someone else," he said as he led her toward the ice cream stand where Jacob was already picking out flavors.

Jake looked at Tor, and glared. "Shut up."

"I didn't say anything," Tor protested, holding his hands up.

"Shut up anyway; I can hear you thinking from here."

"That's scary, Jake."

"No, Elias flirting with my sister is scary. You laughing about it in your head and thinking it's cute that I've gone all big brother about it is scary. Me knowing you're thinking that is just... normal."

Tor raised an eyebrow. "You're panicking," he said gently, like he would when Lug was spooked. "I think you need ice cream."

"Shut up."

***

Jake was enjoying the blow job. He was really enjoying it, his cock pushing hard into Tor's mouth, his hands tangled in Tor's hair, and his balls lifting up tight. He was staring sightless at the ceiling, reaching for his orgasm and feeling it boil in him, surging up and up and almost over, everything tight and bright and ready to explode.

And then Tor lifted his head, fighting against Jake's grip in his hair. He came off Jake's dick with a slurp and said, "So, you're really not worried about it?"

"Fuck!" Jake's hips fell back to the bed and he slapped Tor up the side of his foolish, smirking head. "Will you stop doing that?" It was the third time Tor had stopped, and Jake had had just about enough of that particular game.

Tor grinned at him and kissed the head of Jake's cock, his tongue lapping at the metal ring. "Sorry," he said, utterly insincere. "Just making sure--"

"If you mention either Elias' name or my sister's I swear to fucking God I'll roll over and go to sleep."

Tor licked him. "No, you won't."

Jake growled. "Why are you thinking about either of them when you've got my dick in your mouth?" he asked, not minding the licks or the kisses. His dick didn't care if Tor was thinking about sales tax or the paint on the walls, as long as

Tor's mouth was busy with making Jake come.

"Just to keep you from coming before I'm ready," Tor admitted, and then there were slick fingers shoved into Jake's ass and things were back on track.

"Oh," Jake breathed, the fire stoking him back to a near boil again. "That's better."

Tor chuckled and sucked him again, his fingers going deeper and faster. Jake took it, wanted it, and in seconds he was rocking his way back onto Tor's hand and up into his mouth. He'd have happily done that another dozen times and shot his load down Tor's throat, but as soon as climax was on the map, that nice red X that marked the spot, Tor pulled away, pulled out, and started climbing up him.

Jake groaned in frustration, but willingly spread his legs, lifting one until Tor was in the right place for him to hook up over Tor's shoulder, and then there was just the long slow glide to bliss as Tor took him, pushing in and in and up and down and generally just making himself at home in Jake's ass.

"Ready?" Tor asked, finally as breathless as Jake had been over and over since they'd tumbled into bed.

"Fuck me." Jake's eyes closed and nothing mattered at all except Tor moving over him, in him. Hard and fast, and at some point Jake realized that the headboard really wasn't fastened to the bed frame and he'd have to fix that before they delivered it to the man who'd bought it. It banged and rattled with every thrust and Jake grunted every time Tor did, their voices made for each other, for this, for fucking and loving and then that X was in front of him, written on Tor's hand around his cock.

"Yes!" Jake yelled, his back arching, and then again as he started to shoot, finally, finally.

"Yes!" Tor echoed, his hips slapping on Jake as he sped up, fucked Jake right through it, his cock and his piercing hammering on Jake's gland until Jake thought he'd surely die of it, and it would almost be welcome to go with such perfection around him.

And then, sweating and swearing and with Jake's come on his hand and on Jake's belly, Tor said, "Always," and froze, his climax pouring out of him in and into Jake, so strong Jake could feel it.

It wasn't until Tor was asleep next to him that Jake remembered they had about eight hours before Tor would leave. Five days until he could go home.

Jake sighed and held Tor a little tighter and closed his eyes. It would be all right. In a week, everything would be all right.

Chapter Twenty Four

It was a hard week. Jake spent his days cleaning the house and finishing the donation drop-offs when he wasn't doing last minute things like gathering medical and school records for Jacob. He made a last stop at the lawyer's, spent time with Cath, and tried to ignore the fact that he and Jacob were staying in an empty shell of a home.

He missed Tor. The phone calls he tried to keep to a minimum were either difficult and near-silent or quickly deteriorated into innuendo, depending on how late at night it was and how long it had been since he'd last jerked off. More often than not, they'd have a conversation about once a day and a follow-up call for phone sex a few hours later. He was starting to feel like he was pathetic, but as far as phone sex went, it was pretty good. Tor had a way with words.

It helped him to keep from noticing that the house was cold and barren.

Jacob, on the other hand, seemed to ignore that the house was devoid of everything he'd ever known. He treated sleeping in the tent like an adventure, and even took to ignoring the PlayStation in favor of getting Jake to help him practice his new poker skills.

If Jake had known he'd be spending his evenings playing cards and eating take out, he would have had Tor and Elias take the TV and the PlayStation with them, instead of leaving it for him to wrestle into the car. He got it in, though, along with his bag and the rest of Jacob's things, and then there they were, on Thursday evening, ready to go.

He closed the trunk and looked at the empty house, listening to Jacob and Tressa talking inside. The door was open and he could see them through the living room window, just standing in the empty room. This was the last of Jacob's goodbyes, and then they would go to Cath's for the night, ready for an early start in the morning.

Jake waited by the car, trying not to spy as Jacob and Tressa talked quietly, and quickly looking away when they turned to each other for a hug. He studied the lawn instead, eyeing its color critically and wondering if he should have mowed it once more.

They came out a moment later, Tressa with Jacob's last box in her arms. She handed it to Jake and stood back a step before turning to hug Jacob one more time. "Bye," she said softly.

He nodded, looking vaguely uncomfortable, and she started walking down the driveway. "Tressa," Jacob finally blurted as she reached the street. "I'll call you next week."

She grinned and nodded. "Okay. See you, Jacob. Bye, Mr. Taggart."

Jake waved and looked at Jacob, almost immediately dismissing her from his mind. "You okay?"

"Yeah." Jacob pointed to the box. "Sorry about that, I couldn't pick it up with the cast."

"No problem." Jake opened the back door of the car and fit the box in next to the tent. "Got everything? Want to take a few minutes to look around?"

"Nah, I'm good." Jacob walked around the car and climbed in. "Feel weird, though."

"Weird how? Sick?" Jake asked, starting the car. A flu bug would make travel interesting.

Jacob shrugged. "Sad and excited at the same time. Confused."

"That makes sense," Jake said, nodding. "I'm... more excited and worried. Sad, too."

"What are you worried about?"

"Doing right by you," Jake said. "Hoping I can live up to what your mom would want. But I'm excited about it, 'cause I think you'll like the ranch, and I know the people living near us are good folk. I like you, Jacob, and I'm glad you're going to be with us."

Jacob flushed, an embarrassed smile turning up the corners of his mouth. "I like you, too. And I'm excited about the horses and learning to ride."

Jake smiled back at him. "Good, then. Now, if I can just get you as excited about the joy that is mucking stalls..."

Jacob made a face and Jake laughed, itching to reach out and ruffle his hair. He wasn't sure precisely how it was all going to work out, but it would.

The Silence

Chapter Twenty Five

The drive home was easy and smooth, if a little quiet when Jacob fell asleep about two hours in. Jake let him rest, content to drive with only his own thoughts to keep him occupied. It wasn't quite like being out on horseback with no one around to distract him, but it was close.

When he got off the interstate he debated about taking the main highway into town and looping back toward the ranch, but his need to be home overrode the idea that he could show Jacob around town a little. There would be time enough for that; right then he just wanted to love on his dog and see his horse, and show Jacob his new home. So he switched over to the local road and cut across country, taking only about twenty minutes off the trip but getting there as fast as was reasonable. He did wake Jacob, though, about ten minutes from the spread. "Almost there, kid," he said, reaching over to nudge Jacob's shoulder.

With the ease that came with youth, Jacob straightened up, rolled his shoulders, and blinked a couple of times. Jake would have had an aching neck for hours, but Jacob seemed fine and wide awake within a couple of minutes. He looked out the window and scratched absently at his cast.

"How long?" he asked.

"Couple of minutes. We'll be driving along our land in a mile or so."

"Cool."

Jake glanced at the speedometer and grinned ruefully when he realized he'd sped up again. He wasn't a lot over the limit, but he was definitely faster than he had been since turning onto the local road. A quick look in the rearview mirror assured him he was alone on the road, so he let his lead foot carry them along for a bit.

"This is it," he said quietly, not able to keep from grinning as he pulled in the drive, smiling as he always did at the big iron sign. He had no idea if anyone would even be around to greet them, but he knew for sure that his dog would be there.

Jacob was silent beside him, but was looking around avidly, his feet shifting like he was more than ready to get out of the damn car already. Jake didn't blame him at all; the car was cramped and there was all that space out there to move in and fresh air to breathe.

He pulled up next to the house, the yard empty of trucks and people, and had barely shut off the engine and opened his door when a barking furry mass flew around the corner of the barn and barreled across the yard at them.

"That'd be the pup," he said dryly as Barkley paused to pee on the front tire of the car before launching himself at Jake's legs.

Jacob laughed and nodded, yelping when Barkley climbed right in the car with him and started trying to lick his face. "Friendly thing, aren't you?" he said to Barkley, scratching the top of the dog's head even as he tried to get out of the car and out of the range of Barkley's tongue.

Jake grabbed the dog and dragged him out of the car, pausing long enough for an extended tummy rub before nodding to the house. "Want to go in?"

Jacob nodded, his eyes fixed on the barns. "Yeah, okay. Um, can we take in the box? The one Tressa had."

"Sure." Jake got the box, vaguely curious about what Jacob wanted from it, and headed to the house. He took the steps two at a time and held the door open for Barkley to skitter in ahead of them. "Downstairs first, or your room?"

"Bathroom," Jacob said emphatically.

That was easy enough, and when Jacob came out, Jake took his turn before picking up the box again and taking it upstairs. The door to Jacob's room was open, the sun spilling in and washing the room with light. "This is it," he said, setting the box on the bed. "Hope you can make it your own."

Jacob looked around, starting to smile. "They put the books on the shelves," he said, pointing to the bookcase. "Cool."

"Left your clothes out, though," Jake said, nodding to the boxes on the dresser.

"Scared of my socks."

The room was only half put together, but Jake could tell that Tor had made an effort to do what he could without doing it all; Jacob would have lots of opportunity to get his things where he wanted them.

Jacob sat on the bed and picked up the only framed photo in the room, which had been set on the small table by the bed. "Aunt Cath took this at the zoo when I was ten," he said, holding it out to Jake.

In the photo a much shorter Jacob had his arms looped around 'Lissa's waist, both of them grinning madly. "It's a great picture," Jake said, smiling.

"We were pretending to be tigers." He took the picture back and set it down carefully. With a sigh, he pointed to the box Jake had carried up. "The tiger book she got me that day is in there."

Jake sat down next to him and pulled the box closer. "Want it?"

Jacob smiled a little. "Nah. Maybe later. Can I look around a bit?"

"Yeah, of course. Want some time in here, or do you want the tour?"

"Tour. I'm kinda hungry, too."

"When aren't you?" Jake teased. "All right, fast through up here, then food. If someone shows up with a truck we can take a drive around, too."

"And see the horses."

"And see the horses. Not sure which ones are around, but if Tor has half a brain River will be."

Jacob grinned. "You're kind of attached to him, aren't you?"

"Tor or River?" Jake asked with a chuckle. "They both have their good points. I'm kind of fond of them both, yeah."

"You hide it well." Jacob laughed and stood up. "Come on, let's go. I'm tired of sitting."

"You'll be glad of sitting in a couple of months, I promise. Get you hauling hay bales..."

Jake followed Jacob out of his room and showed him the spare room, then the one he shared with Tor, and the upstairs bathroom, before they went down to the kitchen again. Tor had been grocery shopping, that much was obvious, and within twenty minutes they were well fed and ready to explore the ranch, starting with the stables. Jake hoped the horses took to Jacob as fast as Jacob had taken to the idea of them.

He wasn't terribly worried about it, though. That piece of land was a good place to grow up, and the critters on it were a big part of that. They'd be fine, all of them.

Chapter Twenty Six

"What's wrong?"

Jake blinked and pulled the sheets back on the bed, then looked across to where Tor was stripping off his clothes for the night. "Nothing," he said, sounding unconvincing even to him.

Tor snorted and peeled his jeans off, swatting Barkley in the process. "Right."

Jake shrugged. "It's just..." He shrugged again and took his shirt off, tossing it toward the basket of dirty clothes. "I don't know what happens next."

"Next?" Tor lifted an eyebrow and climbed into bed. "Sleep. Get up. Work. Same as always."

Jake rolled his eyes and finished getting undressed. "You know what I mean," he said as he got into bed. Barkley leapt onto the foot of the bed and turned three circles before settling down.

"Well, not specifically," Tor said patiently. "I mean, there's stuff--get the trust fund set up and figure out how much to set aside annually to pay for his clothes and stuff. There's registering him for school. There's--"

Jake was shaking his head. "That stuff's easy," he said, reaching for the light switch. "I'm more stirred up about the day to day shit. Like what do we *do* now? Neither of us has a clue about kids and you know it. I mean... what time do we send him to bed? How much does he eat--aside from 'a lot'? How much work should he do around the ranch before we cross the line between teaching him responsibility and making him earn his keep?"

In the dark, Tor tugged Jake to him. "We ask him. He

knows how much he eats--and I figure we just get a bunch more food and eat until it's gone. Make more if we need it. He can keep going to bed at the same time he did for the school year--not like he's going to get much chance to sleep in around here. And the rest will work itself out."

Jake sighed. "But what if--"

"Don't even go there, cowboy. Listen to me." Tor pressed a kiss to Jake's forehead. "This is new to all of us. Jacob knows that. All we can do is talk to him. Now, I don't want him to be a maid here or just like one of the other hands any more than you do. He's here because we want him, and we're going to take care of him, yeah? So we tell him that. We teach him about laundry and cleaning up and how to take care of the animals. We give him chores that fit what he can do and give him free time to do what he wants. We teach him to ride and we make sure he's healthy. What we don't do is get lost in 'what if', 'cause that's not going to do any of us any good."

Jake nodded, warm in his bed, and took comfort in Tor's voice, in his arms, and his good sense. "You sure you haven't done this before?" he asked quietly.

Tor laughed. "Nope. Just spent the last two weeks thinking about it while you were away." He kissed Jake again. "Tomorrow, you and one of the boys can take the rental back. I'll take Jacob with me in the truck to check out a few things around the spread, and then we'll see what he wants to do. Until the cast comes off he won't be doing a hell of a lot, but he can tag along with whoever's doing something that interests him, okay? It'll smooth out."

Jake resisted the urge to whine about the rental. More than anything he wanted to get out on River and ride, see as much of his land as he could as fast as he could manage it. "Okay," he agreed, only a little grumbly about it.

"Aw, poor man," Tor teased, clearly knowing what he was thinking about. "Go in to town early, then. Oh, and get Jacob some work clothes and a pair of boots--he's going to need them."

"Yes, sir."

"Sir, now, is it?" Tor tugged on Jake again and tilted his

head for a proper kiss, invading Jake's senses. "I like that."

Jake would have chuckled, but he was too busy kissing back to be bothered.

Barkley gave a low growl and got back off the bed; he was a smart dog and Jake had taught him well. There wouldn't be a chance to sleep on the bed for a while yet, but Jake couldn't quite bring himself to feel sorry for the pup.

He rolled onto his side and pushed closer to Tor, nudging their hips together as they kissed, getting harder. It was good to be home, to be in his own bed; better to be lying there in the dark with Tor.

In a couple of minutes the nudging had become insistent, turning more to grinding, both of them hard and looking for friction. Jake kissed his way along Tor's jaw and buried his head in Tor's neck, one hand rubbing at Tor's chest before moving down. Just as he shifted so he could reach their cocks, Tor moved as well, reaching for the nightstand.

The cap popping on the lube sounded loud in the room and Jake tensed, not sure why. He bit at Tor's neck and held out his hand, palm up.

"Thought I was sir tonight," Tor murmured into his ear, holding the lube back. "Want to fuck you, Jake."

Jake shuddered but shook his head. It wasn't that he really objected to Tor fucking him--and it would be an excellent welcome home--but he wasn't at all sure how well the sound would carry and the bed squeaked. Until they got the frame tightened, he wasn't sure it was such a great idea.

He bit at Tor again and decided the bed was getting fixed before breakfast. "Gimme the slick," he said.

Tor did it, though he didn't seem very happy. He wasn't turning Jake down, though, and Jake had an idea that he'd get Tor warmed up again fast. With a palm full of lube, he gathered their cocks together and started stroking. Too much lube, really, but that just made everything all slick and slippery, and Jake suddenly found himself flat on his back, Tor looming over him and grinning down.

"Not a bad plan," Tor said, and thrust against him. The lube made it fast and more of a glide than a grind, but it was *fun*, in a silly kind of way. The next time he did it, Tor rolled his hips a little and his eyes went wide as he slid too far and Jake's cock suddenly rubbed him behind his balls.

Jake grinned and held onto Tor's hips, guiding him as they started trying to find a rhythm that worked for them both, experimenting with more lube and then letting it dry a bit. They kissed and whispered, and Jake thought he'd never been quite so ridiculously unfocused when getting off before.

Eventually, though, Tor found the spot that really did it for him, for them both, and Jake started biting his lip to keep back the gut deep moans as his balls got hot and tight. It was different from when they shared a house with men; it wouldn't be funny in the morning, there wouldn't be Elias laughing at them from the other side of the table. He couldn't let himself be even as loud as he'd been in the other house; Tor had been the noisy one--not always, but usually--and even so, Jake struggled to mute himself.

"Give it up," Tor whispered to him. "Come on, Taggart. Just relax, will you? Come with me, baby. It's been too fucking long, don't you worry about it, all right? Not now."

Jake stared up at him and nodded, trying to uncurl his spine enough to just get off. He could feel it coming up in him, sneaking and screaming, and he wanted it. He did. He just didn't want to let loose the yell that he was pretty sure was going to come with the orgasm.

Tor shook his head and Jake could've sworn he sighed. "Jake," he whispered. "I'm coming even if you ain't." Then he ground down, slipping and sliding and fitting himself between Jake's legs and growled. "Ah, shit."

When Tor's mouth smashed on his, Jake growled back, letting his shout out into Tor's kiss, giving him the taste of it as he finally found the way to release. His fingers were clamped to Tor's body, his tongue was shoved damn near down Tor's throat, and it was enough. He came, Tor right there with him, both of them pulsing and twitching and the smell of sex saturating the sheets around them.

"Stubborn cuss," Tor called him as he rolled over. But Jake could hear him smiling and he smiled right back, wiping his belly on the corner of the sheet.

"Shut up and sleep," he said, folding himself around Tor's body.

The bed creaked as Barkley, apparently deciding they were done, jumped up on the end of the bed again. He walked his circles, right over Jake's feet, and finally lay down.

"Glad you're home," Tor whispered.

"Not going again," Jake promised.

"Better not. And if you do, I'm going with. Don't want to do this again, Jake."

"Nope." Jake kissed his shoulder and held him a little tighter. "Go to sleep. Real life starts again in seven hours."

Tor snorted but in a few minutes his breathing evened out and Jake smiled. Tor was pretty good at doing what he was told, even if it had taken years to train him.

Chapter Twenty Seven

The two weeks between coming home and the day Jacob finally got his cast taken off were a mix of emotions and changes. The cast itself caused problems because with it on, Jacob was more an observer than a participant in his own life, tagging along with various people as they went about their business and trying to figure out what his chores would be when he could finally do them. On the other hand, he told Jake and Tor, it was good because it gave him a chance to get to know some people and see things before he had to actually do anything.

Two weeks was a long time, though, and Jacob was as itchy to get to the good stuff, as he called it, as anyone else. Not that anyone minded Jacob riding along in the trucks or wandering around the barns, but it would be nice when he could help out instead of just watch.

Jake was pleased that his men seemed to go out of their way to make Jacob feel at home. Elias had come right to the house, first thing, and dragged Jacob off to the bunkhouse to meet everyone, and then disappeared with him into the stables. It didn't matter that Jake had already taken Jacob to meet the horses; in fact, Jake kind of suspected that anytime he lost track of Jacob he'd be found right there, loving on the animals.

There were a couple of trips into town to see the doctor about Jacob's arm, and one to the lawyer's office as well. Jake made sure to stop in at a few places on the way home, and to point out the high school. Jacob seemed to take heart a little then, relaxing a bit when he found out it was a consolidated school. Three other schools fed into it, so he would simply be one of many new faces. Likely, he wouldn't even be the only one who had just moved into the area.

Jake spent the two weeks rushing like mad and trying to find a balance between getting caught up with his ranch and trying to make Jacob feel at home. Tor stood back for a while, letting Jake do as he pleased and helping out when Jake said, but even Jake wasn't surprised when he found himself invited out to the porch for a quiet talk the night before Jacob's cast was to come off.

"You've got to calm down, cowboy," Tor said, sitting back on the railing. "You're going to drive us all shit crazy."

Jake rolled his eyes. "I'm not that bad."

Tor smiled at him and shook his head. "Jake, you're turning yourself in circles and it's not as funny as it was at the beginning. Relax a little, let things take their time. It'll all settle down."

"I just..." Jake waved his hand at the yard. "We're coming on a busy time and I want to make sure he's in okay. That he knows everyone and can find things--"

"You can't make a home by pointing out where the feed is," Tor said slowly. "If he can't find something, there's a lot of folks around he can ask. And that's how he'll get to know them, Jake. By living here, and working here, and growing up here."

Jake fixed Tor with a suspicious look and moved closer to him. "When are you going to go back to being an arrogant, stubborn pain in my ass? It's getting a little creepy the way you're on top of all this."

Tor just grinned at him.

Jake had to concede over the next few days that Tor'd had a point, though. He backed off a little, let Jacob explore more, and spent more time out on River. There were some odd moments, times when Jacob was sullen and a little withdrawn, but going out to the stables seemed to help that. Even mucking out stalls, now that he had the cast off, seemed to make Jacob happy. He was, of course, far happier to actually groom the animals, but as long as he had access to the stable, he seemed okay.

He wasn't as fast to figure out some of the other chores, but Jake didn't much care; as long as the bathroom was clean and the dishes got done, that was good enough for him. Frankly, three men sharing a house meant that it wasn't the neatest place ever, and none of them really cared much. He did, however, draw the line at dishes vanishing into Jacob's room and made sure that came to an end.

Jake wasn't sure what to think the morning Jacob came down to breakfast with a cardboard box in his arms. He looked a little restless, his glance darting all over the room as he set the box down on the table.

"What've you got there?" Tor asked as he buttered toast.

"Just some stuff," Jacob said, a little too casually. Tor's eyes flicked up to him as Jacob set the box down on the table, still favoring his arm. He held it stiffly, like he hadn't quite gotten used to the cast being gone yet.

Jake poured coffee for himself and Tor, waiting to see if Jacob would take the next step and actually open the box. He hadn't by the time Jake got to the table with the mugs, but then Jacob sighed and reached for the folded over flaps.

"I was talking to Tommy," Jacob said quietly. "Well, he was talking to me. He's moving to his own apartment, you know? Talking about packing and unpacking--I think he was trying to make me feel better."

Jake nodded and sat down, letting Jacob go at his own pace.

"And I got thinking..." Jacob stared into the box, his voice getting even quieter. "I mean, I have all my stuff here and all..."

Tor nodded and reached for his mug. "It's your home, kid. You don't have to ask permission to have things around."

"But these are... special things," Jacob whispered. "They... well, some of them are pretty dumb."

"No such thing," Jake said seriously. "Are you going to show us?"

Jacob shrugged. "I guess."

It was still a few seconds before he took anything out, though, and when he did the first item was a pottery mug, obviously hand turned and painted, and clearly something meant for a serious coffee drinker, by its size. "This was her favorite."

Jake glanced at Tor and nodded. "It's real nice," he said slowly. "Should we make sure not to put it in the dishwasher?"

"She always did," Jacob said with a blink. "It's just... it was hers."

"And now it's yours," Tor said firmly, and Jake knew without a doubt that no one would use that mug but Jacob. "But tell me you don't drink that much coffee."

Jacob smiled. "Not often," he said, but he didn't look up and Jake translated that to mean that Jacob had tried coffee but wasn't sure if he actually liked the stuff.

"What else?" Jake asked, reaching for more toast.

"Just some... well, there's a couple of movies." He held up DVD copies of 'Casablanca' and 'Weekend at Bernie's'. "She said they were both classics."

Jake laughed and nodded. "Sounds right. Bet she liked 'Weekend at Bernie's' better, too."

"She did--I think she watched this other one all of twice."

Tor grinned and they sat back in their chairs as Jacob pulled out a few books, a woven blanket, and two more bits of pottery. None of the things Jacob prized found a home before they all headed out for the day, but they were all seen for what they were: Jacob's treasures, and the way he found to make a house his home.

Chapter Twenty Eight

The rest of June was marked by the steady passing of days and Jacob's birthday. They had a cake and presents, which were mostly clothes and music, and Cath phoned. Becky and Susie called as well, which seemed to make Jacob happy, but all in all it was as muted as Jake had expected, and he could only hope that Jacob's next birthday would be happier. Turning fifteen should have been a much more upbeat occasion, and Jake was unsurprised when Jacob spent most of the day alone in the barn or in his room. He was proud of the smiles Jacob managed to work up. Jacob was strong. They both were.

Didn't stop either of them from missing 'Lissa and being angry at the world, though.

Near the end of the month the three of them took to spending the hot evenings flaked out in front of the TV, fans blowing on them and the lights off. It just felt cooler that way. Jake was sprawled on one couch, idly wondering when the weather was going to break, when Tor suddenly stood up from his armchair, crossed the room and grabbed Jake by the elbow, and pulled him up as well. Jake was mystified, but he didn't protest.

"Back in a couple of hours, kid," Tor said to Jacob. "Lights out by ten, okay?"

Jacob nodded, not looking away from the TV screen. "Sure, Uncle Tor." After a moment he added, "Need any help?"

"Nope, me and your uncle have it covered."

"We do?" Jake had no idea what was going on, but he let himself be urged into motion, right out of the living room, across the hall into the kitchen.

"We do." Tor stopped moving and gave him a firm look. "Stay."

"Woof." Jake waited, standing in the middle of the kitchen as Tor went upstairs for a moment before coming back to him. "What are we doing?"

"Going out," Tor said gruffly, taking him by the elbow and urging him once more into motion.

"Clearly," Jake said under his breath as they went out the door. Halfway across the yard he started to get an idea of what Tor's intentions were. "Tor," he protested quietly. "This is a bad idea."

Tor growled.

"No, seriously. It's too fucking hot to go up into the loft."

Tor seemed to consider that and suddenly Jake found himself being propelled toward the apple orchard. "Outside, then."

Jake stifled a sigh. Tor had been getting growly and pissy for almost a week and it looked like he'd had about enough. It wasn't like Jake hadn't seen it coming--there had been too big a shift in their house and their relationship for them to escape rough edges. Didn't mean he liked it or had the first sweet clue about how to deal with it.

Tor wasn't even looking at him. In point of fact, Tor looked more pissed off than anything else, and Jake began to wonder if his original assumption had been wrong. They'd been making do with quick blow jobs in bed and even quicker hand jobs in the shower, but Tor looked too mad to be thinking about fucking.

Unless, of course, he was determined to make sure Jake couldn't ride a horse for a couple of days.

"Tor?" Jake asked cautiously as they drew nearer the trees. "I know things have been a little off lately--"

"Off?" Tor snapped. "No, cowboy, they ain't been off. They've been fucking hijacked. Between working ourselves to death and you jumping at sounds in the night and getting more and more virginal--"

"I am not a virgin!"

"Didn't used to be, no. But I swear to God, Jake, I got further with you when my mother was in the next room instead of Jacob."

Jake rolled his eyes. "And all this bitching and swearing is helping so much."

Tor didn't say anything, but his hand on Jake's elbow tightened a little, his fingers digging in. Jake contemplated breaking away, but then he'd have to stomp off on general principle and he didn't really want to do that. Tor hadn't been having great sex, but Jake hadn't either, and while the current circumstances were far from wonderful, there was still an orgasm in the offering and Jake was just hormone-driven enough to put off the fight until after they were sticky.

He was dumb sometimes, but he was far from stupid.

Tor half dragged and half pushed him through the trees until he found what was apparently a suitable spot, then he let go of Jake's arm and took a deep breath.

Jake physically braced himself, prepared to keep himself upright under the expected onslaught of Tor's aggression--he'd been pushed up against enough walls and trees and beams in his time to know what to do--but it never came. Tor merely stood next to him, breathing. "Tor?"

"Just..." Tor sighed and turned to him, arms opening. "Come here."

A little confused by the sudden mellowing, Jake moved into Tor's space, still half expecting to be overwhelmed.

"I'm sorry," Tor whispered, holding him close. "Don't mean to snap."

Jake blinked a couple of times and rubbed Tor's back. "Understandable."

Tor nodded. "Doesn't mean it's right. But you've been hard to reach, cowboy. Like you've got blinders on, only seeing one part of things. Hard to get to you."

"I'm here now," Jake pointed out softly.

"Uh-huh." Tor's hands drifted down to Jake's ass. "I'm not really in a talking mood, though."

Jake started to chuckle, but before he could even begin to formulate a reply, Tor was kissing him. It started slow and sweet and didn't change into anything like the hungry, brutal claiming Jake had been geared up for; it got deeper and more intense, but Tor's mellowing seemed to have gone right down to his soul, and Jake sank into it. He let Tor's embrace, his arms and his mouth, lull him and soothe his mind and body, and he barely noticed when Tor laid him out on the soft grass as gentle as could be.

"I miss this," Tor told him as he unbuttoned Jake's shirt.

"Sneaking off?" Jake looked up the apple trees, a little surprised. Part of the lure of buying the ranch was that they could stop sneaking out.

"No. Well, that's not to say I don't have plans to haul you out into the barns so we can get noisy again." Tor gave him a wicked grin that went right to Jake's balls. "But I meant I miss taking my time." He spread Jake's shirt open and knelt astride Jake's hips, looking down on him. "Going slow."

Jake could only stare up at him and nod, his mind already a bit hazy. "Oh."

Tor took his time. Jake was a mess in short order, but Tor took his time. He spent an age on Jake's chest, touching and stroking and teasing and licking, and it was almost twenty minutes before he even moved down enough to undo Jake's jeans.

"Please," Jake whispered, for about the hundredth time. His skin was flushed and he was breathing hard, his mouth bruised from kisses and his face scraped by stubble. He never wanted to go back into the house again, not if he could just stay there in the orchard with Tor moving over him, whispering to him, loving him.

"Please?" Tor asked, and Jake could tell by the tone that the man wasn't teasing him, wasn't trying to torture him; Tor was just hazy, too, lost in the creature comfort of exploring and touching.

"Touch me," Jake said, rousing himself enough to help with Tor's clothes. "Long enough, Tor. Get rid of your boots." It was hard to get jeans off with dumb ass boots on--they'd tried it before and it had never gone well.

Tor kissed him again and then they were rolling on the

grass, the night making it damp and cool, and they managed, somehow, to get the boots off. Then everything paused while Tor went back to loving Jake with his hands, holding him and stroking his thighs, and just being everywhere. It was still slow and cool and hot and Jake was beginning to shake with the need for more, but not for an ending. He wanted to crawl right into Tor and stay there for a hundred years, warm and safe, and share the complete focus of their attention.

There wasn't anything in the world other than stars and apple wood and Tor's touch. There didn't need to be anything else; he could live off that, his soul and heart completely happy. Hell, if it came down to it, he could live off the apples and just drown in Tor.

Shaking, almost not noticing, he came with Tor's mouth on him, and rolled like liquid onto his belly, offering. He heard Tor saying something, the tone more important than the words, and then he was anchored and tethered, but soaring all at once.

It wasn't a dream, didn't feel like one, but it was far better. Their connection was something he could never doubt, never forget, though the reminder was welcome. He cried out when he came again, Tor inside him, around him, and he could feel Tor's reply in his blood.

They lay there for almost as long as they had loved, not saying anything at all. Almost all that they'd needed to say had been expressed. Almost.

"Don't want to have to drag you out of the house, Jake," Tor whispered. "Be nice to use our bed again."

"We use our bed," Jake protested, halfheartedly. He knew what Tor meant.

"Not like we should." Tor rolled onto his side and looked at him. "He's fifteen. He's not stupid, and he's not going to be in therapy for years if he hears us on occasion." He held up a hand as Jake opened his mouth. "I'm not saying we get wild-- I'll happily take you to the barn to tie you up, cowboy. But we can actually have sex in our own house and not damage him. Question is, can we do it and not damage you?"

Jake stared at him for a long moment.

"Come on, Jake," Tor said, rolling his eyes. "You're twisted up. I'm asking you to… untwist a little. That's all. He won't break."

Unspoken, was that Tor just might, that he'd come close to losing his temper over something pretty easy to fix.

"It always comes back to talking, doesn't it?" Jake said ruefully, thinking back on how they'd mended their relationship in the first place.

"Sadly, yes," Tor deadpanned. "So what do you say? Be that ornery slut I first shacked up with, yeah?"

Jake grinned. "I'll try."

"Try my nerves," Tor said under his breath, but he was smiling.

It took another hour for them to make their way home, slightly stickier and with a few more grass stains in interesting places. Jake figured it was worth it.

Chapter Twenty Nine

July was, as usual, busy on the ranch. Hay came up for another cutting and Jake hired on day labor to deal with it; Jacob was a help, but he was only one more body, and for a week they needed a lot more than that.

The weather held, though, the rain not coming at all until the hay was in the barn. More than a few bales went in trade for a couple of things they needed, and then damn near the whole ranch fell asleep for two days, everyone recovering with sore muscles, exhausted bodies, and one or two cases of sunburn.

Somewhere in there, in the mix of driving and cutting and binding and hauling, Tor had decided it would be of some use to have Jacob able to drive. He figured it would be a good thing, if only so there was one truck that just went to the barns and back, with no chance at all of someone making a misguided attempt to go to town or on errands somewhere else. So Jake got to watch, shaking his head, as Tor and Jacob took an hour and went on a little forward-only tour of the ranch. He wasn't exactly sure why Tor didn't teach him to put the truck in reverse, but by the end of the day Jacob was able to manage a pretty tight turn and was damn near bursting with pride and the thrill of driving.

Learning to ride wasn't quite so easy, but after a shaky first week--and sore thighs that Jacob made every attempt to deny--Jacob seemed to find his seat. Jake, Tor and a couple of the others made sure to find time to help with lessons, and Jacob spent almost all his time, outside of chores and sleep, on one horse or another. Jake just shook his head again and made sure Jacob took care of the animals in between the fun part.

What time wasn't spent in the saddle was spent with brushes or a shovel and rake.

Jake was almost surprised when he looked at the calendar and realized it was only a few days before school started. July had gone fast, lost in work and helping Jacob settle into life on the ranch. The start of August had gone just as quickly with getting the cattle ready for auction, and suddenly it was time for more shopping. He'd forgotten how fast teenagers grew, and Jacob was well and truly in a growth spurt.

It only took a few hours, really, but it was the strangest Saturday afternoon Jake could recall having in a long time. There were school supplies to get, and he kind of liked that part. There was just something nice about packages of pens and pencils and stacks of paper and binders. They were clean and new and Jake wistfully remembered when learning had been fun; he'd been a lot younger back then than Jacob was now, that was for sure.

Jacob didn't seem to care much about the school supplies, more interested in making sure the new backpack had a pocket for his CD player and dragging Jake over to the electronics to drool over MP3 players.

Jake wasn't exactly sure what an MP3 was, but he figured it had to be something pretty fucking advanced if it needed a tiny player that cost that much. He did, however, make note of the players Jacob really liked; Christmas was coming, after all.

Clothes shopping was faster than he'd expected, considering Jacob was a teenage boy. He just didn't appear to be a particularly fashion-conscious teenager, for which Jake was glad. Jeans, shirts, a new coat for good, and two pairs of sneakers. Another few pairs of sweatpants, shorts for gym, and they were done.

Now all he had to do was survive the actual first day of school.

He only called to check on the time the bus went by once, and he only double-checked with Jacob about the bus versus a drive in for the first day twice. He thought he was doing pretty well until Tor called him pathetic and rolled his eyes.

After that, he shut up and tried to let it go, but he figured he was kind of unsuccessful when both Jacob and Tor made a show of setting his alarm clock for him the night before school started.

Like he was going to sleep anyway.

"What's with you?" Tor asked as they went to bed that night. "It's only school, he's been doing fine. It's not like it's your first day--it's his, and he's pretty relaxed about it."

Jake shrugged and got into bed. "Don't know. Just... want everything to go well, I guess."

"That isn't up to you," Tor said gently. "You're going to give yourself ulcers if you keep this up. And then where will I be? A lame partner with stomach issues, a teenager, and a ranch. Drive me into an early grave."

Jake gave him a sour look, ignoring the way Tor was grinning at him. "All about you, all the time," he bitched.

"Yup. Come here, let me take your mind off it for a bit."

Jake eyed him and then decided it was a pretty good offer. Maybe he'd get some sleep after all. Plus, with Tor going off to the auction in a few days he should kind of stock up on orgasms to get him through the dry patch.

He really was pathetic.

Of course, all the things he'd worried about--Jacob missing the bus, being late, not finding the office or his homeroom, eating lunch alone--were fine. Jacob came home from school with a smile, a pile of homework, the dates for tryouts for the soccer and football teams, and two phone numbers. One was for a guy named Leroy, the other for a girl named Lillian who was in his homeroom and math class.

"She's really smart," Jacob told them as he emptied out his book bag. "She wants to be a doctor. And Leroy was on the soccer team last year; we kicked the ball around for a bit and he doesn't think I'll have any trouble making the team. Can I go to the barn now, or do I have to do my homework first?" The last was called from the fridge where he was gathering what looked to be a full meal.

"Homework first," Tor said, heading back out the kitchen door. "Then horses. And supper is in three hours, so don't eat all that."

Jake smiled as Jacob nodded and put back an apple. He still had bread, cheese, mayo, pickles, chicken, and lettuce out. "So, it was okay?"

"Yeah, it was fine. I don't think I'm behind in anything, but the Spanish book is different from the one at my old school. The math, too, actually, but it looks like the same level." He grinned at Jake. "Are you gonna stand there and watch me do my homework?"

"I think that's my cue to leave," Jake said, rolling his eyes. "If you need help with math, ask Tor. He minored in it at college. History, too, for that matter."

"He minored in both math and history?"

Jake shook his head. "No, sorry. He majored in American history. No idea why." He grabbed his hat and grinned. "Me, I can help with... finding Tor."

Jacob laughed and took his food to the table. "I'll be fine; it's the first day. Not much to do."

"Good enough. Got horses waiting on you." Jake waited long enough to really take in the picture of Jacob at the kitchen table with books spread out in front of him, and then went back to work. It was odd, and not something he'd ever thought would be part of his life, but it felt right.

Chapter Thirty

Jake sat on the porch in the dying light of the day and felt sorry for himself. He hated that Tor had gone to the auction and he wasn't there, too. He hated that they were apart again, even if it was only for four days, and he hated that he was being all girly and depressed about it.

It was too soon after they'd been apart, and it didn't matter that it was necessary. They'd said they weren't going to be apart, and he couldn't quite bring himself around to be reasonable. He knew this was different, that it was the way things had to be and didn't strictly fall under what they'd promised each other, but still. He didn't like it, and alone on his porch he could be as self-indulgent and miserable as he wanted.

That lasted for all of about five minutes before he had to go back in the house; he was making himself growly and irritable. Even more than Tor being gone, Jake disliked being uneasy in his skin, and there wasn't much more uneasy than acting like a kid less mature than Jacob. If Jacob could pull himself together and deal with life, Jake could.

He went into the living room, nodding at Jacob on his way to the desk in the far corner. "Anything good on?" he asked, angling his chin at the TV.

"Nope." Jacob sprawled a little more on the couch. "We got any popcorn?"

"Think so." Jake sat at the desk and opened the middle drawer. He figured he might as well balance the checkbook if he was going to be in a foul mood anyway. He'd start with his personal account, move on to the house account, and if he was really feeling pissy, he'd take a stab at the ranch books.

Tor was going to string him up when he got home. Jake grinned and hunted through the drawer for the calculator. Given the mood he was in, it was a good thing Jacob's money was run through the trust fund. Lord knew what kind of mess he'd make with that account.

"Want some?" Jacob asked, not moving an inch.

Jake looked up from where he'd lined up the checkbooks. "Huh?"

"Popcorn. Want some?"

"Oh. Yeah, okay. Thanks."

"I was hoping you'd make it."

Jake snorted. "Smartass."

Laughing, Jacob rolled off the couch. "What're you doing?" he asked, padding over to the desk.

"Going to balance my checkbook and go over the accounts." God, that sounded dull.

Jacob backed away, still grinning. "Right. I think I'll stick with the crappy TV. I'll put butter on the popcorn, though, just so your night's not a total waste."

"Gee, thanks," Jake muttered, sharpening a pencil. He was going to have to make sure Elias spent less time with Jacob; his sense of humor was rubbing off on the kid.

An hour later, Jake was going over the latest bank statement on the ranch account for the fifth time and fighting down panic. His own checking account had been easy; he'd even managed to find the missing twenty-six cents that he'd held over from the last month. The joint account had been even easier, balancing out in a way that he should have sensed was a warning for things to come.

Two thousand, four hundred and forty-two dollars.

Over.

The bank didn't just hand out large amounts of money, he was pretty sure, but he couldn't find any missing deposits and the debits looked all right. He'd gone through receipts and done the math for four months back, but the statement didn't change at all. It still insisted they had more money in the bank than they did in the check register.

He didn't really notice Jacob go to bed, though he did

vaguely recall telling him good night. Full dark had long settled over the house and the one lamp he had on, there on the desk, was pooling light right on the mountain of paper he'd created. His stomach was knotting up tight. Almost twenty-five hundred dollars. He wondered if he'd feel as sick if they were short that much, and decided he would.

When the phone rang he jumped in his chair, dropping the bank statement. He bent to pick it up, one hand snatching up the phone receiver before it could ring again. "Hello?" he said, almost barking the word. His heart was thudding and his stomach had kind of given a guilty lurch to the left.

"Jake? Wake you up?" Tor sounded amused.

"No. No, I was..." Jake sighed and tossed the statement onto the desk. "We have a problem."

There was a short pause and then Tor's voice lost all its amusement. "What? Jacob? You hurt?"

"No, we're fine. Nothing like that." Jake rubbed a hand over his forehead and stared at the desk, a mess of paper and pencil shavings. "I was doing the books, just balancing the checkbooks."

Tor snorted. "Lonely and bored isn't a good combination for you, is it?"

"Nope. Look, the bank says we got a pile more money than we do. I'm gonna have to go in tomorrow and get this sorted out, find out--"

"Whoa, hold up. More money?"

Jake nodded. "Almost twenty-five hundred dollars, Tor. This is fucked."

"Hang on, let me think a minute. You got the books there?" He could hear Tor moving, could picture him pacing in whatever tiny motel room he and Elias had, walking back and forth between the beds and the bathroom.

"Got the statement from the bank, all the receipts for the last six weeks, the check register..." He moved a few things around and added, "And the payables."

"Get the ledger, Jake," Tor said evenly. "And goddamnit, we're switching the books to the fucking computer. Time you stopped being so stubborn about this."

It was the latest argument, but one Jake wasn't nearly so wound up about as Tor. He didn't care if they got the books on the computer or not, but it would definitely mean they'd need a new computer and they couldn't really afford that until the end of the year. Unless the bank really was giving them a bunch of cash, anyway. The only thing Jake was standing firm on was that they weren't going to buy a computer on credit.

"Yeah, yeah," he muttered, crossing to the filing cabinet and getting the heavy ledger. Instead of putting everything on the desk away to make space he carried it to the coffee table and turned on another lamp. "Tell me you sold some fucking cows today. I need some good news."

"Some. Elias is out closing on another deal, think it'll pan out. Got the books?"

"Yep." Jake flipped the book open and started turning pages, looking for the current spreadsheet. "Oh, hang on, left the statement on the desk." He got up and almost grinned when Tor sighed in his ear. "Okay. What am I looking for? Aside from a huge-ass deposit?"

"You're not looking for a deposit."

Jake blinked. "We got income I don't know about? Little something on the side?"

"Shut up and listen to me." Tor didn't sound amused anymore, just tired, and Jake got the feeling he was missing something a bit bigger than a decimal point. "We went over the books two weeks ago, yeah? Payday? You wrote out the checks for the guys hired on for hay."

Jake nodded. He knew that, and he knew the books had been spot on then. There certainly hadn't been extra money. He scanned the columns for the last couple of weeks and nodded again. "Yeah, everything looks right. But those numbers aren't on the statement, it's backdated. So even if the numbers are right in the ledger, they could still be--"

"Jake, turn the fucking page." The tired was getting growly, but a touch of humor was threading through it again and the knot in Jake's gut loosened a little.

Jake turned the page and closed his eyes. "What the fuck is

that?" he said, proud of how even his voice was. He wasn't going to string Tor up by his balls, because the paperwork of suddenly being sole owner of the ranch was too much trouble and he'd have to do all the cooking. But he suddenly wished Tor was right there so he could slap the jackass up the side of the head.

"Turn back a page and find... damn. Last column over, under 'sundries'. Same total, right? I carried it over, and the total at the very bottom, the actual real live balance, should be what's on the statement, adjusted for the last few weeks' activity."

"Hang on. Actually, call me back. No. Stay there, just... shut up." Jake dropped the phone and went to get the calculator and the register. It was surprisingly easy to ignore the tinny sound of Tor's laughter.

It only took a minute to bring the numbers on the statement up to date and find that the ledger balanced; whatever Tor had been tracking on the back of the current spreadsheet was withdrawals on paper, but not out of the account itself. "Okay," he said, picking up the phone again. "What is this? And why don't I know?" That part kind of pissed him off.

"On the register, see just about two hundred dollars at the start of every month marked as a debit?" Tor asked patiently.

"Uh-huh."

"Marked 'DPS'?"

"Yes, Tornado. I can see it. What I want to know is what the fuck it *is*."

"Calm yourself. You know what it is, Taggart. Dance party savings." Tor said it with such calmness that Jake was sure he was holding all the smugness right there in his facial expression, safely a few hundred miles away where Jake couldn't see him.

"Dance party savings," Jake said dumbly. Dance. Party. "Ah, fuck."

"Uh-huh. Remember the hell we went through paying it off last year? You said--"

"I said we couldn't just pay for something that big without budgeting for it," Jake groaned. His head fell back on the couch, his eyes closed. Not only did he say it, but he'd told Tor to leave the money in the account and just take it off the register.

"You scared me," Tor said in his ear, his voice soft. "Thought something was really wrong."

"I thought something *was* wrong," Jake said, just as quietly. "I forgot, I guess. And then I panicked, and you weren't here and I kinda..."

"Got twisted."

"Yeah."

There was a pause and Jake stayed there, his head back and his eyes closed. He was mostly relieved, but embarrassment was creeping up fast. "I should go to bed," he said.

Tor snorted in his ear. "Running away from me, cowboy?"

"Just a little."

"Stop that."

Jake growled and got up, slamming the ledger closed with one hand and holding the phone with the other. "I hate this. I hate that I can't keep track of everything, I hate that I forget, I hate that you're not here."

"I know," Tor said with a sigh. "But, Christ, Jake. Despite whatever I say in bed, you're not a god. You *can't* manage all that on your own, and you don't have to. Doug never did, and you can't expect yourself to. Partners, yeah?"

"I know," Jake mumbled, putting the ledger back on the shelf. "I do. But it's easier when you're here."

"Yeah. And maybe next time it'll work out better."

It wouldn't, though, and Jake knew it. One of them had to go to auction, one had to stay and run the place. It made sense and it was only a few days a couple of times a year. "Maybe," he said anyway. At the desk he started to gather the receipts into a pile.

"You're still pissy."

"Yep." He was. He should probably start trying not to be, but he'd had a rough hour and before that he'd been working on a good sulk. He was in the groove.

"You know what I'd do if I was there."

"You're not."

"But you know what I'd do."

"Yell back?" That would be good; a nice little fight and then off to bed.

Tor laughed darkly in his ear. "Nope. I'd shut you up, distract you."

"Yeah, well. That's not gonna happen, is it?" Jake tossed the paperwork back in the drawer and glared at the check registers before throwing them in, too.

"It would if you'd shut up and just go with this."

Jake rolled his eyes. "You can't be serious."

"Tell me you're not half-hard anyway. I know you, Taggart. You get riled, you get hard, and then you get off and go to sleep. Wake up bright and cheery."

Jake frowned and glanced down at his jeans. "Shut up. I'm not doing this."

"Not yet, anyway. C'mon, the kid's in bed and Elias isn't here. I can make you feel better," he wheedled.

"I feel stupid when we do this," Jake said bluntly.

"Only until you get into it. Just… sit on the couch, okay? Don't even do anything, just listen to me."

Jake sighed to himself and turned out the lights. He always felt awkward when they had sex on the phone, like he was trying for sexy and missing by a country mile. Tor never seemed to be embarrassed, though, willing to just talk and go on about things that Jake felt but couldn't ever find words for. "The things I do for you…"

Tor laughed softly. "I know. You hate jerking off."

Jake snorted and threw himself on the couch. "All right. Couch."

"Cool. I'm on the bed… well, I will be in a second."

Jake could hear the thumps as Tor's boots hit the floor, and the rattle of the phone as it was set down so Tor could strip. Grinning to himself and shaking his head, he twisted on the couch and stretched out his legs. He wasn't anywhere near getting naked yet.

"Still there?"

"Nope," Jake said. "I went to get a drink of water."

"Funny. You're not going to make this easy, are you?"

There was more than a little hint of a pout in Tor's voice, and even though Jake knew it was most certainly fake, he relented.

"Do I ever make it easy?" he said with a smile. "If it helps, you're right. I got riled, I got sort of hard. Knowing you're naked isn't making that go away."

"Oh, good," Tor said dryly. "Now just shut up, I'm busy here."

"You are?" Jake teased. "With what?"

"Trying to figure out the fastest way to get you panting in my ear. I love when you do that, the way your breath catches. It's even better than hearing you stroke your cock. I can usually judge just how far along you are by how fast your hand goes."

Jake blinked and licked his lower lip. "Oh. Uh."

"Of course, watching is better," Tor went on, his voice dropping a note or two. "I mean, you know what you look like. And when you're jerking off, you get so damn focused. Your stomach gets tight, your legs flex and you just... your eyes, Jake. Your gaze turns inward and everything is right there, everything you want, and you take it, you make it. Your hand on yourself, that fucking ring shining and flicking and then you just do whatever it is you need to get you there."

Jake had no idea what to say. This wasn't the usual 'think about me licking your balls' shit, this was something else. He knew he was blushing. "Tor."

"What? It's true, nothing like watching you, Jake. Even when I'm fucking you, when I'm buried in your ass, I watch. I watch your back, your body, every fucking muscle. When you're in me, all I can do is feel, watch your face and listen to your voice. When you say my name it's like sparks, when you get close to coming you make a noise that's like a rumble I swear I can hear in my gut."

Jake licked his lip again, completely unprepared to realize he'd undone his jeans and had one hand down his pants, fondling his cock. "I like saying your name," he whispered. "Sometimes it's the only thing I can say. Usually it's the only thing I can think."

There was a short pause and Tor took a deep, unsteady breath. "Damn. This is different. I thought I was going to tell you about slamming you up against the wall."

"Yeah." Jake slid his hand up his cock and hissed as his palm grazed the head. He toyed with the ring a second, looking down his body to it, the metal catching the tiny bit of light from the kitchen. "It's working, though. I'm really fucking hard, here." He tugged the ring and hissed again.

Tor gave him a little laugh, thready and darker still. "What are you doing?"

"You can't tell?"

"If I have to guess, I'd say you're tugging on your ring and trying to figure out if you really do have to wiggle out of your jeans to get to your balls. And yes, you do. No room in there for your hand, too."

Jake laughed and lifted his hips. "And you've got your hand around your dick, still loose, and moving faster than when you're serious about getting off." He shoved at his jeans and got them down just enough to give himself some room. "Right?"

"Nope. Got tighter already. Kinda stuck on the image of you with your hand down your jeans. You ever jerk off when you're out on your own?"

"What, when I'm supposed to be watching cows or fixing fences? Of course." He did, too, though not much lately. "I like leaning on the fence posts and taking a break. Sometimes just knowing all that land is ours gets me hard."

"Uh-huh," Tor agreed, *his* breath catching a bit. "Any time I come back from swimming in the river you can be pretty sure I've been having a good afternoon."

Jake groaned. He'd seen Tor swimming, long before they'd gotten together. He'd sat on River's back and watched Tor start to touch himself, laid out on top of a rock, water drops running off his skin and shining in the sunlight. He'd spent months getting off to that image and it had just resumed its place on his list of fantasy material. "That's… good to know," he said, his hand tight as he used a long stroke.

"Wish I was home," Tor said. "Want to see you."

Jake closed his eyes and with his free hand pushed his T-shirt up over his belly. One leg was braced on the floor, the other on the couch, and when he dragged a fingernail over his nipple his hips rolled, shoving his cock through his fist. "Just see?" he said, voice rough.

"No. Want to suck you. I want to hear you, feel your hands on my head when you let go."

Jake knew this part, knew that at this point it didn't matter if he'd felt silly ten minutes ago or not. It might still be ridiculous, but they were in the same place and they were after the same thing, and it was right. There wasn't anything to hide, not from Tor.

"Tor, I'm gonna come soon," he said, more to hear the way Tor moaned than to really warn him. He was sure that Tor already knew. "Think we can do it together?" He had to stop for a second, give himself a hard squeeze just under the head of his cock to keep from going off early. He loved it when they went at the same time.

"Give me... oh yeah. Hang on." Jake could hear Tor better then, the slick sound of his hand on his erection, the sound of skin shifting and meeting. Faster. He could hear Tor moan, in between panted breaths.

"That's it," Jake told him, trying to match his rhythm. "With me. Soon."

"Christ. Tell me you've still got your shirt on."

"Pushed up."

Tor groaned. "Get it messy."

Jake's gut cramped and he curled up. "Tor--"

"Fuck! Jake."

Jake bit his lip, bit back a yell before it could get out, but he knew Tor would hear him coming, could tell by his breath, by the not-silent quiet. Jake knew that Tor would feel it, the same way the pounding of his heart measured out Tor's orgasm.

"Wish you were here," he whispered when he could breathe.

"Wish I was, too," Tor whispered back.

Clearing

Chapter Thirty One

Jake squinted as he went into the kitchen, the light dim compared to the bright glare of mid-morning sun outside. The yard was already filling up with trucks and cars, people arriving early to grab prime camping spots before they settled in for the afternoon of socializing and the evening of music and drinking and barbecuing. At ten-thirty there were already about a hundred people there, including all the little kids, and there'd be a whole lot more in a few hours.

"Jacob?" he yelled, going to the fridge for a bottle of apple juice. There was a line of coolers out on the lawn, but he was pretty sure there wasn't anything in them other than booze and drink mix.

"Stop yelling," Tor said with a grin as he rounded the corner from the living room. "He's doing laundry. What's up?"

Jake rolled his eyes. Jacob was always doing laundry; between clothes for school and clothes for the barn, the kid went through more than his fair share of laundry detergent. "Again? Christ. Tell him he can just throw it in with ours."

Tor shook his head, grin growing. "Oh, no, cowboy. I'm staying as far away from that whole issue as I can get."

"Whatever." Jake shrugged and tossed the cap from his bottle into the sink. "His friend Lillian is here, is all. Turns out her daddy is Pike Kobel."

"I'm pretty sure he knows," Tor said with a wink. "That's why he's doing laundry."

Jake shook his head and swallowed a mouthful of juice. "He's gonna leave her out there while he waits for his favorite shirt to dry? Boy's got messed up priorities."

Tor laughed and leaned on the counter. "Ain't his shirt. He'll be along soon."

"Jeans, whatever." Jake drained the bottle and set it on the counter. "Point is, you'd think he'd get his laundry sorted out the day before the party."

This time Tor's laugh was longer, long enough that Jake figure out he was missing something. "What?"

"Jesus, Jake. Don't make me spell this out for you." Tor was grinning at him and shaking his head in what was clearly disbelief.

"What?" Jake said again, confusion battling with annoyance.

Tor took a deep breath and moved to stand in front of him, his eyes dancing with suppressed laughter. "How old is Jacob?"

Jake glared. "Fifteen, and what does that have to do with the price of bulls? For someone who doesn't give a shit about fashion, he goes through more clothes than--"

"He ain't washing clothes, Taggart. Christ, don't you remember being fifteen?"

Jake's scowl turned into a frown. "I remember getting into a lot of trouble. I remember spending as much time as I could out of the house."

Tor's eyes rolled and he sighed. "Other stuff. What about what your body was doing all the damn time and shit like that."

Jake stared at him. "I'm not following you."

"Oh, for... when *I* was fifteen I was following Kincaid around like a lost puppy and sneaking off every chance I got so I could..." he trailed off and raised an eyebrow.

Jake's brain seized up on him, flooding him with images he'd just as soon never have again. Not of Tor and Kin, but of himself and guys he couldn't put faces to and of being alone in his room doing stuff he'd really rather not associate with his nephew. "Jesus," he said, closing his eyes and turning away really fast, like that would stop him from ever knowing what Tor was trying so hard to make him understand. "Fuck."

Tor grinned at him. "Laundry."

"Shut up," Jake said, scrubbing at his eyes. "God."

"Oh, come on, it's normal," Tor told him in what Jake could only assume was supposed to be a soothing tone.

"I don't care if it's normal, I don't want to know!"

"And he doesn't want you to know, either! So you just let the boy do his laundry and forget about it." Tor grinned and reached for him, but Jake stepped back. "Cut it out," Tor said with a leer. "He's not the only one in this house with needs."

Jake shuddered and backed farther away. "I don't think I'm ever having sex again."

Tor's eyes narrowed. "I think I have something to say about that."

"Ever," Jake insisted. "Or until my brain blocks this whole thing out. God, why didn't you just toss a box of tissues into his room or something? And how long have you known about this?"

Tor shrugged. "Since I noticed he washes his sheets about three times a week. And I keep forgetting about the tissues-- kind of figured he'd get some himself."

"Right, 'cause he does the shopping. It's not like he's going to ask, Tor." Jake closed his eyes again. "What about... fuck. What about other stuff? I mean, should we talk to him about condoms and shit like that?" He ignored the way his stomach tensed at the idea. He never once thought he'd have to have a conversation like that from the parenting end of it, and other thoughts were crowding in, like how Jacob spent just as much time with Leroy as he did Lillian, and there still weren't any posters on his walls. Abruptly, he pulled a chair out from the table and sat down, hard.

"Easy, cowboy," Tor said, laughing at him again. "Want some more juice? You're awfully pale all of a sudden."

"What's wrong with you?" Elias asked, the door slamming shut behind him. "Got any ice in here?"

"It's all out in the yard," Tor said, turning a chair backwards and straddling it. "Taggart here just found out our little boy is growing up and he's taking it kind of hard."

"Fuck off," Jake said weakly.

"What's the problem?" Elias said curiously, going to the fridge and looking in the freezer. "No ice."

"Told you."

Jake waved a hand. "We don't even know if he's into girls or not," he said to the room in general.

Elias shrugged. "That's easy to find out." Before Jake could do anything, Elias walked to the bottom of the stairs. "Jacob!" he bellowed. "Your girlfriend is here! Lookin' pretty, too!"

Footsteps thundered across the floor above them and down the stairs. "She's here? Why didn't anyone call me?" He shot a hard look at Jake and headed for the door.

"Hey, kid," Elias called after him. "Keep it in your pants, yeah? Her daddy's a big man."

Jacob turned scarlet and nodded once before barreling out of the house.

"And that's how you find out," Elias said with a wink. "I'll get him stuff when I'm in town next week."

"Okay," Jake said faintly. "But he's not... I mean, they're not?"

"Not that I know of," Elias said, walking to the door. "But. Don't know about you, but when I was fifteen I was damn sure *trying* to, though."

"I ain't ready for this," Jake said to the top of the table.

Tor's hand landed on his shoulder. "He'll be fine," he said softly. "He knows right from wrong. Trust him."

Jake nodded. He didn't have a whole lot of choice about that, really. He only hoped his day wasn't going to get any worse.

Chapter Thirty Two

Lillian Kobel's daddy really was a big man, and between him following Lillian, and Jake trailing after Jacob, there was quite a parade wandering around the yard until Tor and Mrs. Kobel stepped in.

"You're playing football," Tor said firmly, yanking on Jake's elbow.

"And you're going to sit down here a bit and help me with... not annoying your daughter," Mrs. Kobel said, giving Tor a distinctly sympathetic look.

"We weren't doing anything," Jake protested. He let himself be led away, though, fairly sure that he and Pike Kobel were going to have a chat to compare notes in the near future.

"You were interfering," Tor told him with a grin. "Come on, now, and let Jacob be. Stop looming."

"I don't loom," Jake muttered, letting Tor turn him so his back was to where Jacob and Lillian were sitting with a group of kids their own age.

"Of course you don't." Tor pointed to where a game of touch football was starting up. "Want to join in?"

Jake shook his head. "Not right now. You go. I'm going to... wander a bit. Make sure everyone's got what they need."

Tor nodded, his eyes on the game. "Think I saw Ben and Jeff earlier," he said. "And I know Steve Adleman is here-- might want to talk to him about those horses of his, if you have a mind."

"Horses?" Jake asked, stressing the plural.

Tor wouldn't look at him. "You got a few more good years with River, Taggart. But it might be time to start getting your- self attached to a new critter. I know how you are; just... take some time, you know?"

Jake's jaw clenched, his immediate need to deny that there was any need to think any such thing getting stuck on the truth. River was almost twenty-five and he was feeling fine, but there weren't any guarantees. "I'll talk to him," he said finally. "But I'm not making any promises."

"Not asking you to," Tor said easily. He rested his hand on the small of Jake's back and gave him a quick caress. "I'll find you in a bit. Lots of people to talk to around here today. Try to have a good time, hear?"

"I hear." Jake managed a weak smile. "I'll be stir-crazy by the time the band starts up, bet you anything."

"No bet. Just be glad it's only one night instead of the two the Boss did every year."

Jake shuddered. "Go play," he said, stepping away and catching Tor's hand with his own for a moment. "I'll find you in time for supper. And don't go getting damaged out there."

"Worrywart," Tor accused, his voice more amused that anything else. "Go on, get. And leave Jacob alone."

Jake sighed and rolled his eyes, letting Tor's hand go after another quick squeeze. It was going to be a long day.

***

Jake spent the better part of the day walking through the yard and talking to people, making sure they were having a good time. He played soccer with Jacob and the group of teens until he was breathless and feeling his age, then escaped back to the adults, wondering when exactly hours of talking to people became something he preferred to playing in the dirt. He really was getting old, he decided, and he was damn sure he'd never talked to so many people one after another in his entire life.

"Got a good crowd in," Steve Adleman said as Jake wandered up to him. He was standing in front of a tent and shaking out a blanket, looking like he'd rather be doing anything but making up a bed. "Almost as many as Doug would get."

Jake nodded, his hands stuffed into his back pockets. "Yeah," he agreed, surveying what looked like a sea of tents and piles of blankets all over the front lawn. There were people all over, cooking or sitting and talking in groups, kids running around and dogs barking. "Only down about fifteen families," he said with a nod. He and Tor had found out the first summer they'd tried to duplicate Doug Gillian's guest list that while most people were fine, there were in fact a number of people willing to do business with them but not spend a day socializing. That it was less than a dozen and a half, Jake counted as a blessing.

"Not bad. How's your nephew making out? School okay?"

Jake nodded again. "Yeah, he's fitting in. Got a girlfriend, apparently."

"Ah, that explains why you look like you're going to bolt."

"Nah, that's just me," Jake grinned. "Tor says I'm gonna stroke out if I don't relax."

Adleman laughed and nodded. "Sounds like Rosie. Don't tell Tor I said that, mind."

Jake smirked, imagining the look on Tor's face when he found out he was acting like a middle-aged ranch wife. "Tor says you got some horses coming up for sale," he said, changing the subject.

"Few," Adleman said with a nod. "Boy need something to ride?"

Jake nodded. "He's just new to the saddle, so we need a gentle mount for him. Broke in, not too old, nice size. And I've been told we should look at a youngster for here."

Adleman had been nodding, but his eyes narrowed and Jake cursed the fact that the man had known him for more than fifteen years. "For you, you mean. How old's River now?"

"Old enough," Jake said. "I don't want a new horse, but Tor's right. Wouldn't hurt to have another animal in the stalls, and it's not like it won't get put to work. If we could afford it, I'd say we'd get two for the ranch and one for Jacob, but you know how it goes."

"I do." He flipped out the blanket again and nodded sharply. "Come around next week some time, bring the boy. Got a few you can look at, one in particular I think'll fit."

"All right," Jake said, nodding back. "Think you better find

Rosie--last I saw of her she was looking over the band's play list and planning her dancing."

"Lord help me. That woman's gonna be my death." He was smiling, though, and Jake knew full well that Adleman would be up there doing a smooth two-step as soon as the music started, his arms wrapped around his wife and both of them having a grand time.

Jake grinned and left him there, making sure to find Jacob in the crowd before going to help the band with their gear. He was actually easy to find, kicking a ball back and forth with Leroy as a group of girls watched; it made Jake quake in his boots, but at least he knew where Jacob was. And he had to admit, to himself if no one else, that it was damn fine seeing Jacob in the center of a crowd, having fun. He looked healthy, the sun and work and riding filling him out and tanning his skin. Playing alongside Leroy, who was just as tall but about twenty pounds skinnier with glossy dark hair, they made a striking impression and it wasn't any wonder they had a flock of admirers.

The early evening got filled up with grilling, Tor suddenly appearing and taking over when Jake brought a huge plate of steaks out, the second of three platters. There was food all over, a row of picnic tables set up like a buffet, and in the background Jake could hear the band testing their sound and kids screaming with glee when someone brought out sparklers for them.

"Going good," Tor observed, passing him a bottle of juice and flipping steaks. "You holding up?"

"I'm fine," Jake said, grateful for the juice. "Talked to a lot of folks, though. I don't plan on being social again for months."

Tor smiled at him and nodded. "That's okay," he said easily. "You and me can just kind of hide for a few weeks."

"Promise?"

"You know it."

Jake smiled to himself and went to find Jacob, who'd vanished from sight around the side of the barn. He wasn't too worried, though--he could see Lillian with her mother, uncovering bowls of potato salad. She was a pretty thing, almost as tall as Jacob with short dark hair that framed her face. She caught Jake looking at her and blushed, quickly looking down at the bowl in her hand.

Jake looked away and turned pink himself, wishing for all he was worth that he had the faintest idea how to act toward her.

As dark fell, the band picked up and the sparklers turned into cherry bombs. When the littlest of the kids started nodding off before being put to bed, Jake saw more and more beer bottles and cans coming out and amused himself by seeing how close to the barn he could get before Tor or Elias or Tommy wandered over to check on him, all three sympathetic to his discomfort at knowing that he was there for the duration, but unsure if there was really anything to be done about it.

At one point he actually made it into the stable and he leaned on River's stall, waiting. Sure enough, Tor popped in about three minutes later and Jake grinned. "I'm fine," he said before Tor could ask him yet again. "Go bother Jacob or something."

"Not a chance. He's dancing."

Jake raised an eyebrow. "Is he, now?"

"Uh-huh. He asked Lillian, or she asked him, or something. And the next thing I saw, Pike had his missus up there, right next to him. I think Lillian's going to kill him. Pike, I mean."

Jake laughed. "Christ."

Tor leaned into him and grinned. "You smell good. Like steak."

Amused, Jake nodded and then lifted his chin so Tor could sniff him again. "You like that?"

"Sure," Tor purred at him, leaning closer and pushing him against the wall. "I like everything."

Jake's grin grew. "Wanna mess around?"

"Here?"

"Can't go anywhere else. We can sneak up into the loft for a quickie."

Tor pulled away abruptly but grabbed his hand. "Okay, let's go. Got lube?"

"Nope, gonna have to come up with something else."

Tor snorted but pulled him toward the ladder. "We'll figure it out," he said dryly as he started up. "We've had enough practice."

"Nah." Jake watched him climb, admiring his ass. "Never get enough practice."

Tor grinned down at him and wiggled his butt. "That was damn near sweet. Now, come up here with me and suck my cock."

Jake reached up and smacked his ass. "Bossy. Get a move on."

"Bossy." But he hurried up and vanished into the loft, laughing softly.

Jake scrambled up after him, not wasting time, and had to stifle a surprised cry when Tor grabbed him before he was over the top of the ladder. "Hey," he protested when Tor tossed him onto a hay bale. "These things are hard!"

"Uh-huh, and so am I, so shut up and let's go," Tor said with a laugh, pouncing on him and taking his mouth in a hard kiss.

Jake couldn't really come up with a reason to disagree, so he went with it, wrapping a leg around Tor's and kissing him back, one hand fighting with his belt. It was a lot easier to undo his own with one hand than it was to manage Tor's, so he gave up on groping Tor's ass pretty quickly, concentrating on the kisses and getting their jeans open. "How?" he asked into a kiss as he wrapped his hand around Tor's cock.

Tor groaned and thrust a bit. "Don't care anymore."

"God, you're easy," Jake teased, stroking him again. "Zero to I don't care in less than a minute."

"No time to be fussy," Tor told him, his hips rocking again.

"Oh, if you want fast I can do that," Jake promised, letting him go. "Get off me. God, you're heavy."

"Shut up," Tor said easily, rolling away. "I ain't."

"It must be someone else making me breathless," Jake

said, following him and taking another kiss.

"Better not be. I'm the only one who should make you like this."

Jake grinned and made sure Tor was propped up against a stack of bales before going down to his knees and pushing Tor's shirt up out of the way. "Bossy and possessive."

"You love it," Tor said, sounding a little breathless himself.

Jake had to give him that; he did love it. Not that he'd say as much, not when he could be doing other things, like nuzzle into Tor's hip and lick at his erection a little before tugging Tor's ring with his teeth.

"Tease," Tor hissed.

Jake had to give him that, too. He grinned and did it again, a little lick and a tug, his fingers digging into Tor's hip. Tor smelled incredible, sun warmed and earthy, turned on and musky. He tasted better.

Jake hummed a little as he licked and played, chuckling when Tor's fingers tangled in his hair insistently. He waited until the tug got a bit harder, then took Tor's cock in his mouth and got rewarded with a sigh and the loosening of Tor's grip.

Under his knees bits of hay and dirt dug in, but that was all right. The smell of the barn and of Tor's skin was a heady mix and the feel of denim under his hands and grit under his knees was just fine. He loved what he was doing, where he was, and it spurred him on to suck a little harder, his mouth wet and tight.

He was just really getting into it, the glide up and down and a twist of his tongue around the ring at the very tip of Tor's cock, when Tor's hand tightened again, almost painfully. He froze on instinct, knowing that it wasn't incipient orgasm that made Tor tense like a wire stretched taut.

Elias' voice floated up to them. "Jake?"

Jake relaxed his sucking but didn't let Tor go as his mouth curved into a grin.

"He's busy," Tor called out, his voice only a little rough.

There was a short pause and Jake could hear Elias' boots

scuffing below them. "Where the hell are you?"

"Loft." Tor's breath caught as Jake started sucking again. "*Busy.*"

The second pause was longer, and the boots stopped. "Oh, for fuck's sake... Hurry up. There's people wanting... Christ, you two."

Jake laughed as best he could and curled his hand around Tor's hip as he sucked again and took Tor deep, pulled him in with mouth and hand.

"Just be a minute," Tor said, unable to stifle a groan. "Get out."

"Like I didn't spend years listening to you when you had the room across the hall," Elias muttered, footfalls sounding again. "Still. Think y'all would calm down after all this time."

Not likely, Jake thought to himself as Tor let go and started moving with him, fingers in his hair petting again, curling around the back of his head. Not fucking likely.

It didn't take long after that; Tor dove into him and Jake took him, faster and deeper with less tongue and more sucking, a hand on Tor's ass to keep him going until he could feel Tor get a little harder, taste him leaking. With a moan Jake looked up and met Tor's eyes, staring down at him, his teeth biting at his lower lip.

"Jake," Tor whispered, and Jake winked at him, knowing it was right there in front of him. That seemed to be all Tor needed and with only a gasp Tor came, spilling into Jake's mouth, legs trembling under Jake's hands.

Jake licked and swallowed, but his attention was on his belt, his fingers too frantic to get it open easily. With a curse he finally let Tor go and ripped his jeans open, not sure if he should stand or fall over or what exactly he needed; he just wasn't about to go without, the people wanting to talk to him be damned. He was busy.

Tor solved the whole issue by shoving him back, knocking him off his knees. "Flat," he ordered, diving for Jake's aching erection.

Jake was just as glad for the order, because all ability to think fled as soon as Tor's mouth closed around him. There wasn't anything teasing about what Tor did, nothing sweet or charming, either. It was a damn good blow job, though, indecent and desperate and wet, all tongue and action and the sound of his heartbeat thundering in his ears. He could barely keep quiet as his hips lifted and fell, and when he came he only thought not to yell and not to let Tor get a swelled head about the fastest orgasm on record.

"Damn," he panted, his ears ringing.

"Uh-huh. Damn." Tor was grinning at him, fucking preening. "Get done up, Taggart. We have guests."

"Oh, fuck you," Jake said lazily, grinning back.

"Later. C'mon. Up and at 'em." Tor rolled to his feet and started putting himself back together. "Don't want Elias to come fetch us again, do you?"

"Don't care," Jake said, but he rolled, too, and fumbled with his jeans.

"Right." Tor didn't sound like he believed him. He waited until Jake was dressed and kissed him quickly, tasting like sex. "Back to work."

Jake rolled his eyes but headed down the ladder, unsurprised to see Elias hovering outside the door, gaze firmly on the lawn. He grinned and sauntered over, leaning on the door frame. "Fast enough?"

Elias shot him a dark look. "You're quieter than you used to be."

Jake shrugged. "Got used to privacy, I guess. Doing it in the loft means no yelling."

"Whatever." Elias grinned at him then and nodded out to the yard. "If you stay here, I'll start talking about how damn quick off the mark you are, too. But if you go over to the house, you'll find a crew of men wanting to bend your ear for a bit."

Jake nodded and ignored the way his cheeks heated. He wasn't about to start debating staying power with Elias. "Know what they want?"

"Got an idea," Elias said easily. "But I'll let them explain. Me, I'm going to find a beer and a dance or three."

Tor's shoulder nudged Jake's. "I'll be over in a bit. Gonna

go spy on Jacob."

Jake nodded. "Yeah, all right." He turned his head and kissed Tor quickly, fairly sure they weren't being stared at by most of the ranch. "See you later." He watched Elias and Tor wander off toward the band and the dancing and sighed. He'd much rather just saddle River and head out with Tor, but that wasn't going to happen.

Straightening his shoulders, he headed to the house, wondering who and what he'd find waiting for him. The only thing he could think of was that there had been a fight, or that someone wanted to talk about business; Elias had said there was a crew, though, so that seemed unlikely. A little worried, Jake stepped up his pace, walking across the lane to the front porch.

Sitting on the rail and leaning against the wall was a group of men. He knew them all, and he immediately knew that there hadn't been a fight; or if there had been, it didn't involve any of them. They were friends of Doug Gillian's, all men who owned land or were longtime foremen for landowners, and were among the upper age range of the mass of people gathered. Business men. Serious men who'd gotten past the drink and fight stage a long time ago.

With a strange sense of sudden awareness, Jake recognized these men as his peers, regardless of the fact that they were all about twenty years older than himself.

As he walked up the steps, nodding a greeting to Sam Borden who'd tipped his head at him, Mike Coswell stood up from the bench. "Jake," he said, holding out his hand.

Jake nodded again and shook his hand, curiosity replacing any lingering anxiety. "Mike. What can I do for y'all?" He did a quick headcount and came up with almost a dozen of them gathered there.

To his surprise, Mike looked uncomfortable and there was more than one set of feet shifting restlessly. "Not real sure how to put this to you," Mike said. "So I'm just gonna tell you. See, me and the boys ain't really a bunch for dancing if we can escape our wives, and we don't really sit and drink much anymore. Too hard on a body these years."

There was round of chuckles and a few rueful nods. Jake tilted his head, waiting. He had no idea what he was supposed to do; he wanted to be a good host, he really did, but he didn't really know how, given the situation.

Mike shook his head and looked down at his boots for a moment. "See, the thing is, I--we--know you, and we all know that you'd usually left the party by this point. So you're probably in the dark about what Doug had going for us older folk. And we're kinda hoping that if we just fill you in, we might be able to... well, do what we do when the music gets loud and the rest of them all blow off steam."

Jake felt his mouth open and closed it again. "Okay," he finally said, mystified.

Mike grinned at him. "Well, see, usually around now Doug would kind of open up the kitchen to us--not everyone, just us--and we'd get a few good hands of poker in."

There was a series of nods and surprisingly hopeful looks, the shuffling stopping as to a man a dozen people waited for Jake's reaction.

Jake stared at them. "You mean to tell me that for more than ten years I hid in the bunkhouse and there was a poker game going on?"

Sam Borden cleared his throat. "To be honest, the first couple of years we didn't ask you along because we knew why you were hidin' and this isn't entirely a dry game. Then we kinda didn't know if you'd want to play with us, and then... well, Tornado took to keepin' you company. But now Doug's gone, you're the boss and can't disappear, and we just kinda thought..."

Jake shook his head, a slow smile turning up the corners of his mouth. "Well, shit," he said, pointing to the door. "Too many of us for one table and I only have one set of chips."

"Got it covered," someone said, holding up a box that rattled. Another two held up cards, and there they were, trooping past Jake as he held the door open for them, each one saying thanks in his own way and every man grinning broadly.

Jake followed along after the last of them, watching as they moved through to the kitchen and rearranged his furniture to make room for the card table. They knew what they were doing, where to sit, and where the fridge was. The way they set themselves up, it was clear that they'd been doing this for years, and were glad to get back to it. Jake found himself smiling as they made themselves at home, beer going in the fridge, mixing bowls full of potato chips and pretzels taking over the counter.

"Sit, Jake," Mike said, pointing to a chair. "Your party, your deal. But don't think we're gonna take it easy on you. Heard stories about you and cards."

Jake carefully blanked his face as he sat down and picked up the cards. "All lies," he said calmly. "I don't play poker."

Hoots of laughter greeted that, and Jake grinned. This was going to turn out all right after all. Provided he didn't bet the ranch and lose.

He wasn't sure how much time had passed before a hand fell on his shoulder and Tor said, "What the hell is this?"

Jake jumped, but didn't look up from his hand. He was working on a full house, jacks high, and he was fairly sure he was going to win the hand and the five bucks in the middle of the table. "It's a card game," he said. "Poker. Maybe you've heard of it?"

Tor laughed and squeezed his shoulder. "Shut up. Who's winning?"

A chorus of groans came from the other table and Jake looked over to see Sam raking in the pot. He'd been winning all night, more than Jake, even. "Go bother them," he said to Tor. "I'm busy here."

"Yeah, okay," Tor said, moving to the other table and taking a vacant chair. "Jacob's gone to sleep, out on the lawn."

"Already?" Jake asked, raising the bet at his table.

"It's after midnight."

A dozen men looked at their watches, then carried on playing cards and talking. Someone got Jake some juice from the fridge when they fetched a beer, and Jake smiled to himself. All was right in his world, and he kind of thought that if this wasn't as good as heading out to the meadow with Tor for the night, it was an acceptable alternative. He'd have to call Doug

Gillian and let him know that his seat at the table would be waiting for him if he came for a visit for the next year.

Chapter Thirty Three

Jake drove to town with the speedometer firmly fixed on the speed limit, not a mile over or under. His hands were curled around the wheel at ten and two, and not once did he let go, not even to turn up the air conditioning.

If he let go, he was going to fucking kill someone and that wouldn't be a good thing.

He pulled into the school parking lot and waited for a group of kids to move out of the way, not sure if he was vibrating from the restless stir of the truck or from anger. It was lunchtime, and there were kids all over the place, most of them looking at him. It wouldn't have taken long for word to spread, and he was sure they all knew who he was and why he was there.

He parked and spent a minute rearranging things in the cab, stalling for time as he composed himself. He couldn't go in there as pissed as he was. He almost wished he'd let Tor come with him, despite the argument they'd had about it. Almost, but not quite. He had to deal with this on his own.

He took a breath and steadied himself, then climbed out of the truck. The door slammed louder than he'd intended, but he ignored it as he walked into the school. It was harder to ignore the kids lining the halls, eating lunches and chattering, watching him with either wariness or open curiosity. Just outside the office, Leroy and Lillian were standing next to the bulletin board, eyeing him anxiously.

"He's okay," Leroy blurted out and Lillian nodded frantically.

"Let's hope he stays that way," Jake growled, walking past them. He stopped and went back to them, knowing it wasn't their fault. "Look, I'll let him call you later, okay? Right now, just… go eat your lunch. Get back to class."

Lillian nodded but didn't move. "We know why," she said, lifting her chin. "Everyone does. And if he hadn't done it, I would've."

Jake sighed, his suspicion confirmed. "Don't take this on," he said gently. "It'll wear you down. And I don't want you getting in trouble, too, hear? There's better ways."

"Someone has to," she said firmly. "Or it'll never stop."

"It isn't going to stop this way," Jake said. He didn't think he'd be able to make her see that, but he had to try. "This is just going to make it worse."

She frowned at him and shook her head, her hair bouncing. "It isn't right."

"No," Jake agreed. "It isn't. But beating the crap out of them isn't right, either."

"Mr. Taggart?" a voice said behind him.

Jake turned and nodded at the secretary, then looked back at Lillian and Leroy. "Go on now. He'll call you later."

They finally moved off, looking worried and upset, and Jake turned into the office. He wasn't really sure what to say, so he just waited.

The secretary smiled at him sympathetically. "Go on in, they're waiting."

Jake nodded and took off his hat, following her nod to the open door of the principal's office. Inside, he could see Jacob and another boy sitting on chairs against the wall and a man in front of the desk. Behind the desk, Mr. Sutherland looked grim.

Jacob looked up at him, his eyes bleak and his lip swollen; his shirt was ripped at the neck and dirty everywhere else. He looked better than the other kid, though, who had a nice shiner coming up under a bag of ice.

"Mr. Taggart," Mr. Sutherland said, standing up. "Thanks for coming in."

Jake nodded and sat down in the free chair, next to what he assumed was the father of the boy Jacob had been fighting. "Sorry I had to," he said quietly. He looked at the boys carefully, trying to see if there were any more injuries than the obvious. "Y'all hurt more than I can see?" he asked, and they both shook their heads at him, neither of them meeting his eyes.

He turned back to Mr. Sutherland, sparing a glance at the man next to him. "What happened?"

Mr. Sutherland held up a hand and then turned it over, palm up. "Jacob and Nicolas had words in the yard, and it escalated to a fist fight. This is Nicolas' father, Darren Candanoza."

Jake nodded at Candanoza but said nothing, waiting.

"I was just about to explain what happens next," Mr. Sutherland went on. "For fighting that consists of pushing and shoving, we usually manage an in-school suspension. However, in this case, there were punches thrown and injuries sustained. That is a more intense level of violence, and in our district that dictates that the boys' discipline be firmer."

Jake turned to stare at Jacob, unable to help himself. He had no idea what he'd do with him if Jacob got kicked out of school. "For one fight?" he said, his voice hollow. He noticed that both boys suddenly looked terrified and that the look on Candanoza's face was probably the same as his own.

"For any fight," Mr. Sutherland confirmed. "We cannot treat violence lightly, nor bullying. But as I say, we also have to be realistic. Neither Jacob, who admittedly threw the first punch, or Nick, who pushed him verbally, are habitually problem students. They are not, generally speaking, a danger to other students." Mr. Sutherland stood up and crossed his arms behind his back. "The bullying is as much of an issue as the fighting."

Jake and Candanoza exchanged glances, then Candanoza cleared his throat. "Maybe you better fill us in," Candanoza said.

Mr. Sutherland nodded slowly. "I've spoken to both of the boys and a few of the other students who were there. I know that this may not be easy to hear, but Nick was being fairly vocal about the relationship that Mr. Taggart has with his partner, and Jacob took offense. To be completely honest, Mr.

Candanoza, your son was being somewhat more than rude, and the things he was saying are not tolerated any more than fighting is. He was deliberately provocative, crude, and malicious. Jacob retaliated inappropriately, and here we are."

Jake closed his eyes and tried not to swear out loud.

"You what?" Candanoza said in a low voice, and Jake could hear the chair beside him creak.

Jake opened his eyes to see Candanoza looking at his son with an unreadable expression. "I can't believe you--God, you know better than that, Nick." He looked at Jake and his expression changed subtly, the muscle in his jaw twitching. "I raised him better than that, Mr. Taggart. He don't get that kind of crap in his head from home, I can tell you that much."

Jake nodded, believing him, or at least choosing to for the moment. That kind of crap came from all over, and it didn't really matter where Nick had learned it, or when he'd chosen to believe it and throw it back into Jacob's face. It had been done, and this wasn't Jake's fight, not this time.

Nick didn't say anything at all and Mr. Sutherland cleared his throat. "I've told Nick that it's unacceptable to say such things while he's at school. And I've told Jacob that violence is an unacceptable reaction."

"What happens now?" Jake asked, looking only at the principal and making sure that his hands were curled around his knees and not bunched into fists. He wasn't going to hit anything; not his fight.

"You can take the boys home with you. They're being suspended for three days each and the incident will be noted on their files. As this is Tuesday, they'll be allowed back on Monday and we expect that they'll have kept up their assignments and any extra work they have due."

Jake and Candanoza both nodded and stood up, the boys scrambling to their feet a moment later.

"Get your stuff," Jake said evenly.

Jacob nodded, not meeting his eyes, and fled the office.

"You got anything to say?" Candanoza said to his son.

"I'm sorry, sir," Nick said softly, looking at the floor, ice bag still on his eye.

Jake wasn't sure who he was talking to, and apparently neither was Candanoza.

"For what?" Candanoza demanded, and Jake held up his hand.

"For..." Nick looked up, misery written on his face. "I'm sorry I said what I did, and I'm sorry for fighting."

Jake glanced at Candanoza. "Isn't me who needs an apology, and you'll be getting one from Jacob after I talk to him. This shouldn't have happened."

Candanoza nodded. "Go on," he said to his son, gesturing to the door. "I'll meet you at the car. And you make sure you don't forget anything, I can't take time off work to come back."

Nick left in a rush and all three men in the office sighed.

"Damn," Jake said under his breath. He turned to face Mr. Sutherland and offered him his hand. "Sorry about this."

"It's been a hard year for Jacob," Mr. Sutherland said sympathetically. "If it helps, I think this is a one time thing; they're both good kids, just need to sort some things out."

Candanoza nodded and shook Mr. Sutherland's hand as well, then turned to Jake. "I'll talk to him," he said, holding his hand out to Jake. "I'm sorry this happened."

Jake shook his hand, and shook his head again. "This isn't my fight," he said, and it felt good to say it out loud, though it ran less true than it did when he was thinking it. "But it's not one I want Jacob fighting, either. He shouldn't have hit your boy."

Candanoza shrugged. "In his place, I probably would have done the same thing, which might be part of the problem." He sighed again and looked suddenly weary. "And now we take 'em home for a three-day vacation. Sleeping in, doing homework, and watching TV."

Jake snorted. "Not Jacob. I got a ranch to run, and that boy's going to work his ass off."

They left the office together, walking through the hall and ignoring the looks they got from the assorted groups of students. Jake was glad to see that Lillian and Leroy had vanished, although he suspected that they were with Jacob as he gathered his things.

Jake and Candanoza stepped out of the school and Jake put his hat back on, digging for the keys to the truck and squinting into the sun.

"Can I ask you something?" Candanoza said, standing next to him and pulling out his own keys.

Jake nodded, glancing back into the school to see if Jacob was coming yet. "Sure."

"Just thinking about these days. Me and Nick's mom, we both work. Can't really take time off to make sure he's not sleeping all day and playing video games."

Jake nodded again, not really sure what that had to do with him. He could understand where Candanoza was coming from; he had no intention of letting Jacob laze about.

"Need an extra hand out at your place?" Candanoza asked, apparently serious.

Jake considered it for a moment, turning the idea over in his head. If he had to, he could keep the boys apart. If he wanted to, he could shove them both into the barn and make them muck stalls. "Always need another hand," he said slowly. "He know his way around a barn? Ride?"

Candanoza damn near grinned at him. "He can ride. He can rake stalls. He can lift shit until his arms fall off."

Jake smirked. They were on the same page. "We start early," he said. "Probably too early for you to drop him off. But I can have one of my hands pick him up on his way out in the mornings; got two that live in town. Bring him home for supper."

Candanoza nodded, the smile breaking free. "Perfect. School work, too."

"Before breakfast." Jake felt himself smile as well, but had to wipe it away as Jacob came out, loaded down with his book bag and a few extra folders. "Truck's over there," he said, handing him the keys.

Jacob nodded, but said nothing. He took the keys and walked away, shoulders hunched from the books and what Jake suspected was a mix of embarrassment, lingering anger, and general dejection.

Jake watched him go and shook his head. It was going to be a long ride home. "I'll call you tonight," he said to Candanoza. "Let you know who's going to pick him up and what time. I'll warn you though, it'll be around six."

"He'll be ready," Candanoza said firmly, gesturing to Nick as he came out of the school as laden down as Jacob had been. "He might not be happy about it, but he'll be ready."

Nick looked at them both, his gaze a mere flicker over Jake. There was shame there, and a healthy dose of it, too, and Jake couldn't quite make himself be unhappy about that. "Ready for what?" Nick asked.

"You're spending your suspension working for Mr. Taggart," Candanoza said, one hand on Nick's shoulder as he guided him away. "Think of it as character building."

Jake missed Nick's reply but he caught the smile Candanoza threw back at him. "Talk to you tonight," he said.

Jake nodded and headed for the truck. Tor was possibly going to have a fit. Maybe two.

Chapter Thirty Four

"You did what?" Tor yelled, slamming the front door closed and stepping out on the porch.

"Easy," Jake said under his breath as Jacob flinched.

Tor gave him a hard look and took a deep breath. "All right. Okay. Calmly. You got in a fight. And got suspended. Why?"

Jacob's misery was almost palpable and Jake took a breath with him as Jacob's eyes filled for a moment. "He was calling you guys faggots and saying all kinds of horrible things. Laughing. So I hit him."

Tor's back stiffened and he looked at Jake, who nodded. "Shit," Tor muttered, pushing a hand through his hair.

"Go on in the house," Jake said softly. "Get a start on your homework, have something to eat. I'll be in after I talk to Tor."

Jacob nodded but didn't move. "I'm sorry," he whispered, looking down. "I just... I couldn't." His voice cracked and Jake pulled him into a rough hug.

"Shh," Jake said into his hair. "Go on in. It'll be okay."

Jacob nodded and pulled away, reluctance betrayed by the way he managed to both move and lean into Jake at the same time. "Sorry," he said again. He went into the house, closing the door gently behind himself.

Jake and Tor looked at each other for a long moment and Jake sighed. "I don't know. I just don't. I mean, I can understand, but... shit."

Tor nodded and leaned on the post by the steps. "Between what James did, filling his head with crap, and what he's been going through, it must be a mess in his head."

Jake looked out across the yard glumly. "The other kid has a nice shiner. His father's pretty upset, embarrassed. Seems like a good guy."

"Kids pick up this stuff from more places than home," Tor said with a nod.

Jake took a quick breath. "Don't flip out at me, okay?"

Tor tilted his head at him. "What?"

With an inward cringe Jake said, "I'm letting the kid Jacob was fighting with work his suspension here. I'll get Tommy or Fred to pick him up in the morning."

Tor stared at him. "Are you nuts?"

Jake shrugged one shoulder. "Maybe. His father didn't want him slacking off for three days, and we can use the help. Maybe it'll help, if he comes out here and sees we're just like everyone else."

"And maybe Jacob and him will get into it again and everything will go to hell."

Jake turned to look Tor in the eye. "So we keep them apart. Fuck, Tor, I'm doing the best I can, here. Don't give me shit for this, back me up."

"Hey, I'm on your side," Tor said, but his eyes sparked. "Just don't know if this is such a great idea. What's this kid's name?'

"Nick Candanoza," Jake snapped.

Tor gave him a hard look. "This Nick's got some ideas I don't particularly agree with, is all, and I don't like inviting that into my home."

"You think I do?" Jake looked back at the yard again. "This ain't for us, Tor. I won't fight Jacob's battles for him, but I don't want him fighting ours, either. Maybe this can turn it around. One more person growing up knowing we aren't evil because of what we do in the privacy of our own home."

"Our home," Tor repeated. "So help me, if this kid makes trouble on our land, I don't know what I'll do."

"You'll hold your tongue and we'll talk to his parents and he can spend the rest of his suspension away from here," Jake said firmly.

Tor laughed, the sound rough and sharp. "You parenting

me now, Taggart?"

"Do I have to? I think I have enough going on with the one in the house."

"Fuck." Tor shook his head and stepped off the porch. "I'm going back to work. You do what you have to. I just hope this works the way you think."

Jake watched him go, hoping right along with Tor. He had no idea if it would or not. With a sigh, he turned and went into the house, the silence oppressive and laden with his own upset and Jacob's anxiety.

They hadn't really talked much on the drive home, Jake unsure what to say and Jacob clearly willing to put off any discussion for as long as possible. Not that Jake could blame him.

He went into the kitchen and found Jacob sitting at the table, his unopened books piled up in front of him. "Did you eat?" he asked, going to the fridge.

"Are you really mad?" Jacob asked, his voice low.

Jake thought about that as he got out some leftover chicken. "I'm upset," he said, reaching for the bread. "I understand why you did it, but I don't like it. Don't like that it happened at all, don't like that you had to hear anything like that. Pissed off that you got in trouble at school."

There was a long silence from the table and Jake looked over to see Jacob staring at the table top. "I don't know what else I could have done," he whispered. "I was just so mad."

Jake nodded. "It's hard, I know." God, did he know. He'd never been able to walk away, either. "It's done," he said firmly, starting to slice up the chicken. "Now we just have to deal with the aftermath. And you have to get it set in your head that if it happens again, and it might, that you let it go. I don't want you getting in trouble for this shit. Doesn't solve anything at all, Jacob. People are going to think what they think, and punching them isn't going to change their minds."

"I know," Jacob said in a small voice. "What's going to happen?"

Jake built a sandwich and put it on a plate. "Well, Nick's coming out here. His dad didn't want him sleeping in and taking it easy, so he's going to pitch in and help out around the ranch. So are you. School work, ranching... this isn't a vacation, and you'll both know it."

Jacob nodded. "Thanks," he said when Jake passed him the sandwich. "You going to make us work together?"

Jake shrugged. "We'll see how it goes. Depends on how the two of you act. I won't put up with shit from either of you, and Nick won't be spouting off while he's here. If he does... well, he'll be going home and I think his dad will be harder on him than I could be."

Jacob ate for a few moments. "He's... he never said anything before. I knew he didn't like me much, but he's never been like he was today."

Jake shrugged. "Sometimes people just say shit, not getting what it does to people. Showing off, talking crap. Pushing for the sake of pushing. I don't know."

"It sucks," Jacob said succinctly.

Jake nodded. "Yep. It does." He gestured to Jacob's pile of books. "Get some work done and come on out to the yard. I'm going to go see what we can find for you to do. And I need to talk to Tor."

Jacob grimaced. "He's mad."

"Oh, yeah," Jake agreed. "But not at you."

Jacob sighed and took another bite of his sandwich. "Okay. I'll be out in a while."

Jake stepped back and nodded sharply, not really looking forward to the next couple of days, or talking to Tor about it all. He hoped that after Tor cooled off a bit he'd let things lie, but he suspected not.

Shaking his head to himself, he headed out the back door and went to the stable, walking slowly. He could hear the radio in there turned up loud, and voices talking over it, at least three. He stepped in, nodding to Elias, who was going over what looked like a receipt with Tor, and waved Fred over to him.

"Need a favor," Jake said, taking Fred outside, away from the radio blaring.

"Sure, what's up?"

Jake quickly explained what had happened and asked if he'd mind bringing a passenger out in the mornings and back with him at supper. By the time he'd gotten to the part about Nick Candanoza's dad wanting his boy to work, Fred was grinning. "I can do that," he said with a nod. "Want me to put the fear of God in him, too?"

Jake blinked and shook his head. "Shit, no. Not that I wouldn't want to give him a shake if I was fifteen, but I'm not and you aren't either. None of that, all right?"

Fred sighed, still grinning. "Yeah, yeah, okay. Call me at home tonight and tell me the address. Oh, and let them know it'll be just before six and I don't have time to hang around waiting."

Jake snorted. "I think Candanoza will have the kid outside waiting on you. He was kind of unhappy."

"Good," Fred said, kicking at the dirt. "Suppose you want us to keep our opinions to ourselves around Jacob?"

"I'd appreciate it," Jake said. "Won't help any if he starts thinking anyone approves of him fighting."

Fred nodded again and slapped his thigh with his gloves. "You're the boss."

Jake grinned. "I am. Don't suppose Tor's calmed down any?"

"Not a lot," Fred admitted. "He's the boss, too, and I kind of want to get back to work, you know? He's a little cranky at the moment."

"Great," Jake said under his breath but not in the least surprised. "Think I'll go check the survey pegs for the new corral. Kind of… stay out of his way for an hour or so."

"Good plan," Fred said, grinning again. "Maybe if you feed him well at supper he'll be in a better mood."

"Maybe," Jake said, though he doubted it. Tor wasn't going to settle until they'd cooled their tempers and talked reasonably.

It was going to be a long day.

***

"Are you going to sleep at all?" Tor said in the dark.

Jake rolled over and looked at the clock. "God, I hope so. It's after midnight." He'd been lying there for an hour, waiting for sleep to come, but it seemed as far off as it had when he'd gone to bed. It didn't help that Tor had been damn close to cheerful all evening. It made him nervous.

"What are you thinking about?" Tor asked, an arm slipping around Jake's waist.

"What do you think?" Jake knew he sounded surly, but that was how he felt; his back was starting to ache from keeping it all inside.

"I think you're going over a huge fucking lists of 'what if' and second-guessing absolutely everything. Stop it."

Jake rolled his eyes. "Right. Just stop. Like that'll change anything. Like that'll keep shit like this from happening again, like no one will ever say things to Jacob again. Like it'll change the fact that living with us makes him a target."

"Hush, now," Tor said quietly, shifting beside him. "You're getting too worked up."

Jake gritted his teeth. "I hate this."

"I know. It sucks. But you said it yourself; you can't fight his battles for him. All we can do is raise him to know right from wrong. Fighting is wrong, I think he's got that sorted out. If it happens again, we'll deal with it again. And again."

"But it shouldn't happen at all," Jake said, staring into the dark. "He shouldn't have to pay for what we are."

"No, he shouldn't. And neither should we. Come on, you're sounding like you're ashamed of us, and I know that ain't right."

Startled, Jake rolled over to face him. "No," he insisted. "Not that. There's nothing to be ashamed of. I just... I'm wondering if we're actually doing him any favors."

"Because living with Cath and having the stress of her traveling would be better? Because letting your bitch of an aunt have a say would be better than this? Look, he stood up for himself; he wouldn't let this Nick kid get away with it. Sure, he chose the wrong way to deal with it, but it just shows that he's not going to let anyone push him around. That what James did, filling his head with hate, didn't take. Shows that we're doing a decent job."

Jake closed his eyes and rested his head on Tor's chest. "I know," he whispered. He did, really, even if he was finding the wrong words to talk about it. In his heart, he knew that having Jacob with them was the right thing to do. "Are you still pissed at me for letting Nick come here?"

Tor's hand smoothed over his shoulder. "Nah. It'll be fine. I think we should keep them apart tomorrow, though, kind of feel things out. I don't like inviting trouble to visit, but I've cooled down a bit. He's a kid. Kids do stupid things. Fuck knows I did."

Jake nodded, his back relaxing marginally. "His father seems okay. Said he laid down the law and that if there was any trouble or attitude to call him and he'd come out. I think Nick knows that it'll be worse for him if that happens."

Tor pressed a kiss to Jake's forehead. "Relax," he said softly. "Nothing you can do about anything right now. Let go, cowboy. You've really got to stop taking everything on yourself."

Jake sighed and closed his eyes, nuzzling in a little more. "I'll try," he said, almost meaning it. It was hard, though, keeping things out. It went against his nature.

"Don't want you slipping into an early grave," Tor whispered. "I like you right here."

Jake smiled. "Like it here."

"Then prove it and go to sleep. We'll get through this. You don't have to take on the world by yourself."

"I know." Jake made himself relax a little more, made himself push everything but the awareness of Tor's skin away. It still took him a long time to sleep, but he got there eventually, surrounded by the one thing that was more important than anything else.

Chapter Thirty Five

The next morning Jacob was sitting at the kitchen table, bleary-eyed, but with books open, when there was a knock at the door. Jake set down his coffee cup and nodded sharply as he pushed himself away from the counter. "I'll get it," he said, leaving the kitchen. He thought he heard Jacob say something under his breath, but it was easy to ignore.

He opened the door and looked at Nick, who stood there holding his books and looking vaguely terrified. He was about the same size as Jacob, though his hair was darker and longer and he had a beauty of a black eye.

"Morning," Jake said, holding the door open. "Come on in. Don't mind the dog," he added as Barkley pushed his way in along with Nick, probably looking for breakfast.

"Okay," Nick said quietly, following him in and letting Barkley sniff at his fingers.

"Jacob's already working on his homework," Jake said, leading him into the kitchen. "Have you eaten yet?"

"Yes, sir," Nick said, hovering by the door.

Jake picked up his coffee cup again and pointed the dog to his cushion in the corner. "All right, this is how it's going to work. It's almost six-thirty and I have work to do. Tor's already in the barn, along with the rest of them. You two have until nine to do your schoolwork--Jacob, you can make your own breakfast today. I'll be around, in and out until it's time to get you two sorted with chores."

Jacob nodded, toying with a pen. Nick nodded, too, moving his bag to the other hand, but said nothing.

"I expect you to be civil to each other. At nine we'll go out and get you started. Have a seat, Nick, I'm sure you've got stuff to do."

Nick took a breath and stayed where he was. "I'd like to apologize first, sir," he said. "Jacob, I had no call to say what I did. I'm sorry." He said it fast, in one breath, and it sounded rehearsed, but it was an apology.

Jacob looked at him, shifting in his chair uncomfortably. "I'm sorry I hit you," he mumbled. It sounded just as rehearsed, but Jake nodded anyway. It was a start.

"Good," Jake said, draining his mug. "Get going, boys. I'll be in the living room for a bit, doing invoices." He waited until Nick moved to the table and pulled out a chair before leaving them.

"Your eye looks like it hurts," he heard Jacob say quietly. Jake listened, but didn't hear any sort of pride in his tone, just neutral observation.

Nick made a noise and his bag thumped on the floor. "Nah, not anymore. My mom flipped out, made me put all kinds of stuff on it." There was a pause and then he added, "It was a damn good punch. You move fast."

Jake waited, not sure if he should go back or not, but Jacob snorted, the sound half laugh. "Yeah, I guess. Hurt my hand."

Jake kept walking, missing the rest of the conversation. If they got loud, he'd worry. An hour later he finished with the invoices and went to the kitchen, smelling bacon. Jacob was at the stove, making up three plates.

"Told him he needed more than cereal," Jacob said, nodding toward Nick, who was bent over a notebook. "Is Uncle Tor coming in to eat? We'll need another plate."

Jake went to the window and looked toward the barn. "Not sure. Want me to go find out?"

Jacob waved toward the carton of eggs on the counter. "I'll just make 'em all."

"All right. Thanks," Jake said, checking the coffee pot and deciding to skip putting another pot on. He watched Jacob crack eggs into the pan and smiled to himself, proud of how much Jacob was doing around the house, how far he'd come since his mother's death. Cooking, working on the ranch, doing laundry for whatever reason… he was coming along just fine, barring the current problem.

The eggs were just landing on the plates when Tor came stomping in the backdoor. "Is that food for me?" he called, tossing his hat on a peg.

"Some of it," Jake said, taking two plates to the table.

"Good enough." Tor came in and nodded to Nick as he crossed the room to wash his hands. "Coffee?"

"One cup left, but it's old," Jake apologized. "My fault, sorry."

"Instant'll do," Tor said, turning on the kettle. He shook water off his hands and came to the table, sitting across from Jake.

Nick and Jacob cleared their books away by making piles on the floor and Jacob brought the other plates over, then the carton of juice.

"Thanks, kid," Tor said, picking up his fork. "Morning, Nick."

Nick picked up his own fork. "Good morning, sir."

Jake grinned as Tor almost choked.

"Tor. God, please. You call me 'sir' and I won't know who you're talking to."

Nick nodded, his face pinking. "Okay."

"Now, Taggart--you can call *him* 'sir'."

"Shut it," Jake said evenly. "Eat up, we got work to do and they got math."

"Yes, sir," Tor said, earning himself a grin from Nick, a laugh from Jacob and a glare from Jake. "Invoices done up?"

"Yeah," Jake nodded. "What's the plan for the day?" he asked, scooping up eggs.

"Got Elias and Tommy out on the fence--breaks to the east. Stalls need raking, and need some shifting done in the loft. Fred, Kip and Kirk are out with the herd, might need help later or tomorrow. The rest of 'em are getting ready to fix fences and dig postholes for the new corral."

"'Kay," Jake said, reaching for the juice. "I'll start in on the barn chores, Nick can help out. When Jacob's done with his homework maybe y'all can help with the postholes? The sooner they're done, the sooner we can get that up."

Jacob looked unenthusiastic, but Tor nodded, chewing more bacon as he got up to make his coffee. "Right. When?"

"Told them nine, that's more than two hours with the books."

"Should do," Tor said, pouring water. "Lunch?"

"I'll stick a roast in. Be hungry for a hot meal by then." Jake finished his breakfast and picked up Tor's empty plate. Jacob was shoveling it in almost as fast, but Nick was a fair bit slower and Jake grinned. He'd put money on him eating his lunch just like the rest of them, starved after a few hours of work.

"Ready?" Tor said, putting a lid on his travel mug.

"Yep." Jake looked at the boys at the table and hoped he looked firm rather than pissy or scary. "Finish up, come on out when you're done with your homework. And don't be giv- ing the dog any bacon, hear?"

Jacob nodded and Barkley looked displeased.

"You're getting fat," Jake told him and Barkley managed to look faintly embarrassed before getting up to follow Jake and Tor out of the house.

"He is, a little," Tor said, watching Barkley bound off to the bunkhouse. "I think he's getting food from that lot."

"Wouldn't surprise me," Jake said. "Oh, hell. I meant to find extra gloves for Nick."

"There's some in the barn," Tor said, looking around as they walked. "New ones, even. How'd it go in there?"

Jake glanced back at the house. "Well, they apologized to each other. Didn't hear any yelling, so I count that as a plus."

Tor laughed, nodding. "I'll take it. You gonna keep an eye out?"

Jake gave him a flat look. He wasn't about to actually in- vite a lecture, and he knew full well Tor would have one ready.

"All right," Tor sighed, smirking at him. "Just don't fuck- ing hover."

"I don't hover." Jake ignored Tor's snort of laughter and hurried up to the barn. Maybe he could actually get something accomplished before it was time for the boys to join in.

He got the horses in the stable turned out and went back to the house where all was silent save for the scratching of pens. He had no idea if Jacob and Nick were being precisely that studious when he wasn't around, but decided not to worry about it. He went in twice more, giving Tor a stiff finger when he caught him smirking again, and finally tossed gloves on top of the books.

"Okay, let's go," he said with a grin. "There's stalls needing done and holes waiting to be made."

Jacob groaned and picked up his gloves. "How come I have to dig holes and he gets to clean stalls?" he asked, dragging out his boots.

"Because you actually like cleaning stalls," Jake said with another grin. "Don't worry, everyone will get their turn. Could be worse, you know."

Jacob gave him a sour look.

"It could be raining," Jake said cheerfully.

Nick shuddered and looked down at his feet. "These okay?"

Jake nodded. "Yeah, boots are fine. I hope you don't have a strong attachment to them, though. They're gonna get messy."

Nick sighed and held onto his gloves. "All right. Ready."

Jake looked at them both, pathetic and already wilting. "Cute," he said, raising an eyebrow. "But you haven't actually done anything yet. You look like that around four tomorrow afternoon, and I'll buy it."

Jacob rolled his eyes and they both straightened up a bit. "Postholes."

"Postholes. Your uncle's waiting."

Jacob nodded and headed out, only dragging his feet a little. "Have fun, Nick," he said over his shoulder. "Hope you're good with a rake."

Nick looked warily at Jake. "Um, how many stalls are there?"

Jake grinned and held the door open for him. "Enough to keep you busy for a while."

"I was afraid of that," he sighed, trudging out.

To Jake's approval, Candanoza hadn't been exaggerating

when he said Nick could clean a stall. Jake showed Nick where everything was and where to put the dirty straw, and left him to it for an hour or so, the radio turned up. Up in the loft, he starting shifting bales around, listening to Nick sing along to every song that came on. At least the kid wasn't full of attitude; he had a decent voice, too.

Stalls done, Jake and Nick went back to the house and got things going for lunch, then headed back up the loft. Jake spent the morning finding little picky jobs for Nick to do, things that weren't all that important and thus got left and put off. They sorted tack, cleaned tools, and made sure the horses' water buckets were all cleaned out. They swept up, split up a bale of hay into flakes out in the old paddock, and finally rounded up Tor and Jacob for lunch.

The afternoon passed mostly the same, with neither Jake nor Nick making a great deal of effort to talk to each other; Jake wasn't sure what to say and Nick seemed to be concentrating on doing all his tasks just right, which Jake frankly appreciated. He hadn't known what to expect of Nick, but this wasn't it, not really.

He thought about that, after Fred had left in the evening with Nick almost asleep in the passenger seat. Jake had kind of assumed that Nick would be more aggressive, more ornery. At a bare minimum he'd expected him to show some obvious discomfort around Jake and Tor when they were together, but he hadn't even given them a speculative glance. And he'd been all right with Jacob, too, if not exactly friendly.

He thought about it more, all through supper and dishes, until Tor finally nudged him and rolled his eyes.

"Can smell you thinking," he said. "Spill."

Jake merely shrugged. "Went better than I'd hoped, is all. I'm a bit confused."

Tor nodded and made a face. "So maybe tomorrow will be hell on wheels."

"Oh, thank you so much," Jake said, smacking him on the arm. "Now you've jinxed us."

Tor looked at him incredulously. "Jinxed? Are you twelve?"

"You tell me," Jake said with a grin, squaring his shoulders.

Tor looked him up and down and leered. "Nope. Not twelve."

"Hello, minor in the room," Jacob said as he came in.

"You can leave again," Tor said, leaning in to kiss Jake quickly.

"But I'm hungry," Jacob said, reaching for the potato chips.

Tor laughed at him and Jake stepped neatly away. "All that hard work."

"I got blisters!" Jacob said indignantly, holding up his hand to show them.

Jake nodded sympathetically. "Wrap 'em up before you start tomorrow," he said. "They'll toughen up, but you don't want them to bleed."

Jacob made a face and left, taking the chips with him.

"I don't think he liked making postholes," Tor said mildly.

"That's okay. I *hate* making postholes. Does he know why we need a bigger corral yet?"

Tor shook his head. "Not unless you told him."

"I think we can wait on that. At least until he's back in school."

"All right," Tor agreed, moving closer again. "Now. Where were we before the eating machine came in?"

Jake grinned and reached for him. "You were admiring me and were about to suggest we take a walk."

"I was?"

"You weren't?"

"I was. Let's go for a walk."

Jake winked and allowed himself to smirk before leading Tor to the door. He had a feeling he was going to sleep better than he had the night before.

Chapter Thirty Six

The following day started much the same as the first, although Nick ate more at breakfast. He and Jacob settled into their homework easily while Jake and Tor did up the breakfast dishes, and by the time Jake headed out to the barn, Jacob was getting Nick's help with a chemistry question.

"As long as we don't go back in there to find them bleeding," Tor said as he helped Jake turn out the horses, "I'll be happy."

"I'll be happy if we get some real work done today," Jake said, looking around the tidy barn. "It looks nice, but I feel like I lost a day."

Tor grinned at him. "Y'all can help with the postholes."

Jake glared at him but he knew full well that he'd be working on them before the day was out. They had a powered posthole digger and auger bits, but only one; it actually went faster if they had one person working the machinery and two or more digging more holes by hand. He didn't hold out much hope of sweet-talking Tor into letting him run the digger.

He was right, of course. By noon all four of them were digging holes, Jacob and Nick taking turns with the machinery while Tor and Jake worked by hand. It didn't seem quite fair to Jake, but the way both boys were developing blisters there wasn't a lot of choice. Over lunch he thought furiously about what else he could do, but the determined look on Tor's face said that he wasn't getting out of digging damn postholes.

"When we finish expanding the corral," Jake said, leaning on a shovel, "we're never doing this again."

Tor flashed him a grin and nodded, sweat shining on his arms and staining his T-shirt. "Next time, we make the hands do it."

"Hell, yes," Jake said emphatically. "Tomorrow, they're doing this. I'm going out on River. This sucks."

Two heads swiveled toward him. "Can we come?" Jacob asked, his eyes pleading. Nick didn't say anything, but matched Jacob's look with one of his own and added an air of utter exhaustion that almost looked genuine.

Jake sighed and looked at Tor. "Fences?"

"The fences should be fine," Tor grinned. "They don't break *that* much. Could always take them out and check the back pasture, though. See if it's ready for us to move part of the herd."

Jake nodded slowly, rolling his eyes when Jacob whooped and Nick grinned. "All right, settle down," he said, trying not to smile.

Jacob and Nick went back to digging their hole with renewed enthusiasm, certainly more than Jake had. The breaks all four of them took became more frequent as the day wore on, and at about four o'clock Elias and his crew rode into the yard, looking dusty and dry.

"Hold up," Jake said to Jacob and Nick. "How about you two go help with the horses, yeah? That's enough digging." He didn't have to tell them twice, and he caught Tor looking at him with a grin as the boys hurried into the stable. "What?"

"Nothing. Except you're getting damn soft. They had another half hour in them, at least." He winked and glanced down at the hole he was working on. "This is my last for the day, Boss."

"Oh, shut up," Jake said mildly, shaking his head. "See you in a bit."

"I'll be here."

Jake wandered into the barn, nodding with approval as he saw both Jacob and Nick helping out with saddles and tack. "Not bad," he said as Elias came up to him.

"Yeah, they know what to do," Elias agreed. "How's the digging going?"

"Slow. Hard. Annoying as ever."

"Not my favorite job either," Elias grinned. "How many

left?"

"Only a half dozen or so. We can start on the posts and boards next week." For the next few minutes Jake and Elias talked about what needed ordering and what work had to be done, sketching out a rough plan for the following week and double-checking who was going to be working on what over the weekend.

When they were done, they stood for a moment watching Nick and Jacob taking care of Shelby, laughing at something one of them had said.

"Getting along pretty good for a couple of yahoos who were trying to kill each other day before yesterday," Elias commented dryly.

"I was just thinking that," Jake said. "I was also wondering why some smart ass who hates queers hasn't so much as blinked at me and Tor."

Elias nodded slowly. "Gonna ask him?"

Jake thought about that for a moment. "Shouldn't."

"Nope. But you're gonna."

Jake shrugged one shoulder. "Maybe. But not like that." He made a slightly more honest attempt to convince himself to leave well enough alone. "It's not really my business."

Elias snickered and gave him a long look. "Maybe not," he said, taking a step back. "But it might be an idea to make sure *they* get to the bottom of whatever started this."

Jake was still thinking about that when Tor came in, wiping his face off with the sleeve of his shirt. "Jacob," he called. "C'mere a second."

Jacob nodded and came to stand with them and Jake raised an eyebrow. "What's up?"

"Nothing," Tor said, looking hot and exasperated. "Christ, you worry. Just need a hand unloading the truck; Tommy's back."

"Oh. All right." Jake looked away and Tor sighed.

"Hey, relax," Tor whispered in his ear as he walked behind Jake. "You'll get ulcers." He kissed Jake's cheek, high up by his ear and kept on going, Jacob following in his wake after giving Jake a rueful smile.

Jake rolled his eyes and looked back at Nick, who started petting Shelby again, studiously not looking anywhere else. "Pretty much done for the day," Jake said, keeping his voice low and mellow.

Nick nodded and gave Shelby a final rub before coming out of the stall. He looked around the barn for a second and then asked, "Anything else you want me to do?"

"Nah," Jake said. "Can go sit on the porch, if you want. I'll find something cold for us to drink."

Nick nodded but didn't move and Jake stifled a sigh. "That bothered you?" he asked after a long moment.

Nick shook his head and then looked up at Jake. "Actually, no. It was... y'all are..." He narrowed his eyes, looking frustrated.

"Normal?" Jake suggested.

"Married," Nick countered, his eyes glancing away. "You act like my mom and dad, most of the time, but with more cussing."

Jake laughed, not able to stop himself. "Sorry," he said, and Nick shrugged and grinned. "Bad language kind of gets to be a habit."

Nick nodded and they started walking toward the far end of the stables. "As long as I don't do it around my mom, I'm okay."

"Moms can be that way," Jake agreed. "You and Jacob seem to be getting along," he added on before he could stop himself.

Nick nodded and Jake could see his face flush. "Yeah. I was a real jerk to him."

Jake could hardly argue with that. "How come?" he asked, slowing their pace a little. "I mean, even before just now, you weren't exactly looking to puke every time me and Tor were in the same room. You don't act like you got that kind of hate in you."

Nick stopped walking and looked at his boots. "I don't, I guess," he said quietly. "I was mouthing off, and I just didn't stop. I couldn't... I was angry and I kept talking and pushing."

Jake stood facing him, knowing those feelings. Not being

able to shut up, aggression pouring out. "How come?" he asked quietly.

Nick sighed and didn't look up. "He walked in there on the first day of school like he owned the place. Everyone's always going on and on about him, how sad it all is. And it is, I know that. But he just... took over. Plays soccer, gonna make the football team easy, smart and friendly. Everyone likes him, wants to know him. And then Lillian..." He looked toward the door, and Jake could see how red his face was, how the muscle in his jaw twitched as he ground his teeth.

"Left you in the dust, huh?" Jake said sympathetically, understanding growing.

Nick nodded sharply. "That's about right."

Jake wanted to sigh again and thanked everything there was that he wasn't a teenager anymore. "That's what this was about?" he asked, trying very hard not to sound like he was being dismissive. "Shit, Nick. There's going to be lots more happening with girls that you're going to have to deal with."

Nick looked at him with frank disbelief and Jake couldn't keep a grin back.

"What, you think that because there's a girl involved I don't know anything? It doesn't have anything to do with being gay or straight, it's about relationships. And when it comes to relationships, it doesn't matter what kind of bodies are involved, trust me. Men can be just as hard to figure out."

Nick eyed him. "Wouldn't it be easier?"

Jake laughed and shook his head. "I don't really have a lot to compare to, so I could be flat out wrong, but at least the women I know will tell you exactly why they're pissed off. A man will just walk out and leave you sitting there wondering what the fuck just happened."

Nick snorted at him. "That's what girls do. Sorry, man."

"See? Just proves my point. That's relationships, Nick. A whole lot of 'what the hell?' mixed in with the good stuff. There's good news, though. The older you get, the better your brain works and you figure out how to deal with stuff."

Nick winced. "Better than being an asshole?"

"Uh-huh." Jake nodded at him. "Better than that. You see

Jacob walking in and taking over. I see a fifteen-year-old kid whose mother died. A kid who had to leave his friends, his home and his team, and had to start over. Move to a new state to live with uncles on a ranch, when he couldn't even ride a horse. You see where I'm going with this?"

Nick looked at the floor again and nodded. "Yes, sir," he said quietly. "I'm *sorry*."

"I know you are," Jake said. He did. "But you better make sure Jacob really gets that. What you did was wrong on all kinds of levels. What he did was wrong, too, I won't deny that, and I know I'm biased as all hell, but I can see where he's coming from a little better."

Nick nodded again and swallowed. "Yes, sir."

Jake nodded as well and took a breath. "Let's go get something to drink, okay?"

"Okay."

They left the barn and Jake sent Nick up to the porch, wandering over to Tor as they crossed the yard.

"You look pleased with yourself," Tor said, meeting him halfway.

Jake grinned. "Fixed it, I think."

Tor's eyes narrowed. "Did you, now?"

"Had nothing to do with us, under it all," Jake said. "Just new kid in school gets the girl shit. Want something to drink?"

Tor tilted his head and nodded after a long moment. "Sure. We'll be up in a few minutes."

Jake grinned again and headed to the house, looking forward to iced tea and a day spent riding, even if he did have two teenagers tagging along. There were worse things in the world.

Chapter Thirty Seven

The first Saturday after the corral was expanded and two stalls made ready, Jake and Tor hitched the horse trailer to the truck early and went back inside to find Jacob almost vibrating while he made breakfast. He might not have gotten the idea when the corral was being worked on, but when he was in the middle of readying more stalls than they had horses for, he figured it out.

"Easy," Jake said with a grin, taking the spatula from him. "Don't burst yourself."

Jacob grinned and nodded, then bounced toward the table, almost tripping over Barkley. "Do you know which one you're going to get?" he asked, falling into a chair.

Jake shook his head. "Nah. Doesn't much matter to me; I'll decide there. Called last night; the one you liked is still waiting."

Jacob beamed at him. "Excellent. What time do we leave?"

Tor laughed. "Right after breakfast. And don't choke getting it down; you still have to wait for us."

Not surprisingly, breakfast was quick and Jacob talked them into letting the dishes soak instead of washing them up right away. "C'mon," he urged, hustling them into their boots and hats and then into the yard. "Fast there, faster home."

Jake and Tor both grinned at him, and Jake even caught a little of his excitement. He wasn't all the way up to looking forward to getting himself a new horse, but he was at least in a decent mood about it. The half hour drive was spent talking about new saddles and what they could get for the money they had; Jake could have easily made do with the one saddle, but Tor pointed out that every horse they had, barring poor

Cotton and maybe Jacob's, would be a working animal. Saddles all round would make the most sense, because no matter how often Jake had one horse out, someone would be on the other. Just because River was aging didn't mean that he was being retired just then.

When they arrived at Steve Adleman's place, the three of them piled out of the truck and stopped in the drive long enough to pet the dogs who came to greet them, and then Adleman himself came out of the stable, calling out a cheerful, "Howdy."

Jake and Tor exchanged good mornings with him, turning down the offer of a cup of coffee when Jacob almost whimpered at the implied delay. It made Jake roll his eyes and Tor grin, but they both relented and let him loose, watching with shaking heads as he went into the stable, leaving them in his wake.

He went right to the stall he wanted, the same horse waiting there as the first time they'd been around. "Hey," Jacob said softly, letting the horse push at his hand. "Remember me?"

"Looks like he made his choice," Adleman said dryly.

Tor nodded as Jake wandered through the barn, close enough to listen and take part in the conversation. "He's talked about only him," Tor said. "Don't think we could change his mind if we tried."

"So don't try," Adleman said with a laugh. "Think it's the other that'll need talking around, anyway."

Jake rolled his eyes. "Don't fret, I'll get it sorted," he said, looking back at them.

They both grinned at him and then Adleman went to where Jacob was loving on the six-year-old gelding. "Want to take him around the ring?" he asked, pointing to the saddle over a stall wall.

Jacob nodded almost frantically and Jake watched as Tor helped him saddle up the horse, everyone smiling. In a few moments, Jacob was leading his horse out of the barn and Tor was talking price with Adleman as they followed him out.

Jake spent about twenty minutes looking at the horses in

the stable, his choice already narrowed down to two before they'd even arrived. One was a four-year-old mare with white markings, the other a gelding who was a bit bigger, though not as big as River. They were both a rich brown color, darker than the one Jacob had picked, but while they were perfectly fine horses from good blood, Jake couldn't make up his mind. Finally, he decided it didn't really matter and went out to watch Jacob ride, putting off the choice for a while longer.

He found Tor by himself, leaning on the fence and watching Jacob ride in the large, fenced-off ring. "Where's Adleman?" he asked, leaning on the fence close enough to brush shoulders with Tor.

"Went in the house to find the horse's file. Be back soon." Tor leaned a bit and nudged him. "You pick?"

"Nah, not yet," Jake said, his eyes on Jacob. "I will."

Tor nodded and they stood there for a few minutes, just watching. Jacob was riding at an easy walk, his face split by a huge grin. He stepped up the pace a bit as he came around the near corner and more or less pranced past them, showing off and grinning even more, making them both laugh back at him.

"Kid needs a proper cowboy hat," Tor said as Jacob slowed again as he cross to the far end of the ring. "But he looks damn good in the saddle. Took to it easy, didn't he?"

Jake nodded, eyes on Jacob. "He did," he said softly. "Took to it all pretty smooth." He swallowed and sighed. "Wish his mother could see this. He looks so fucking happy."

Tor's arm slid around his shoulders for a moment. "She'd be proud of him," he agreed. "I think she'd be pretty pleased with you, too."

Jake shrugged. "It's hard," he said softly. "Being happy for something that came out of hell. I miss her. He does, too. He hardly talks about her anymore, you know? But he still feels it."

"Of course he does," Tor said. "You both will--we all will--for a long time. But you're both doing it, don't lose that. You're doing better than surviving. Look at him, Jake. He's happy. He's healthy. He's a good kid."

Jake nodded and sighed. "I know. And he's our family and

I would only trade that to get 'Lissa back."

Behind him, he could hear footsteps, so he cleared his throat and turned his head, nodding as Adleman came up to them. "Looks like we're buying a horse," he said with a smile and a nod at Jacob, who was passing them by again.

"Good thing," Adleman said. "Think I'd have that boy here every day after school if you weren't."

They filled out the sale form as Jacob rode once more around the ring and finally dismounted alongside them, grinning. "He's mine?" he asked, one hand patting the horse on the neck.

"Oh, yeah," Tor said with a grin. "You can relax now."

Jacob beamed and turned to the horse. "Hear that, Cobi? You're moving to our place."

Tor and Jake exchanged a look. "Cobi?" Jake asked carefully.

Jacob flashed him a grin before turning back to the horse. "Uh-huh. For Cobi Jones."

Tor cleared his throat. "Who is...?"

"Soccer player. Jeeze, you don't know who Cobi Jones is?"

Tor snorted at him. "I do now. All right, Cobi it is, and he's coming home, so you might want to take him to his stall and get his tack off."

Jacob nodded and petted the horse again, then started to lead him away. "Which one are you buying, Uncle Jake?" he asked, making an obvious effort to get out of his own preoccupation.

Jake shifted his weight uncomfortably. "I'll get that settled, don't worry."

Jacob and Tor both rolled their eyes, but Adleman grinned at him. "I've got one more you might want to see," he said, eyes crinkling. "Just got here last weekend, thought you might be interested."

Jake tilted his head. "Didn't see one in the barn that wasn't there last time," he said, wondering why Adleman was being coy.

In response, Adleman merely pointed behind them, across the lane between the ring and another, smaller corral. Jake turned and Tor huffed a laugh, muttering something to Adleman that might have been "sold".

Jake looked at the lone horse standing near the fence and started walking slowly toward her, moved like he was tied to a lead himself. "How old is she?" he heard himself ask, though his thoughts were all on how much she looked like River. Maybe a hand or two shorter, but big and strong, and damn, the markings were even close to being the same.

"Three. Barely broke, lots of spirit, but healthy and good natured. She likes people, likes being ridden; just got a lot of energy."

Jake nodded and climbed the fence, standing still as the filly eyed him and stepped forward. "Hey, darlin'," he crooned as the horse came near. "What's your name?"

Adleman cleared his throat. "I didn't name her, so you can't blame me, all right?"

Jake glanced back at him. "Okay," he said slowly. "That sounds... frightening." He turned back to the horse and reached out to her, patting her nose gently and letting her snuffle the cuff of his shirt.

"Well, you gotta know that the guy who named her never met River."

Tor snorted and Jake looked back again to see him reading a second file. "Tell me," he demanded, moving around the filly carefully, soothing her with his hands.

Tor grinned at him. "Well, you'll be interested to know that she's a great niece of River's. She's got good blood."

Jake nodded, wishing she was saddled and making do with giving her a pretty careful once over. "Name?" he asked again, admiring the sleekness of her coat.

"Creek."

Jake glared at Tor. "Are you shitting me?"

Tor shook his head, looking like he wanted to laugh his ass off. "Nope. Her name is Creek."

"That's gonna change," Jake muttered to himself.

"Told you," Tor said, sounding satisfied. "Now, let's talk price and leave the man with his horse."

"Hey, I didn't say I was going to buy her," Jake said,

though he had to admit that even he wasn't convinced by his tone of voice. "I haven't even ridden her yet."

"Saddle in the barn, knock yourself out," Tor said, closing the file. "Me and Jacob will let you know when it's time to load her up."

Jake glared at him, but he didn't say much else. He forced himself to wait until Tor and Adleman had turned to walk away before he took hold of Creek's halter and started guiding her to the barn. He was going to ride his new horse and then he was going to tell Tor to shut up. After the horses were loaded. And probably unloaded.

He wondered idly if Jacob would help him pick a new name, but then he thought of Cobi and winced. Maybe not.

Chapter Thirty Eight

He really should have noticed that things were going too well.

Jacob was doing well in school again, hadn't gotten into any more trouble, and was spending more time than ever on the phone with Lillian. It made Jake glad that neither of them were old enough to drive yet, and he pretended not to notice that the dip in Jacob's laundry coincided with extra purchases of tissues with the groceries.

The new horses were settling in well, and Jake made sure that he spent as much time as he could with Creek, getting her into shape for work. River was still his mount of choice, of course, but Jake had to admit that Creek was a fine addition to the ranch, even if Tor did join forces with Jacob to keep Creek's name. When a name plaque appeared on her stall door he finally gave in and let her keep it, despite his feeling that horses named River and Creek was kind of silly.

It had been a good season, all told. The crops had worked out just about to expectation, the auctions had done a little better, and even with the added expense of two horses plus everything that went with them, they were doing all right.

That didn't mean he couldn't check the books again to make sure, though, and that was right about the time that it was brought to Jake's attention that all wasn't exactly as bright in his life as he'd thought.

It started with Tor's sigh as Jake got the ledger off the shelf. "What are you doing?" Tor asked. "It's Friday night."

Jake shrugged one shoulder. "Still gotta get up at six. Just another night, isn't it?" They'd go to bed at the usual time, get up at the usual time; Jake didn't really see how Friday could be any different from Tuesday, really. Even the shows on TV were better on Tuesday. "Where's Jacob?" he asked, crossing to the desk in the corner.

"Kitchen. I think he's on the phone again."

Jake rolled his eyes and flipped the ledger open, then dug in the drawer for the check register. He'd balance things out, maybe make some popcorn later and see if Tor could be put in a better mood by some couch time.

"You're seriously going to do that?" Tor asked sharply.

Jake glanced over at him and nodded, a little confused. "Just going to make sure that things are right," he said in what he intended to be a soothing voice.

"Don't fucking patronize me," Tor said, standing up. "Of course they're right, you did them three days ago. And four days before that. What the hell do you think is going to happen every seventy-two hours, Jake?"

Jake stared at him and carefully closed the check register. "What?"

"Yeah, 'what'?" Tor glanced back to the kitchen and lowered his voice. "I'm sick of this, Taggart. Just stop trying to control every single thing all the damn time, all right?"

Jake opened his mouth but couldn't find anything to say that made sense. So he said what he thought, instead. "What the fuck?"

Tor glared at him. "You're doing it again. Only way fucking worse, and you don't see it at all. You've gone beyond your whole Bossman routine here, cowboy. It ain't just me you're trying to fix all the time anymore, it's everything."

"What the hell are you talking about?" Jake said, standing up as well because sitting down with Tor fucking towering over him wasn't exactly the way things should be. Not when Tor was pissed, anyway.

"I'm talking about the books, damn it. I'm talking about you fixing everything with Jacob, even his own battles--the ones you said you didn't want to fight for him. I'm talking about you taking over every single thing you can in everyone's life and working yourself to fucking death on me."

Tor had made it back up to yelling and Jake could hear the

silence in the kitchen like it was a weighted blanket, stifling and smothering. He hissed a quick "Shut up," at Tor and watched the door, waiting for Jacob to appear.

"I will not shut up," Tor yelled. "We're having this out and we're doing it now, goddamn it."

"The hell we are," Jake said bluntly. There was no way in hell he'd have Jacob listen to this. No way at all Jacob would have memories of them fighting, not like Jake had of his parents screaming and cursing at each other. He headed for the door himself, and kept on walking. Right past Jacob, sitting silent at the table with the phone to his ear, and through the kitchen into the yard.

He could hear Tor coming after him, the screen door swinging shut with the same bang it always made, only this time it seemed louder, sharper. Not willing to have Tor yell for him to stop, Jake did it himself, turning and waiting as Tor came to him with heavy, quick steps. "Don't you ever yell at me when Jacob can hear."

"Don't you ever tell me to shut up," Tor snapped back, his eyes flashing.

Jake nodded stiffly, waiting for the next round of Tor's aggression. When it didn't come and the look on Tor's face didn't soften at all, he said, "Well? You got something to say, do it now. No sense in getting pissy and not finishing what you start."

Tor growled at him. "What the hell is up with you?" he demanded. "I thought we got this sorted out years ago. You don't try to fix everything; you don't take everything on yourself. And here we are, you working fourteen-hour days and worrying at every fucking thing you can think of and making up extra ones on top."

"I do not," Jake snapped, his own anger finally showing up and focusing on the crap Tor was saying.

Tor's eyes narrowed. "Then what happened this morning?"

Jake felt his argument slip away like it was sand in a downpour. He tried to find a way to twist, to get off the hook, but he'd been caught up and he knew it. He clenched his jaw and stood there, though, not willing to just give in and let Tor win.

But Tor wasn't about to back down either and he pressed forward with gaining momentum. "This morning," he said, standing in front of Jake like a dark force of nature. "In the shower. Or has it slipped your mind? Couldn't have, you pick up on details and store them all. Crop prices, cattle stocks, who's working where and when. You know it all, don't you, Jake? It's a damn sure thing you didn't forget this morning."

It occurred to Jake that Tor was really pissed off, more than he'd ever been before, maybe. "That what all this is about?" he asked, crossing his arms over his chest. "Is that what this comes back to? Damn it, Tor, can't you ever get angry over anything that doesn't have a direct effect on your cock?"

For a moment he thought Tor was going to hit him, then he saw the flash in Tor's eyes dim a bit. That was all there was, there wasn't a slump in his shoulders or a gentling anywhere else, and Jake knew he was wrong. It was about a whole lot more than a derailed blow job.

Tor took a breath and turned to look the other way, off to the right. "You were fucking worried about River and Creek, Jake. About if they were getting enough of your time and if their feelings were hurt. I was on my fucking knees and you were thinking about the fucking mental health of your horses." He looked back and met Jake's eyes, the glint back, shining and bright. "It was just the last thing, though."

Jake suddenly felt exhausted, the weight of all those fourteen-hour days that were probably more like sixteen pulling on him. "I can't be anything but me," he said finally.

"But you're not you," Tor said firmly. "You're some obsessive thing, scurrying from task to job to worry and back again. You're chasing things that don't need you chasing them, and you're not you at all. Not one little bit. The Jake Taggart I know, the one you really are, has a damn room full of Lego you ain't looked at in months. The Jake I know reads more than ledgers and sophomore homework and notices from school. The one I know and love is a cowboy who actually enjoys his life and his work." He took a step back and shrugged. "Don't know who you are. But I'm getting my Jake back."

Jake stared at him as Tor turned and walked back into the house and then he stared at the house for a while longer. He had no fucking idea what to do with that, no idea what it meant. He thought about going in, but couldn't see what good it would do, not until he had some words to explain what he was doing, what he was working for. A life for Jacob, for himself and Tor. For their ranch, their men. He was doing the best he could, and he wasn't sure how his best could be so far off from what Tor seemed to want.

Confused and upset, he eventually made his way to the stable, but the horses were restless with him there when it wasn't the right time, and he left them after a short while and went into the house. The lights were all off, the TV silent, and the clock glowing in the kitchen said it was almost time for bed.

Knowing he'd be unable to sleep, he sat in the dark living room and waited for morning or for Tor to come looking for him. He fell asleep before either happened.

Chapter Thirty Nine

Jake woke up before dawn, his back stiff from sleeping slumped on the couch. With a grunt and a bit of a moan, he got up and stretched, grateful that he was awake before Tor or Jacob. He really didn't want to have to explain what the hell he was doing on the couch when there was a perfectly fine bed upstairs.

He put the coffee on and took a shower, coming out of the bathroom just as the alarm went off in his and Tor's bedroom. He heard the buzzing stop and with a sigh went into the room, shutting the door gently behind him.

Tor was sitting up in the bed, sheets pooled around his waist, and looking at the empty space beside him in confusion. "Slept on the couch?" he asked, sounding more than a little hurt.

"Not on purpose," Jake said, almost making it an apology. "I meant to come up. Just didn't make it."

Tor nodded, apparently accepting that at face value. As Jake got clean clothes from the dresser Tor climbed out of bed and stood next to him, reaching for his jeans. "I was thinking about something as I fell asleep," he said in a low voice. "Think I have an idea."

Jake raised an eyebrow, not surprised at all that neither of them was actually saying they were sorry for anything; chances were, neither of them was sorry for anything other than the yelling and it would take some more time before they got around to talking about that. "About what?" he asked, keeping his voice down as well. Jacob didn't need to hear anything more than he had the night before.

But Tor shook his head and reached for a T-shirt. "Still

turning it over. Let me think on it, talk to Elias. See you at lunch?"

Jake nodded, vaguely annoyed at Tor's unwillingness to share, but curious as well. "Yeah," he said. "I'm going to be helping Kirk with the horses this morning, and checking on some things around the barn. Are you going out with Bobby and Tommy?"

Tor nodded, then shook his head. "Not sure. I'm supposed to, but if this idea of mine will hold water, I might not need to. Either way, I'm supposed to help with getting the fencing into the other truck and take a look at the bunkhouse roof. Need some new shingles, gotta see how many."

"All right," Jake said, doing up his jeans. "I'll get breakfast going. Coffee's already on."

Tor nodded and leaned forward suddenly, kissing his cheek. "We'll get this sorted," he promised in a whisper. "You may try my nerves, but I'm keeping you."

Jake smiled despite himself and said nothing, pretty sure there wasn't really anything to say to that. Tor let him go and Jake headed back down to the kitchen, pausing to knock on Jacob's door as he passed. He waited until he got a grunt in reply before going down the stairs to get breakfast going, feeling a little better for a man who'd slept on the couch.

***

At noon, Jake and Jacob made lunch and then Jacob went up to his room to toss some clothes into his school bag. Leroy and his dad were going to pick him up by one so the boys could go to town, and then they were spending the night at Leroy's. Jake was just as happy that Jacob was going, not sure if there was going to be a repeat of Tor's tantrum.

But when Tor came in for lunch, tossing his hat onto the hook just inside the back door, he seemed more thoughtful than anything else, and certainly not angry at him anymore. "What's for lunch?" he asked, going to the sink to wash his hands.

"Leftover beef. Want it hot with gravy? Got potatoes on."

Jake poked a boiling potato and decided they were well past done. "Jacob, food's ready," he called.

Tor thought hot was better than cold, so by the time they'd heated the meat and got everything ready for the table, Jacob was back and getting drinking glasses down. The three of them sat and ate in near silence, Jake wondering if Tor's idea had turned into something or not and Jacob looking back and forth between them uneasily.

"Relax, kid," Tor finally said, finishing his potatoes. "Me and your uncle might holler once in a while, but it doesn't mean anything other than we have to sit down and talk."

Jacob nodded and relaxed a bit but Jake had to force himself not to sigh. No matter how long they did it, talking never came easy. Still, if it would avoid scenes like the one they'd just had, he'd try a bit harder. He had a smug little voice in his head that wanted to point out that he hadn't been aware that a discussion had to happen; that was all on Tor, and it had been Tor who hadn't been talking this time.

Not that it mattered, his more rational mind pointed out. They were still going to have to talk. And it was probably going to happen sooner rather than later.

Elias knocked at the back door and came in when Jake waved to him, stopping Jake from brooding over the matter for the time being. "Hey, Jacob. Car just coming up the lane, should be your ride," he said, taking off his hat.

Jacob scrambled up and took his plate to the sink and then dashed to where he'd dropped his bag. "See you tomorrow," he called, thundering down the hall to the front door. Jake and Tor barely had time to call out their goodbyes before he was gone, slamming the door behind him.

Jake shook his head to himself as he started clearing the table. "Coffee?" he asked, gesturing to the pot.

Both Tor and Elias shook their heads and sat at the table, watching him as he put the dishes in the sink and started running water. They didn't say anything at all, just watched him. After about two minutes of that, he turned and glared at them. "What?"

"Cranky," Elias said, glancing at Tor. "You're right."

"Told ya."

Jake growled at them. "Right. Cranky, bossy, and not my-self, I'm told. What about it?"

Elias slid another look at Tor and stood up. "Do it," he said, picking up his hat. "If you don't, I just might." He nod-ded at Jake and grinned. "You follow his lead, Jake. It'll be fun."

Jake glared at him again as he turned and left, then trans-ferred the look to Tor. "What's going on?" he demanded, lean-ing on the counter.

Tor stood up and walked to him, stood close enough to touch, but didn't. "We're going on a little vacation, you and me. And before you start calling me names and pointing out that we don't have time, hear me out."

Jake snapped his mouth shut, his protests about time dying before they could be vocalized.

"I'm talking about a working vacation, sort of," Tor went on, shifting his weight just a little. "Thing is, I don't think I'd mind you working so fucking hard if I knew you were having fun, if you were doing it because you loved it and not because you're running scared of making a mistake. So you and me, we're going to be cowboys for a few days. The way we're supposed to be, not going over fucking paperwork and homework and running the place. Just... cowboys."

Jake frowned at him. "What do you mean?"

Tor gave him a tentative smile. "The herd's gotta be moved," he said hopefully, inviting a response.

"Uh-huh," Jake said with a nod. "We're going to be work-ing on that for the next two weeks. Men and horses and trucks and trailers." They had the bulk of their stock in one well-tended area, but it was time to get the animals to fresher pas-tures; for the size of their herd and where the best land was, that meant splitting the herd up. It was a huge job, by times confusing and stressful if everyone didn't know exactly what group of animals was going where.

Tor's smile grew a little. "Lot of cows to shift," he said agreeably. "And you and me are taking thirty head and put-ting them down in Stuck Jump."

Jake blinked at him, confused. A small part of the stock had to go to an area which they couldn't reach on truck at all, and had to be moved the old-fashioned way with horses and dogs and hard work. It was called Stuck Jump among the hands, though the name didn't turn up on any maps. Jake figured it got its name because by the time the cattle got there they were stuck, and the hands were ready to jump off the nearest cliff. It was pretty easy to keep an eye on the cattle, though, once they were there, and for some reason the whole area had always been pretty free of predators and problems. The only real drawback was the getting the cattle there.

"We were going to do that anyway," Jake pointed out, not seeing where Tor was going with his plan.

Tor's smile grew even more and he shook his head. "You were, yes. With about three other guys. And you were going to ride back to the house at night, the four of you trading shifts on who had to stay out there with the cattle over the three days it'll take to get them there." He waited for Jake to nod and then kissed the tip of his nose. "What I'm telling you is that you and me are doing it alone, and we're not coming back until it's done. You, me, three horses, and that damn dog of yours. Three days, two nights, and the open range."

Jake laughed, utterly amused by the absurdity of it, but Tor didn't laugh with him and with a choke he started shaking his head. "Oh, no," he said, not quite believing that Tor was serious. "You and me. Away from the--"

"The ranch, the house, the stables, the headaches, the books, the nephew," Tor confirmed. "For three days and two nights." He nodded sharply and stepped back two paces. "Elias can run the show, we'll take the radios because we're not stupid, and Jacob can either put himself to bed or he can stay in the bunkhouse, his choice. The boys will make sure he eats, and he's old enough to do his homework without us nagging him. If he doesn't, it's his problem."

Jake shook his head again, speechless.

"We're goin'," Tor said firmly. "Monday morning. You might want to have a last look at the books on Sunday night, follow that seventy-two hour thing you got going on." Then he picked up his hat and headed out, sparing Jake one more grin as he opened the door. "Hey, you might even like it," he called as he walked outside. "Camping and shit. It'll be fun."

Jake watched him go, still trying to come up with objections, but he didn't hold out much hope of settling Tor down without a fight, not when he was being that unrelentingly cheerful about messing up Jake's order. There wasn't much he could do until he had some time to think about Tor's grand plan for getting him back to the way he was supposed to be. Whatever that was.

Chapter Forty

By the time Monday morning dawned Jake still hadn't been able to come up with anything logical to say against Tor's idea and a whiny 'I don't want to' would likely just get him a pat on the head. So he said nothing and made sure that he had a change of clothes ready to take along with his toothbrush. His revenge would consist of letting Tor take care of all the details. Food, supplies, blankets, a kettle to boil water and a pan to cook in… all of it he happily left up to Tor.

It was particularly frustrating that Tor took care of it all with a grin and obvious enjoyment. He even made sure that Jake saw him packing the lube away in his blankets, the bastard. "Okay, hot breakfast and we're out of here," Tor said, plunking a plate of bacon and eggs in front of him.

"I wanted toast," Jake said under his breath.

"I know," Tor said, dropping three slices of hot toast on top of the eggs. "There you go."

Jake pointedly ignored the way Tor was smirking and Jacob's laugh and ate his breakfast without giving them any more reason to tease.

He saw Jacob off to school and then reluctantly followed Tor out to the barn, where most of the hands were gathered. He was, by that point, unsurprised to find both River and Creek saddled up and with their saddlebags packed; Tor wasn't giving him an out, or a reason to bitch and complain.

Within a couple of short hours the entire move had been organized, the cattle Jake and Tor were taking rounded up, and Elias had sent everyone off to their jobs for the day. Jake and Tor sat on River and Lug and made a final check of their overall plan, double-checked the radios with Elias, and then they went to work.

Jake found it amazingly easy to put aside any distractions. There was a job to do, work he was made to do, and his head didn't have space for any pondering right then. He wasn't really upset to be there in the first place, although he wasn't thrilled with the way Tor had strong-armed him. He was still a little baffled about what had spurred Tor into his fit of temper, but out there with the cattle and the sun shining on him, it wasn't something he was going to concern himself with. There were more important things to deal with.

He whistled Barkley up and rode out; one of the nice things about cattle was that if they took it into their heads to wander off from where they were wanted, they were pretty easy to urge back into the herd. Really, he and Tor weren't moving that many either, and between the nice weather and the scenery, it was actually kind of like the vacation Tor had promised.

He caught Tor grinning at him a time or two, and by late afternoon Jake had finally given up the last of his resistance. Their land was beautiful, spread out all around them. The wind tossed the grass, the cattle kicked up dust, and everything under the huge blue sky was perfect. They rode and called out to the cattle, urging them up a rocky slope and then down the other side, letting them take their time getting to the small patch of level land.

The cattle milled around them and Jake waited for Tor to make his way to him, Lug nudging cows out of the way and Barkley standing on the top of the rise they'd just come over like a proper cattle dog, looking very pleased with himself.

Jake squinted into the sun as Tor reached him and nodded. "We'll get to the first stop site in under an hour, I think," he said, looking around. "We made better time than I thought we would."

Tor smiled and shrugged. "Nice weather, fresh start... we'll probably be right on time tomorrow, and dragging our asses in on Wednesday."

Jake snorted. "The real drag will be the ride back to the house."

"Yeah, but it's days off," Tor said, flashing him another grin. "You settled in your skin, now?"

Jake nodded slowly. "Getting there," he admitted. "This idea didn't suck, I guess."

"Why, thank you," Tor laughed, looking as pleased as Barkley on his hill. "Lucky for you, I do. So we should get these cows, moving, yeah? Before I change my mind about rewards for good behavior."

Jake rolled his eyes, but he moved River into a walk and whistled for Barkley. He wouldn't do just anything for one of Tor's blow jobs, but he wasn't stupid enough to turn one down if it was in the offering.

He was almost dead on with his assessment of how long it would take them to get to the first camp; they rode into the field in just under an hour, the cattle funneling through a short gully and into a pen that had been there for as long as Jake had worked the spread. It wasn't big, but it would keep the cattle where they were supposed to be for the night. He and Tor rode through them, leading Creek and pushing their way to the far end and out the gate. They'd camp there for the night, and in the morning it would just be a matter of opening the gate and herding the cattle on out.

"You better be riding that girl tomorrow," Tor said, eyeing Creek who was tossing her head and looking very put out that she'd just been led around most of the day.

"Yeah," Jake agreed, ground tying River and going to her. "Her turn. I'll take her in the morning, then we'll switch around. Between the three of them we'll--" He broke off with a laughing gasp as Tor pounced him, dragging him away from Creek almost before he could make sure she wouldn't wander. "Aren't we going to set up camp first?" he asked as Tor tugged him by his belt.

"Nope." Tor grinned at him and pushed him to the ground, fingers working at the buckles of Jake's chaps and his belt at the same time. "Goddamn, I love chaps."

Jake laughed and looked down, his cock stirring as Tor undid the buckles and started in on his jeans. "They're a bit in the way," he pointed out.

"Don't care," Tor said, leaning over him and kissing his mouth hard, one hand holding his weight and the other massaging Jake through his jeans. "Well, well, what have we here?" he teased, rubbing a little harder as Jake firmed up even more.

"If you don't know, you ain't been paying attention."

"I think it requires closer inspection," Tor said, his eyes crinkling as he grinned.

Jake really didn't have any objections, and he even helped out a bit by wriggling when Tor finally got his jeans open. Tor moved down his body, hand wrapped around Jake's cock and tugging with far too light a touch, teasing. Jake watched, his erection leaping as Tor tossed his hat off and bent his head over Jake's groin.

"Looks like it belongs here," Tor said, his breath puffing across Jake's hot skin.

"Cut it out," Jake pleaded.

"If you insist," Tor said, his tongue darting out to lap at the head and flick at his ring.

Jake moaned happily, the wet heat from Tor's mouth a pleasure he never really got enough of. He let his head fall back and saw nothing but sky, starting to darken in the east, and suddenly all his senses felt jacked up. He could hear the cattle and the horses, the wind rustling, and even Barkley sniffing around the fire pit. He could smell the country, a mixture of scents that he'd always associated with freedom: grass and cows and horses and sweat. He could almost taste it, wild and comforting at the same time.

And all he could really feel was the dirt under him, small rocks in the soft grass, and Tor's mouth on him, licking and sucking and taking him to full hardness. He lifted his head again, his hat falling off, and looked down to see Tor watching him, brown eyes hot and dark and somehow knowing.

"It's good," Jake whispered, tangling one hand in Tor's hair. "So good."

Tor made a noise that might have been agreement, might have been something else, and winked at him. Then his mouth got tight and wet, his tongue pushing on just the right spot and Jake gasped, arching.

Tor's hand curled around the base of his cock, the heel pressing on his balls and jerking him off a little with shallow strokes as Tor took him deeper into his mouth. He spent almost too long playing with the spot just under the head that made Jake crazy, but just as Jake was about to tug his hair, Tor dove down, sucking hard and doing that special thing with his tongue that even after years of experiencing, Jake had never been able to manage to duplicate.

"Fuck," Jake groaned. "Oh, God." He felt his balls pull up, knew that Tor could tell how close he was. "Come on, do it. Please."

Tor made a noise around him, the vibration traveling out and spreading through Jake's body, and then he did it again. A suck, a lick, and a swirl of his tongue and then Jake was crying out to the sky and spilling down Tor's throat in long, ragged pulses, his eyes closed tight.

"Come here," he said when he could, petting Tor's hair. Tor had his head on Jake's thigh and was breathing just as hard as he was. "Come here."

Tor nodded and crawled up to lie next to him, smiling. "Hey."

"Hey," Jake said, wrapping his arms around Tor and pulling him down for a long, wet kiss. He could taste himself on Tor's tongue and he moaned happily, his hands tugging at the back of Tor's shirts.

"It's okay," Tor said into the kiss. "Um. Really."

Jake pulled away and glanced down at Tor's crotch, then grinned. "Bring extra jeans?"

"Hell, yes. I'm not stupid." Tor grinned right back at him, apparently not worried at all about ruining a pair of jeans on the first day out.

Jake laughed and kissed him again. "I didn't. I'd appreciate it if you kept that in mind."

"Keep your dick where I can get at it, and it won't be an issue," Tor promised.

Jake shook his head and looked at the sky, smiling. He sure as hell hadn't been thinking about his horses that time.

"Ready to set up?"

"Just gotta start a fire. Hungry?"

Jake nodded. "Yeah, I could eat. We've got to water the horses, too. You want to take them to the stream or do you want to start the fire?"

Tor shrugged. "Doesn't much matter. You relaxed yet?"

Jake considered that, took it for what it really meant. "Getting there," he said honestly. "Tomorrow night'll be better."

Tor nodded at him and kissed him again before rolling away. "You got it, cowboy. Tomorrow night."

Chapter Forty One

The second day was as good as the first, although Tor was right about the timeframe. They were going over terrain that had a rougher patch in the afternoon, two hours of being a bit slower and watching the cows carefully, the horses dancing over loose soil and rock, the cattle plodding.

Jake took more than a little pleasure from sinking into his work, doing what he did best. He rode easier, the sun warming him and the sound of the herd and Tor's voice as they called back and forth soothing him to his bones. They had to work with one stubborn beast a little, finally gathering the herd into formation and moving along at a better pace, and Jake realized he'd been grinning for so long his face was starting to ache.

He felt better in his skin, his body relaxed and soothed so much that he wondered just how long he'd been holding himself stiff and tight. Even his bones felt better, his gestures wide and sweeping, his joints all unrestricted and slack. He was fairly sure that if he were walking instead of riding he'd be sauntering along, so unwound he'd be a rolling puddle.

They made camp that evening in easy silence, both of them smiling as they settled the horses for the night and got the fire going. It was an easy quiet, Jake not at all worried about the lack of conversation because it wasn't necessary. They worked together like they should, two halves just doing their part and knowing that the other was taking up the rest. They'd get everything done that needed doing, and then they'd eat, the world working the way it should.

Tor made supper, crouched down on the far side of the fire, and Jake sat on a rock, watching him. Tor looked as re-

laxed as Jake felt, glancing up every now and again to give
Jake a smile or a wink, his hands careful as he cooked over
the low flames. Jake returned every smile, unable not to, and
when they ate it was side by side, close enough that their
thighs were pressed together.

Tor put the kettle on the coals while Jake rinsed their
bowls out, making a bit of weak tea for them to have while
the sun set, then shook out their blankets. Chaps were shed
and Jake took his belt off, too, knowing it would just be in the
way eventually, and grinned when he saw Tor do the same.
He knew there would be talking first, but it didn't matter.
They were going to get naked and sticky at some point fairly
soon; it was that kind of night.

Jake settled himself next to Tor and considered the coals a
moment before leaning forward to stir up the fire and toss another few sticks of found wood on top. "You were right," he
said, glancing at Tor and tugging the blanket up over his
shoulders. It wasn't cold yet, but it would get there.

Tor gave him a lazy smile. "I know. Feels good, yeah?"

"Yeah," Jake agreed. "Damn fine. Didn't know it had gotten that bad."

"I told you," Tor pointed out, not unkindly. "You worry
me, Taggart. So damn stubborn."

Jake shrugged a shoulder. "I guess," he said. "Don't know
how to stop it, though. I just… this is what I do, what I am."

"Only part of it," Tor said, leaning closer. "You always
take care of what's yours, yes. And me and the ranch and Jacob, we're all yours, no mistake. But the last few months,
you've been way over the top, cowboy. I ain't kidding when I
say you're going to work yourself up to ulcers."

Jake sighed. Talking was getting easier, but it was only
because he was alone with Tor, miles from everything, that he
could force the words out of his mouth. "I'm scared, I think,"
he said, looking at the fire. "It's so fucking much. Ranch. Being the boss and making sure people have jobs. Jacob." He
swallowed hard and turned to give Tor a fast look. "My sister
died. She just… died. Anyone could. You could. Can't control
that, can't plan for it, can't stop it."

"Jake," Tor breathed, a hand suddenly, gently, on Jake's face. "That what this is about?"

Jake nodded sharply, pushing into Tor's hand. "Think so," he admitted. "Kind of stupid, but there it is. I'm running everything because I'm running nothing, not really. Everything's tethered so fucking poorly. One accident and the world ends."

Tor didn't say anything, just kissed him, kissed his jaw, his mouth, his cheeks. Tiny, rapid little kisses, not breathing at all, and all the while, pulling Jake closer to him, manhandling him until Jake was wrapped in blankets and Tor, so tight he couldn't get free if he'd tried.

"I'm sorry," Jake tried to explain, tried to take some of the pain away. "I didn't see it."

"Hush." Tor's voice was rough, and he started breathing again, mostly in harsh gasps. "Right here, I'm right here, and I'm not ever going to leave. No accidents, no walking away."

"Can't promise me that," Jake whispered, twisting until he could touch Tor back. "Can't."

"I can," Tor insisted. "Have to. There's nothing that'll tear me away from you, Jake. Not one fucking thing. Can't be."

Jake knew that was wrong, that it wasn't a promise that could be kept, but it didn't matter. Even if Tor couldn't stop it from happening, the fierce determination in his voice, the way he loved Jake with every heartbeat, that was important. That he would stop the universe in its tracks if he could so he could make things whole for Jake... that mattered.

It mattered that Tor was damn near choking, his breathing still rough and uneven. It mattered that when Jake reached up to him, touched his cheek with work-scarred fingers, they got damp. There wasn't anything more powerful than that, the promise there in Tor's eyes and not in the words.

"Okay," Jake said, curling himself into Tor and letting him clutch at Jake as much as he wanted. "Ain't gonna happen." His heart tripped up and he could feel them both shaking more than a little.

"Won't let it," Tor insisted and Jake smiled.

"Stubborn," he said in a low voice.

"Damn right. You and me, take on anything. We can

outstubborn anyone, anywhere and anytime."

Jake's smile turned into a grin. "Probably," he agreed.

After a few moments Tor reached out and snagged a belt from the pile of leather, chaps and belts all tangled up, then tossed it back with a muttered, "Wrong one." Then he pulled the other one to them, and held it up. "Now, what are we going to do about this?" he asked, breathing steady again and his fingers caressing the belt holes. "You're tightening up another notch, don't think I didn't notice."

"You notice everything," Jake said, batting his eyelashes.

"Stop that, and don't change the subject." Tor gave him a stern look. "You're needing to take better care of yourself. Don't make me get all pissy again."

Jake sighed and took the belt from him, touched the dent where his buckle now sat. "Yeah, I know," he admitted. "I'll try."

"Let go? Stop checking the books, stop hovering over Jacob, let the rest of us take on some of the worry?" Tor pressed.

Jake nodded. "Yeah."

"Play with Lego, ride for fun and sleep better? Eat more?"

"I eat." God, how he ate. Apparently stress burned a lot of food.

"Keep eating," Tor amended, his fingers on the belt with Jake's.

"All right," Jake agreed. He kind of thought he'd agree to a lot of things if Tor kept holding him and touching his hands like that. Sneaky bastard, taking him out in the wild and treating him right.

"Okay, then," Tor said with a nod. Then he rolled them over and pushed Jake to the ground, a tangle of blankets and limbs. "Good man."

"Do I get a prize?" Jake asked, liking his new position rather a lot. He wiggled under Tor and grinned up at him, appreciating the hard ridge of Tor's cock nestled on his hip. There was the prize right there.

"I think I have something for you, yeah," Tor said, grinning back. He moved too, but it wasn't random wiggling like

Jake; he shifted with purpose, his hands stroking down Jake's arms to his wrists and then grasping them firmly. "We're all alone out here," he said expectantly.

"Noticed that," Jake said, looking at the nothing all around them, save some livestock and an exhausted dog curled up near the fire.

Tor's grin grew a sharp edge. "Can make some noise," he said, dragging Jake's arms up over his head and looping the length of Jake's belt around his hands and wrists.

Jake nodded, suddenly having a harder time breathing again. "True," he said, all parts of his body reporting in. His back was happily on the blanket, his cock was getting close to rigid, his legs were parting without him telling them to, and his hands were flexing, testing the belt.

Tor laughed at him and rolled his hips, pushing against Jake in a slow, hard grind. "Gonna keep being a good man? Do what you're told?"

"If you want me to," Jake said, his tongue darting out to lick suddenly dry lips. "If you don't, then no."

That got him a chuckle. "So I win, either way? Sweet."

Jake tossed his head and tugged at the belt, his boots digging into the dirt as he met Tor's grind with his own. "You don't have other jeans," he pointed out.

"Aw, always thinking of me." Tor kissed him, tongue pushing in and tasting. "Stay," he said as he rolled away. "Where's the lube?"

Jake's body clenched tight, relaxation fleeing. "Don't know," he said, looking around. "Saddlebag."

Tor got up and went to find it, stripping off his shirts as he went and tossing them to the side, away from the fire. Jake watched him, his skin smooth and catching the light from the fire and the orange glow of the sky. His breath caught again, and with bound wrists he started tugging at his own clothes. He had no trouble with his fly, but his shirts were hopeless so he abandoned them to concentrate on his boots.

"Stop," Tor said, grabbing at his hands. "Leave 'em." He shoved Jake back and followed him down, kissing him hard enough to bruise Jake's mouth, his hands pushing under Jake's shirts and rubbing over his belly. Calluses dragged and scraped, and Tor moaned, his hands seeming to be everywhere.

Then they were gone, leaving searing trails on Jake's skin, and Jake could feel Tor fumbling with his button and zipper. One pair of jeans opened and then the other, fabric yanked aside as Tor bared them, pushed them together.

The heat from Tor's body was stunning, overcoming the glow from the fire even, and Jake moved against him, unable not to. They were making noise, not the cries and yells that were likely still to come, but grunts and moans and muttered fragments of words as they turned and twisted. Two pairs of boots kicked up dust, and Jake struggled with his arms, bound up and keeping him from doing what he wanted.

That he couldn't touch as much of Tor's naked back as he wanted to made his cock swell and throb. That Tor knew it and made all the more effort to keep him pinned down had him gasping even harder than he normally would.

"Christ," Jake swore, nipping at Tor's jaw in growing frustration.

"Uh-huh." Tor ground against him, distracted him with a kiss that went on until Jake's lungs ached, and then fingers dug into Jake's hips turning him, rolling him.

Jake swore again as Tor's rough and wet fingers probed at him, the angle awkward and wrong, and that annoyance piling on top of the frustration. He didn't think he'd been harder in his life. It was perfect.

But Tor was snarling, too, and then he was gone, up and over and jerking Jake over onto his belly, yanking him back up onto his hands and knees. Jake wasn't sure that he'd be able to hold himself up, his balance shot by the way his wrists were bound, his attention caught by the clink of his belt buckle on the rocks and the tail of it tickling the inside of his arm.

"Better," Tor growled into his ear, his chest laid out over Jake's back. "So much better." He panted, smoothed lube over and into Jake and then gasped as he pushed in, his ring breaching Jake first. "God damn."

Jake nodded, his head hanging low. "Come on," he said, words almost lost as he inhaled sharply. He was trembling, his legs feeling weak already and the head of his cock catching on his shirt as it hung off him. Every whisper of the fabric tore through him, bolts of fire rushing through his body. "Hurry."

Tor grunted and pushed in, hot and hard and filling him with an almost brutal thrust, and froze.

Time stopped, the seconds stretching out to frame years, and Jake could see it all. Tor owned him, body and soul, and there wasn't any way Jake would change that. He breathed the air around them and drew Tor into his lungs, into his blood, and it was better than right, it was living. He was grounded on the solid flesh of an imperfect man, and only the thundering sound of his heartbeat was louder than the air gusting past his ear in an irregular rhythm.

"Tor," he said softly, loudly, the word stretching out and up and filling the camp, the pasture, the land, the sky.

"Jake."

And then they moved, only by instinct and without any finesse. If Jake had wanted to gather his head enough to really please Tor, to work some magic of his own, he couldn't. It wasn't needed, it wasn't even particularly wanted. They were free to do whatever they wanted because they were there, in that place and together.

His shirt caught at him again and he couldn't twitch it away, couldn't use his hands for anything other than keeping himself upright, and it was enough, not being able to move as much as the insistent cling of his now damp shirt, and it made him scream Tor's name to the sky again, made his fingers dig into the grit and dirt as he came.

The cattle spooked, the horses kicked up a fuss, and Jake felt Tor go, heard his name, and ignored everything but Tor spilling and saying what Jake had always known to be true. Some truths had to be spoken to be real, but not that one.

It made it precious, though, those few times they said the words, like a gift. A glittery treasure they shared between them, something no one else could see, so when he heard it, Jake did what he always did when he held that gift. He savored the words, tasted their color and memorized the way they sounded, and then he gave them back. Lying on the ruined blanket, his land under his nails and Tor heavy on his back, he said, "I love you, too."

Epilogue

Fair Weather

Cath came for Thanksgiving, taking a few days extra on either side of the holiday between business trips and extending the weekend. When she drove into the yard in time for a late lunch, Jacob bounded out to her, already talking about Cobi before she was even out of her car.

"So, you're telling me you really want to show off your horse?" she teased, gathering him into a tight hug.

"Yes!" he said, then immediately looked chagrined. "Um, after you've said hi to Uncle Jake and Uncle Tor, I guess."

Jake shook his head, grinning. "Hey, you," he said when he got his turn to hug her. "Good drive?"

"It was all right, yeah," she said with a nod, turning to Tor. "You look good. Finally got this one to settle down?"

"Yup," Tor said, chuckling. "Only took a few months."

"That's why I let you do it," Cath said with a wink. "I would have brained him."

"Hey, now," Jake said mildly. "I wasn't that bad."

All three of them stared at him in frank disbelief.

"Oh, shut up," he said, rolling his eyes. "Okay, coffee is on. But I think you should go to the barn and let Jacob introduce you to the animals. Tor and I'll take your stuff in for you, then we'll give you a proper tour after you've had something to eat."

Cath looked at Jacob, who was almost quivering, shifting his weight from foot to foot. "Oh, all right," she laughed. "Lead on." She tossed her car keys to Jake and started after Jacob, shaking her head. "Oh, hey," she said, turning back with a gleam in her eye. "Elias around?"

Jake blinked at her and Tor almost choked on a laugh. "Behave!" Jake told them both. "That's not funny!"

Cath smirked at him. "Wasn't trying to be," she said, chasing after Jacob.

Jake glared at Tor, who was trying to look innocent but was still laughing. "She scares me."

"Elias is a fine man," Tor said, finally managing a straight face.

"Doesn't mean I want him with my sister," Jake muttered, getting Cath's bag from the trunk of her car.

"Can I tell him that?" Tor asked, grinning again.

"Hell, no."

"You're kind of hot when you pull this big brother stuff, you know."

Jake snorted. "When I do it to you, you bitch and call me bossy."

"It's not hot when you do it to me," Tor said patiently. "Just annoying."

"You're weird."

Tor smiled at him and pulled the door open, waiting for Jake to go in first. "In a good way," he said as Jake passed him. "I'll get lunch. If they're not out of the barn in ten minutes, you can go fetch 'em."

Jake nodded and went up the stairs, putting Cath's bag in the spare room. They'd redecorated it again, using pastels and whitewashed furniture to make it as bright and warm as they could. It wasn't the same as when they'd decorated what had become Jacob's room for 'Lissa and Cath and Becky, but he hoped Cath would like it and feel welcome.

They had lunch, toured the house, and then Jake took Cath around part of the spread in a truck, after unsuccessfully trying to get her to ride with him on River.

"I haven't ridden in years," Cath protested. "Next time, I promise."

"It's easy," Jacob assured her. "Really. Okay, your thighs hurt a lot for the first while, but then it gets easier."

Cath raised an eyebrow at him and pointed to the truck.

"That has drink holders and won't hurt my thighs."

"Shouldn't have mentioned that part," Jacob said mildly. "Oh, well. See you when you get back--I'm going out on Cobi."

"Don't be late for dinner," Tor and Jake said at the same time, sighing when Cath laughed at them.

Later that night, after the grilling and the evening chores, after Jacob had carried himself off to his room for the night, Jake sat out on the porch sipping his apple juice while Tor joined Cath in a cold beer. He was vaguely surprised Elias wasn't there, and said so.

"He'll be around," Cath said with a wink. "Just letting family visit for a bit first."

"Elias is family," Jake said, conceding to himself that if Cath and Elias did anything more than flirt just to tease him it wouldn't be the end of the world. As long as Elias didn't leave the spread, anyway. "I'll call him in a couple of minutes."

Tor nodded, settling deeper into his chair. "So what do you think, Cath?"

Cath smiled at them both, looking relaxed and rested and healthier than Jake had hoped to see her. "It's a great place. You've done well here, guys. Jacob seems happy."

"He's getting there," Jake said softly. "He's got his moments--we all do. But he's busy and trying new things, and I think he's dealing with things okay. School's good, he's got friends, that horse... I think he's doing okay."

Cath nodded and lifted her bottle. "He's grown damn near an inch and a half. Does he always eat that much?"

"Yes," Tor laughed. "Eat and sleep and ride. That's Jacob."

Cath laughed. "Good. And you two? How're you doing?" She looked at them, her gaze growing more speculative, searching their faces.

"Adjusting," Jake said with a shrug. "We're fine. Fitting things together. It's different than what we're used to, but it's working."

Tor nodded slowly. "It is. It's working fine."

Cath looked across the yard, then back at them. "It's... interesting, looking in on this. I mean, not what anyone would have figured--Jake being the one out of all of us to be settled like this. A home, a piece of land, and married with a kid. Of the four of us, I don't think anyone would have picked you for this." She smiled at him and reached for his hand. "I'm glad it's you. You've done good, Jake."

Tor smiled and nodded at him and Jake looked out over his ranch, his throat tightening. "Yeah," he said finally. "I guess I have."

He had it all. He'd never expected it, never dared to hope for it, but there it was. Family, a home, and land to work on. More than he'd had any right to dream for, but it was his and he wasn't ever going back to less than that.

He looked at Tor and smiled back at him. Luckily, he wouldn't have to. They had it all, and they were keeping it.

Natural Disaster

Printed in the United States
87930LV00004B/101/A

9 781934 166635